ALREADY GONE

BRIDGET E. BAKER

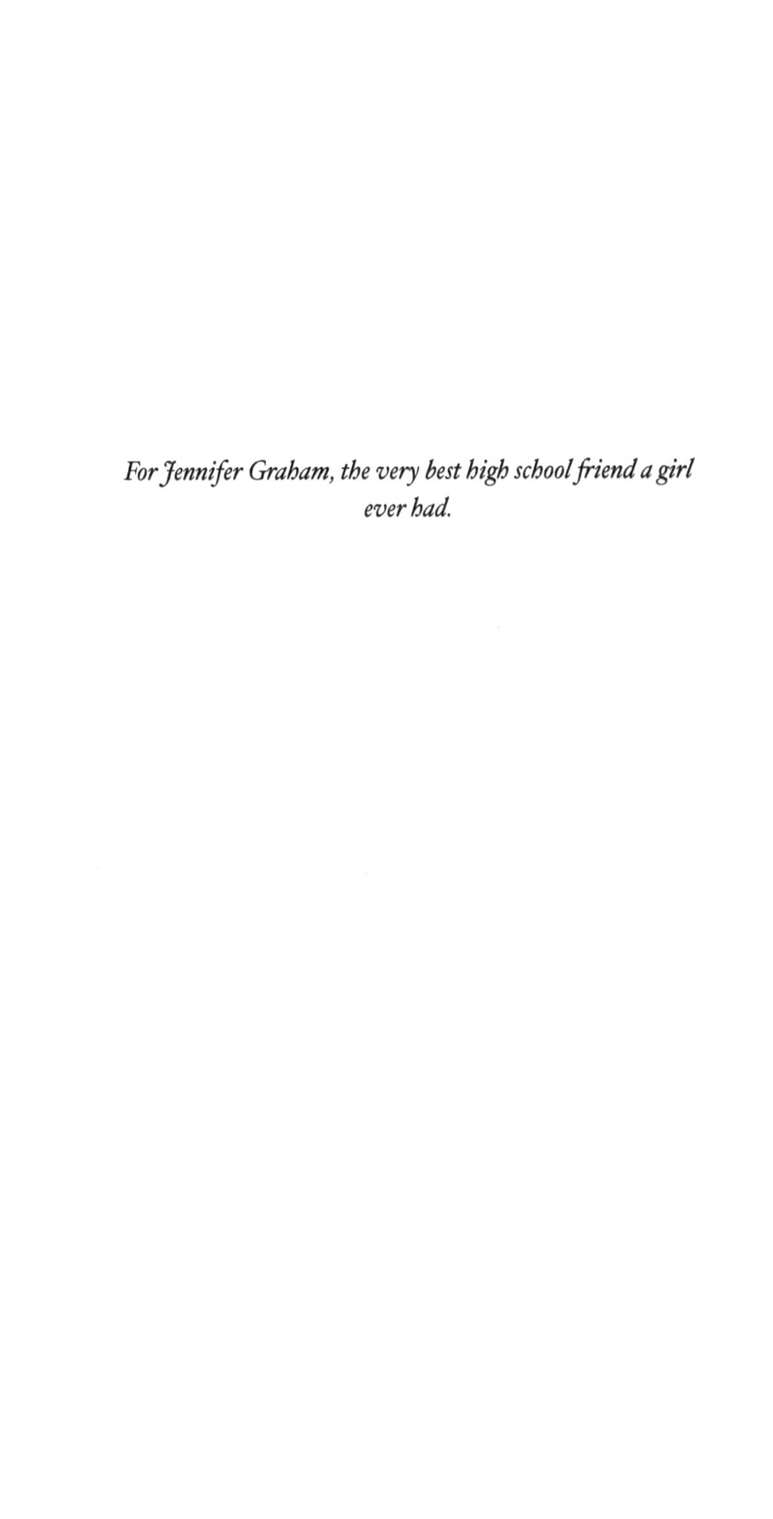

*For Jennifer Graham, the very best high school friend a girl
ever had.*

Chapter One

LACY

Time's a fickle trickster.

If I'd been born a few weeks earlier, I'm pretty sure it wouldn't have happened. If my vivacious little sister had been born a few weeks later, it might not have taken place. If Mason had shown up just one day after he did, it probably could've been avoided. If the principal had waited a few minutes that day, well, I don't know. Sometimes I think if I could've scraped together a handful of leftover seconds, we could've saved her.

She might still be alive.

Chapter Two

LACY

It's Hope's fault that I'm here, but I can't focus on that, not right now.

I'm supposed to sign in when I arrive at the shrink's office. The little white sheet with blank spaces stares at me accusingly, like it knows what I've done. I want to sign in with a beautiful curly script, as if somehow that will make things better. I can't do it though, because there isn't a pen or pencil in sight. What kind of crappy, rundown office doesn't have a pen by the sign in sheet?

When I lean over to pull one out of my backpack, I unzip the front pocket too far. Pens and pencils scatter all over the faux-wood, scuffed laminate floors.

I want to swear, but I bite my tongue instead. Who knows what this secretary might tell the doctor? I really need him to write a positive evaluation for the court. Pens and pencils scattered all over the place, one shiny yellow number two pencil broke about a third of the way down. I stare at it dumbly, transfixed.

I broke it. Like I break everything.

The secretary walks around the counter to help me, and

I notice she's wearing the exact same orthopedic sandals as my grandma. I wish Granny could still work in an office, instead of just laying in bed in a nursing home.

"Oh dear," the secretary mutters. "I do this kind of thing all the time. Here, let me help."

My conscience kicks me when she crouches down and starts gathering my clumsily scattered pens and pencils. I don't deserve her help. I don't deserve anyone's help.

I lean over to pick them up myself. "It's your fault this happened. Who doesn't have a pen out for the sign in sheet?"

She straightens up and glares at me. "Excuse me for helping."

I sigh. I should be thanking her, not yelling at her. My hands shake as I gather up the rest of my writing utensils, but I can't force out an apology. It's a good thing my mom's not here. She'd be furious.

I pick up the broken pencil and scrawl my name on the white sheet with it, scrunching my fingers to make the little nub work.

"I am sorry I didn't have a pen out." The secretary holds out a blue ink pen and when I reach for it, she smiles. I notice she has lipstick on her teeth. I tap meaningfully on my tooth with the pathetic shard of my yellow pencil while she's looking at me. She inhales quickly and rubs on her tooth. "Did I get it?"

I shake my head.

"I'll just duck into the bathroom for a second."

I raise my eyebrows at her leaving me here unsupervised but don't stop her. After all, I know I'm not really a lunatic.

While she's cleaning the lipstick off, I glance around. The larger, shattered end of my pencil lies on the floor alone. I ought to pick it up and stick it in my bag. With a little sharpening, it'll be fine.

I wish people could be repaired as easily as writing utensils. Resharpened when we get dull, a little pink cap slapped on our heads when our factory erasers run down. I could use a little sharpening, too. In their own way, humans are more fragile than a pencil, and when we break, you can't just sharpen the shards and keep on writing.

The desk plaque for the younger-than-Granny secretary reads: Melinda. There's a stack of office supply order forms in front of her and I think about checking a box for some new pens as a joke. When I lean over it, something beneath it catches my eye. It pokes out from under the order forms, and I can barely make out the font at first. When I tilt my head, I realize it's a rèsumè, Melinda Brackenridge's résumé. I know why I want to escape this tiny office, since my butt was court-ordered to come in the first place, but why does she want to leave?

I hear the bathroom door and jump, straightening guiltily.

"How long have you worked for Dr. Brasher?" I ask to distract her from the guilty trembling of my hands.

"Oh, years and years now. First we were at a group practice, but they made him take a lot of patients he wasn't too happy with. He likes helping kids and teens. He started his own practice so he can do what he wants. You'll like him. Everyone does."

Somehow I doubt if he left a group practice to be a do-gooder. I bet he got fired or something and tells people he left to help kids. Sounds a lot better. "So he's what? A saintly shrink?"

Melinda's eyebrows draw together and her lips compress. "Dr. Brasher is the best child psychiatrist in the state."

"Then why do you want to leave him?"

Her jaw drops.

I point at the résumé.

Her face blanches. "I don't want to leave, I swear. Please don't say anything. He's such a good guy, and an amazing doctor."

I raise my eyebrows.

"I haven't had a pay raise in years and my son, well, I need a raise." She gulps.

If she meant to say that out loud, I'll eat my broken pencil, but I kind of like her more now. "Family should always come first."

She nods.

Family is complicated.

If it weren't for my little sister Hope, I doubt I'd be in this fusty old office, waiting on a shrink whose evaluation will determine whether I'm capable of being released into the world as an adult. And yet, the thought doesn't make me nearly as angry as it would have last week. I don't think I realized how much time I wasted being angry with Hope.

So many seconds thrown away. I wish I could gather them up and hug them close. I wish I realized then that you can't hug people forever.

Melinda snags the clipboard and reads my name. Or she tries to, I think. So much for making a good first impression. "Angelique Vincent?"

I clear my throat. "Umm, I should be on the schedule. Lacy Shelton? I have a three-thirty appointment."

She squints at the tiny words on her paperwork. "Shelton. Yes, there you are. Let me see if he's ready." She ducks through the doorway that I assume leads to Dr. Brasher. When she opens the paneled wooden door again, she waves me over.

Melinda looks frazzled and guilty when I walk past, which is one emotion I recognize easily. It's obvious she doesn't want to quit, and I'm guessing she can't bring herself to ask for more money either. I wish I could help, but I don't have time to worry about her problems. Mine are about to slap me between the eyes.

For a moment Dr. Brasher meets my eyes silently. I stare right back. He's a tall man to be wearing that particular sweater vest. Before he sits down, I notice it isn't quite long enough. His hairy belly isn't something I particularly wanted to see, but I imagine he spends all day staring at people he'd rather not. I guess we all do junk we don't want to.

He looks down at a file sitting on his desk, and I follow his gaze to a photo of me and Hope, both of us smiling on a blanket on the beach. It's torn down the middle, and taped back together. I know who taped it. And I know she's gone now, never to return. Like a pencil in a wood chipper, irreparably damaged.

All my fault.

I gulp and sit down on the hard wooden chair across from Dr. Brasher's desk. My eyes veer away from the photo and right into a pink notebook. Hope wouldn't use a black and white speckled composition book, no. She made mom buy her a special English journal, with sparkly bling and a splashing dolphin. Sometimes she acted like she was nine years old.

My heart stutters. Why does Dr. Brasher have Hope's stuff? Did the judge send it here? My fingers itch to reach for it, but nothing I do seems to go right, so I force my hands into fists at my side.

This has to go right.

"Ah, I see you've caught me," Dr. Brasher says. "I was just studying up on your case, a little last minute maybe."

I start to speak, but I can't quite get words past the frog lodged in my throat. I cough to clear it and then force myself to croak a few words. "Why do you have Hope's journal and that photo?"

"Please," he says. "Sit down."

I do, but I can't help another pointed glance at the journal.

"Does it bother you that I have it?"

I stomp down on the surge of emotion. I just have to survive the next hour. "No, I'm just curious."

"I see in the file that you're only eleven months older than her. Irish twins, as it were."

I've explained this so many times, the words fall out without thought. "Since I was born in early fall and she came along the very next year at summer's end, we started kindergarten the same year."

"That's awfully close in age. Did you mind having a sister when you were little? Were you ever jealous of her?"

I don't snort at him, or tell him to look at the photo. I don't tell him that everyone was jealous of Hope. I don't tell him she ruined my life. I don't tell him I hated her sometimes. And I don't bother telling him I loved her, too. I loved her enough to keep giving and giving when all she did was take take take.

"Even if I was jealous, that's normal, right?" I ask. "Textbook, even. Half the kids in America are jealous of their new baby brother or sister."

He holds up the photo, one side of it flopping forward along the scotch tape fault line. "She looks a little different than you do."

Thank you Doctor Obvious. My brown curly hair looks nothing like Hope's long, blonde locks. Our eyes are the same shape, but different colors. My pale, lightly freckled arms and legs inspire vampire jokes galore. Her limbs are tanned and muscular from swimming. My angular face and bony body look even more gaunt when compared to her perfect curves.

I guess it's safe to say Hope didn't steal my looks, but she's taken most everything else I've wanted over the years, sometimes without even trying. When we were babies, she snatched pacifiers I wasn't ready to give up, my favorite stuffed animals, my snacks, and even my cutest clothing. As we grew, so too did the list in my head of stolen goods. I kept track of them all.

Not that I plan to confess that in an interrogation ordered by a judge.

"You're right. Only our face shapes look the same."

"Can you describe your relationship?"

I glance at the clock. "We've only got an hour, right?"

He smiles. "We have as long as you need, Angelica."

I shudder. "Don't call me that. My name is Lacy, okay?"

He makes a note on his yellow pad. It doesn't inspire confidence that he needs to write down my name, like he knows he won't remember it otherwise. Or maybe wanting to use a nickname tells him something about my brain. What does it tell him? I want to stand up and demand that he tell me. I want to know what's going to happen. I want to take everything back. Instead I clench my fists and try to school my face into a façade of calm.

I can't survive much more of this mock serenity. My head will explode. "For today we only have an hour, right?"

He nods. "I have another patient scheduled after you, but you can come back tomorrow and the next day, for as long as we need. We may be seeing each other a lot for the next few weeks."

My heart rate spikes. Weeks? I don't have that much time. Why would this take that long? I always finish tests in the first fifteen minutes. I write five page papers in half an hour. Why would it take that long to be evaluated?

Then it dawns on me. "Shrinks are all paid by the hour, right? So the more time it takes for you, the more money you make. Got to pay for that Porsche for the wife somehow, am I right?"

He shakes his head. "My wife drives a Subaru, and she paid for that herself. Would it interest you to know that psychiatrists are actually the worst paid doctors in America?"

I shrug. I don't really care much one way or another, but that might explain Melinda's dilemma.

"Speaking of," I say, and then stop. She asked me not to say anything, but maybe Dr. Brasher could do something about it. He might want to do something. It's not like I promised her I'd keep quiet. Things that can be fixed should be fixed. Before it's too late.

"Did you have something to tell me, Lacy?"

I look down at my feet and then back up to meet his eyes. "Do you like your secretary, Melinda?"

He raises just one eyebrow. "How is that related to psychiatrists being poorly paid?"

"I'll explain, but I need to know. Are you happy with her work?"

"Of course I am. I've been working with her for years. She's my secretary and also my office manager. She keeps things running."

"I get that you're not well paid, but she needs more money. She's got a son who's, well, I don't know exactly what his deal is, but if you don't give her that raise you can't afford, you might be looking for a new office manager."

Melinda's face had bleached white when we spoke earlier, but Dr. Brasher's doesn't grow pale. His cheeks flush crimson.

"Look, if it helps, you can write down that we spent as

many hours as you want. I won't say a word." Happy shrink, better eval, right?

Dr. Brasher splutters. "I would never falsify my hours. And how could you know that Melinda needs money?"

I shrug. "I notice things." At least, now I do. "You only get one shot to get things right sometimes." Familiar tears well up in the back of my throat, my eyes misting. I take a big, ragged breath to head them off. "But whatever. You're the one with the fancy degrees, so I'm sure you know better than I do."

He steeples his hands in front of him and studies me. "Now you've gone all teenager on me, but you don't need to. I have an MD, yes, but I still appreciate insightful advice from any quadrant. Your file says you're in line to be Valedictorian, and I can see why. I feel as though I should set the record straight. For court-ordered evaluations, I'm paid on a flat fee basis."

Great, and my suggestion that he pad his bill makes me look like an idiotic teenager at best, a chronic liar at worst. Another spastic misstep. Heat floods my chest and spreads up to my cheeks. "That sucks for you, but it means you want to wrap this up as fast as you can, right? I'm on board with that."

"It takes as long as it takes," he practically growls. This could definitely be going better. He breathes in and out a few times before saying, "How did you feel about your little sister when you were growing up?"

"I loved her, of course. Everyone loves Hope. I'm pretty sure it's involuntary, like pupil dilation, or breathing."

Dr. Brasher scoffs. "Pupil dilation?"

I shrug. "I got tired of being the smart one sometimes, okay? It sucks, being the plain one, the boring one, but it's not like I could do much about it. If I bleached my hair and tried to swim or something, I'd have looked like a pathetic wannabe, a disappointing, washed-out clone. So I focused on my strengths and just tried to love her for hers."

"Did you ever like the same guys?"

My hands start to sweat. I didn't expect him to have her journal. I have no idea what it says in there. I don't like unknowns in mathematics, and I despise them in real life.

"Hope was on homecoming court, okay? She's swim team captain, so she meets a lot of jocks. The kind of guy who likes her is usually good looking, funny, smart, athletic, or popular."

Basically, anyone who's breathing.

"And what about you, Lacy? What kinds of guys like you?"

"Up until this year, the closest I got to having a guy's undivided attention was when I read Hemingway or Chaucer."

"What changed this year?" He steeples his hands again.

It's starting to annoy me. "I bet you've already read all about it."

"I don't know your side of things," Dr. Brasher says. "That's why you're here."

"If I walk you through what happened and you write your report, then we'll be done, right?"

He nods.

"Where should I start?"

"Where do you think it all started to go wrong?"

He already knows what happened and he's got Hope's journal, so he's probably figured out that it's all my fault. Things went about as wrong as they could have gone. Fights. Missed school. Police. Drugs. Juvie. Possible expulsion. And the one bad thing no one ever seems to want to talk about.

I can barely breathe and I look away. Sniff and wipe my eyes.

She died.

The rest of the stuff doesn't even matter compared to that.

But looking back on all that mess, in the cluster my life has become, no one's asked for my side of the story. Not the judge, not a single teacher, not my best friend Drew, no one. It's like they're all afraid of the answer.

And maybe they should be.

It all started the day I met Mason. Is it ironic that the first truly great day of my life was probably also the very thing that set in motion the events leading up to the worst? Or does life always work like that? Mom lost Dad right after Hope was born. Maybe bad always nips at good's heels like a moronic, overeager puppy, shredding everything and peeing in the corner.

Dr. Brasher still stares at me expectantly and I realize I haven't spoken a word. "I guess it all started with Mason."

Dr. Brasher rifles through a pile of papers on his desk and then he looks back up at me. "Mason Montcellier?"

I nod my head, impressed when he pronounces the difficult last name correctly. "Yep."

"Why don't you tell me about him."

I bite my lip. I don't want to talk about Mason. It hurts. Not crippling pain, like when I think about her, but thinking about Mason hurts in a different way. Plus, I honestly don't even know how I feel anymore. I cared for Mason more than I thought possible, and now I have no idea how to feel about him. Do I love him? Do I blame him? Do I feel anything at all?

I clear my throat. "It was your typical story, I guess. Outrageously attractive boy meets nerdy girl. It was the 'happily ever after part' where things started to break down."

Chapter Three

HOPE

Dear Diary:

I'm totally not the kind of girl who writes in a diary. I suck at writing, but Ms. Littleton said she'll give me extra credit if I write five pages or more in this one at least three times a week until the end of the year, and boy do I need it. My grades are not good. I wouldn't really care actually, except that I can't swim if I fail any of my classes, and I'm like a teeter-totter in English. Passing, failing, passing, almost failing.

Eligibility.

It's a dirty word on swim team. Probably with any sport in high school, but definitely with Brazosport High School's swim team. I'm the captain this year since I'm a senior and pretty much the best swimmer we've got. I thought it would be awesome to be in charge, but I do a lot of paperwork, which blows. I have to take attendance, check eligibility (ugh), and plan out our practice outlines. It's not even the same practice plan for everyone, since the swimmers in distance events have a completely different (and more boring) workout focus than sprinters.

I'm a sprinter, obviously.

I have no idea how those distance swimmers can just plonk their faces in the water and not resurface for like two whole hours. I think I'd fall asleep. Or go crazy. Maybe both. I want to get somewhere as fast as I possibly can, then pop up and look around to hear people cheering. I swim freestyle mostly, but I'm also pretty good at backstroke and butterfly. It makes me helpful in filling holes in relays. Now that I'm captain, I have to worry about that kind of crap.

Today's meet should've been perfect. It's a Thursday in the winter, so I worried some of my best swimmers would be sick, but when we checked in, they were all present. Plus, everyone had all their stuff: swimsuits, goggles, and parkas. We all made it to the bus on time. The bus worked like it should and there was no traffic. We even got there five minutes early. I knew it would be a hard meet, swimming against one of the powerhouses in the greater Houston area, but we were ready.

I'd gotten on and looked at the Friendswood website, so I knew they had dozens of championships behind them compared to our zero, but our team was ready this time. We sucked hardcore a few years ago, but we've come so far since then. I've stolen a half dozen great athletes from dance team, of all places, and a few more from track. Although, when I stole a promising new (former) runner two weeks ago, the track coach Mr. Benitez went to the principal. Apparently I can't hang out around the high school track after swim practice any more. But the point is, Friendswood and Brazosport are almost the same size, so we both had a lot of talent to draw on. Friendswood High School may be richer, but I figured we were as ready as we'd ever be to take them down.

I was an idiot.

I'm sort of dating my co-captain Dave, which might have been my first mistake I guess. I tried to tell him to move Anna to the medley relay, but he just smiled at me and did what he wanted. I told him we needed a pre-meet pep talk, but he said that was a waste of time.

"We aren't cheerleaders," is actually what he told me.

I tried to make everyone keep their parkas on when we unloaded, but he said to let them do what they want, warm muscles don't matter. Coach Collins lets us manage the little things. He says it helps us grow together as a team. He's as big an idiot as me. Although if I'm being honest, probably none of that would've made much of a difference anyway.

I was in the first relay, the meet's very first race. When my turn came, I felt completely calm. I stood up on the starting block, goggles in place. My foot placement was perfect, my right front foot at the edge, my toes curling over the block. My left foot was about a shoulder's width behind, and my hands had a firm grip when Vivian approached me swimming the breaststroke. I didn't jump in too early and disqualify us, but I flew forward the second Vivian tapped the wall.

We were slightly behind Friendswood when I leapt into the water, but by the time I finished my fifty meters of fly, we had a pretty good lead. Faith kept that lead and we won. Dave pulled me in for a hug, since he was standing behind me waiting for the men's relay. He swims backstroke, which means he's up first and he starts in the water. I should've been watching Dave reaching up and grabbing the block. He's sort of my boyfriend and he's really good looking, too. He has blonde hair and light green eyes. He's also got a long, lean swimmer's body, in spite of the fact that I poached him from track just last year. Maybe Coach Benitez had a point.

I wasn't looking at Dave as his relay started. No one from our team was. It was the first time I'd ever seen *him*.

The race started and I wasn't even cheering. I was conscious of the fact our team was winning, but my focus was split. Dave got out of the water just as I saw *him* mount the block. Dave was looking for a high five, a hug, or really any kind of congratulations I think, but I ignored him, my eyes glued to our competition. Dave huffed and walked off, talking to one of his buddies behind me.

I couldn't stop looking at one of the largest guys I'd ever seen at a high school swim meet. He had to be more than just a few inches over six feet tall, and his skin was dark, as though he'd been in the sun every day of his life. His size, his shaggy black hair, his enormous muscles, they were all impressive, but what drew my eye was a huge, black, whale tail tattooed across his shoulders and down his back that rippled with muscle as he moved. Above the whale tale was one word in black block letters. Moby.

Our team was still winning. And just in case you don't know Ms. Littleton, seconds count in swimming. In fact, split seconds matter. They often make the difference between winning and losing. So it'll tell you something when I say his teammate reached the wall, and before he bothered to jump in, this guy looked back over his shoulder and winked at me through his goggles.

I gasped, I know I did.

Then he leapt straight out over the water. He had the most beautiful entry, and then the most gorgeous butterfly I've ever seen. If you've seen someone swim butterfly badly, you probably thought they were drowning, but if you've seen it done right, it's a thing of, like, really amazing beauty. I've seen videos of Matt Biondi from the Olympics in the eighties and nineties and his butterfly is so perfect it almost made me cry.

Biondi had nothing on this guy.

Our boys' team lost the medley relay. Badly. Because of that hulking whale man. Once I got over ogling him, I really couldn't stand the fact that he existed.

Dave hated him too. Probably more than me since he didn't like swoon when he saw him or anything. I ignored Dave's cursing and focused on the races, keeping a silent tally in my head. We were tied after the women's medley, but our team pulled ahead in the 200 free, winning both first and second in the women's, and landing first and third in the men's. I knew we had a tough meet ahead of us because Friendswood has a bigger team with more swimmers to call on, but we were still doing well.

I was helping one of the freshman girls stretch a stiff shoulder when I noticed my little green-pea track recruit warming up for his first race. Dave was watching, I saw, and he knew. I should have let it go since he kind of runs the boys and I run the girls' side, but I just couldn't. I walked over to talk to him.

"Why are you wearing swim trunks, Adam?" I asked, even though I knew the answer. No new swimmer, especially someone who used to run, wants to wear a speedo. They just don't. As some kind of stupid rite of passage, the guys never tell them *why* they actually need to wear one. They always say it's the drag. Wearing trunks will slow them down, they say.

"I'm fast enough," he said. Because the baby swimmers always say that. The reality is, they'd rather lose than wear a tight little suit.

I should've left it alone. It happens every year, but most new swimmers are freshmen and they all dive in together, which means their swim trunks all peel off at the same time. Everyone laughs at all of them, usually in the same race. This poor kid was a sophomore, and we were in the middle of the season. "You may be fast enough." His times were pretty good in practice. "But you don't just wear a speedo because it's faster."

He frowned. "Huh?"

I leaned in and whispered in his ear. "Those trunks will fall off the second you hit the water."

His cheeks flushed and he ran to the locker room to change.

"Why'd you tell him?" Dave asked. "That was going to be so freaking funny."

I rolled my eyes. Sometimes Dave's a jerk.

He wasn't laughing when Moby smoked us in the 200 Individual Medley. It sparked my first real fight with Dave. Ever. I guess we'd never really cared about anything enough to fight about it before.

"Why do you keep staring at him?"

"At who?" I tried to play dumb.

"That Moby freak. Geez, you're supposed to be cheering for our team. You should be looking at me."

I shrugged. "If I was staring, it's because he was destroying you."

"He's only one guy. Swimming's a team sport."

"Their entire team is good, Dave. It's going to be a tough meet. We knew that when we signed up."

I picked up my clipboard and tallied the points. Friendswood was already ahead, not by a huge amount yet, but by enough it would be hard for us to catch up. When the race ended, I barely had time to update the totals before Dave sat down right next to me and slung his arm around my shoulders.

"Watch it," I said. "You're flinging water on my paper."

Dave rolled his eyes. "Your paper doesn't even matter. It's just so you can obsess over every little thing during the meet."

I shoved his arm off. "What's your problem anyway? Since when do we sit around all snuggled up?"

"You're my girlfriend. If I want to put my arm around you, what's the big deal?" He glanced to the right just then and I followed his gaze. Moby was looking at us, smirking. It pissed me off, so I yanked Dave down for a kiss right there in the middle of the meet.

Coach Collins cleared his throat and I pulled back.

"Sorry Coach," I muttered.

"I didn't think I needed to review proper behavior for a meet with my team captains." Coach Collins leaned over and grabbed my clipboard. "Maybe instead of locking lips you two could, I don't know, get ready for your events?" Coach pointed.

I swore, because I was up.

I scrambled to find my goggles and reach the block in time. I won the fifty free anyway, but it was my worst time in over a month. Afterward, I barely had time to stretch out before I was up for the hundred fly. I didn't like doing events back to back, but we had agreed to forgo diving which would normally give me a break, and our team needed the points from a few more first places. I figured the fly was my best bet.

I was back in my groove by the time the race started, and I beat Friendswood's best swimmer by a solid two seconds. I was in the free lanes cooling down from my sprint and working the lactic acid out of my muscles when I saw him. Moby was standing at the pool's edge watching me. I rolled over and backstroked until I reached just below where he was standing, staring at me rudely. I flipped him off with both hands and turned back over. I hoped Coach didn't see it, but it felt good to show him that his team didn't scare me.

When I went back to our risers to relax until my last

event, the 200 free relay, I noticed that both Dave and Moby were ready for their next race too. Both were doing the 500 freestyle, the longest event at a high school meet. I walked by Dave and squeezed his hand before I took my seat in the risers, sliding into my parka to keep my muscles warm.

I'd seen Moby swim twice at that point. I knew he was the best swimmer at the meet. I thought he might be the best swimmer in the greater Houston area. Still, nothing had prepared me for watching him swim the 500 free. I should explain about freestyle. Most people think that the crawl stroke, where your legs scissor kick and your arms slide up and around over and over, is actually the freestyle stroke. That's not true. Actually freestyle just means you can swim however you want. Of course, everyone does the crawl because it's the fastest stroke for the least effort, so it's a no brainer.

Except for Moby.

I swear he smiled at me before he leapt in again, but instead of swimming the crawl with the other seven guys swimming, he swam butterfly for the first hundred yards. It wasn't just me staring. Everyone stared. Butterfly is exhausting. No one swims it during a freestyle race. We all watched, transfixed, at his perfect form for the fly. Then he switched to backstroke for the next hundred. He swam breaststroke, usually the slowest swim stroke, for the next hundred. The worst part is that, even swimming those alternative strokes, he pulled so far ahead the other swimmers, Dave included, that he lapped them. Twice. When he finally switched to the crawl for the last two hundred yards, he pulled ahead even further, so far that no one could believe it. He finished the entire thing in under four and a half minutes. To give you an idea, the high school record is something like four minutes and thirteen seconds. That's for someone who was at the end of a taper, not in the middle of the season, and doing the crawl the entire time.

I hated Moby in that moment. Hated his arrogance and how he was beating us so badly, and I was jealous. And I hated that I was jealous. But I also kind of fangirled a little. I couldn't help it.

When he stepped out of the pool, he saw me staring with freaking starry princess eyes and he knew. He knew I was completely blown away, and I hated that he knew it. His eyes found mine immediately and he grinned.

Dave came in almost a minute later. When he stomped his way over to me, clearly embarrassed and upset, I tried to act outraged. How could a freak like Moby exist? Luckily I didn't have long to fume, since I was anchor in the next relay. Our girls team won again. I recorded it and headed over for my last cool down. Moby was in the water, still cooling down from his race.

I slid into a cool-down lane, one over from him. I waited to push off until he was halfway down so we'd only pass sporadically. Within one lap he had matched me, and we were swimming in sync. Almost every time I came up for a breath I saw him, smiling at me. I finally pulled up against the wall and he did, too.

"Are you swim-stalking me?" I asked.

"I was in the water first, lady. You picked the lane right next to me." He arched one eyebrow. His glorious muscles rippled when he pulled up and sat down on the concrete edge of the pool. "I think that means you're the one stalking me."

"Why are you still cooling down, anyway? A little worn out from showing off?"

"You haven't even seen me show off yet." He smiled. "But no, I didn't start until after your medley."

I started with surprise. "Why?"

"I like watching you. You're the best swimmer here." Other than him, obviously. His grin said he already knew that, so I didn't acknowledge it.

"I doubt my boyfriend appreciates your flirting with me." I pulled out of the water then, and I should have stood up and gone back to the risers, hoping to catch the end of Dave's race.

I didn't.

"I don't see him here," he said. "Must be busy losing another one."

I stood then. "You're a jerk."

He shrugged, still smiling. "Sometimes, but I'm a jerk who always wins."

I didn't know what to say to that, so I walked back to our risers and tallied Dave's most recent second place win in the hundred back. Even though I won every single race, we were still losing and I was pissed about it. When the last event was called, I watched as our girls teams took second and third. I tallied the races and even with the additional six from the last race, we still had less than seventy points. No matter what our boys 400 freestyle relay did, we couldn't win.

It still pissed me off to watch Moby's team destroy Dave's by over five seconds, all of them thanks to Moby. I guess it pissed Dave off too. When he finished his cool down laps, he came back to where I was getting my things together. He normally would have grabbed the box with the meet stuff, clipboard, extra supplies, back up timers, a few kickboards and other random crap.

He just walked off instead, leaving me to lug my bag and the box of random crap alone. "Thanks a lot, Dave," I muttered. Then I slid my bag strap over my head and settled it across my body. Finally I leaned over and heaved the box up.

"What'd you say?" Dave turned back to me.

"I said, thanks for leaving me to carry everything for the whole team." I meant the box. Mostly.

He dropped his bag and stomped back to where I stood. He tried to yank the box out of my hands, but it was too late now.

"No way." I pulled the box against my chest. "Don't do me any favors."

"Fine, I won't." He turned to walk to the bus, still fuming, presumably over our loss. He'd seen the same score tally I had. My name was all over the card, two sixes for first place, and part of two teams scoring eight points for relays. His was on three times, but only in first once. This wasn't new. Almost every meet I did better than him and he'd sulk a little, but by the next day he'd be back to normal and we'd be mostly fine. It had been like this ever since October when we started dating off and on. I wondered whether he was more jealous of Moby or of me.

"Wait," Moby said, taking the box from me smoothly. "Who did you say was the jerk?" He smirked and fell into step beside me, walking me out to our bus.

We didn't make it more than a dozen steps before Dave turned back and saw him. His face flushed and he swore. "What do you think you're doing?"

Dave jogged back toward Moby, but I stepped out and put my hand on his chest. "He's just being nice." Like you weren't, I thought.

"I don't know how they do things in Brazosport," Moby said, "but in Friendswood, guys don't let beautiful ladies carry huge boxes out to the bus."

"Just the ugly ones?" I asked.

Moby looked momentarily confused before he smiled. "We don't let any girls carry big boxes, no matter what they look like. Not if we can help it."

"Put it down." Dave said. "It's not a heavy box, which I know from carrying it after every meet this year, and my girlfriend doesn't need your help. Neither do I."

Moby hunched over and used a low voice to mock Dave. "Me man. Me say you no carry big box for my woman." He grunted.

That pissed Dave off pretty bad, but before he could do anything about it Coach Collins showed up. He held his hands out, palms facing out, and spoke in a loud voice. "Drop it, Dave. You will be civil, and you will carry that box the rest of the way to the bus."

"You've seen him, Coach. He's been all over Hope since we got here, and now he's-"

"I won't say it again," Coach said. "Take that box and go to the bus."

Dave scowled, but he yanked the box away from Moby and stomped off toward the bus. He stopped at the steps and looked back at me. "You coming?"

I nodded my head. "In a minute."

He sighed with disgust and carried the box up the stairs and through the double doors.

"Thanks for helping," I said awkwardly, very aware Coach Collins was standing between Moby and me.

"He's going to be helping us a lot in the future," Coach Collins said.

"What does that mean?" I asked.

"It means I'm moving," Moby said with a smile. "My family's relocating to Surfside beach tomorrow. We're going to be teammates."

His interest in me and in our team made so much more sense. He's going to be joining us.

I broke up with Dave on the bus on the way home, and I didn't even mention why.

Chapter Four

LACY

"Tell me about Mason," Dr. Brasher says. "Why did he change things?"

"Well, he stood out right away."

"How so?"

"He looked different, for one. Very different."

Dr. Brasher raises an eyebrow.

"This should be easy," I say. "Just think of the hottest guy you've ever seen. Channing Tatum, or you know, you're old so maybe Brad Pitt. I don't care, take your pick. I promise you, Mason Montcellier is hotter. He's like a supernova. You almost can't look right at him. Black hair and light brown, almost golden eyes. Flawless features, perfect symmetry. A few freckles so you believe he's a real person instead of a cyborg, and sun-kissed skin all over."

Dr. Brasher sits back in his seat and regards me quietly before he says, "You seem very concerned with his looks. Why do they matter to you so much?"

I raise my eyebrows. "You're a doctor, so I know you're smart. This should make sense to you immediately."

He simply looks at me.

I sigh. "Didn't you take honors classes when you were in school?"

He shakes his head. "I actually struggled in High School. I didn't really buckle down and worry about scholastics until college."

"Well, let me paint you a little picture then. Brazosport isn't a huge high school, but it's pretty big. There are maybe two thousand students in all, but I'm in all Advanced Placement classes, right? College level Calculus, History, English, Spanish and Physics. In those classes there are a lot of bright people, even at crappy B-port high. There are tall kids. There are short kids. You'll see freckled kids, dark kids, pale kids, even a few perfectly tan kids, since some of us live in Surfside. You'll find science geeks, with the Dow plant so close, and kids who read obsessively. There are others who study history in their free time. My classes have kids of almost every race, and almost every shape, but there's one thing you never see. Never. There are no genuinely, naturally attractive kids. Maybe because no one in there focuses much on their appearance, I don't know."

I pause and Dr. Brasher stares at me blankly. I sigh and continue. "You obviously never took speech and debate, because even compared to the AP classes, it's a microcosm. The people in there care about presentation, but not in the way popular kids do. In fact, most of us are hiding there because we interact better with adults than with other kids. I'm nothing to look at, and I'm Jennifer freaking Lawrence in there."

Dr. Brasher snorts. "What you're saying is that when you met Mason for the first time, he stood out."

"That's an understatement. Anyhow, my first class of the day is speech and debate. They arranged varsity speech and debate first so that it's not such an inconvenience for one of us to step out every morning and miss class to do the school announcements. That someone has been me for the past three years."

"Do you miss it?" he asks.

"What? Doing the announcements?" I roll my eyes. "I've missed a great many things since everything went down Dr. Brasher, but doing the school announcements isn't on that list." I switch into my announcement voice. "Hello, students of Brazosport High. Today is January fifth. First, please stand to say the pledge of allegiance. Now, the Texas pledge. Now, let me tell you all about the dumb awards our basketball team won. And let me close with a message from our school counselor. Drug usage has been on the rise, and we all know how bad drugs are for you. Please make sure if you see anything strange or out of the ordinary, or any suspicious behavior, you report it immediately to a principal."

Dr. Brasher smiles. "You sound pretty good at that, actually. But, what does that have to do with meeting Mason?"

"I'm getting there." I think back to that day. "I finished the school announcements and then I walked two hallways over, up the stairs and down to the far end of the hall. Speech class is banished to the furthest corner of the school."

I look down at my black Converse sneakers, and I can see it all again in my head just as it happened that morning. My beat up sneakers, my worn jeans, my puffy Adidas bunched under one arm and my suit in a bag, slung over my shoulder. A day like any other until I walked in the door, prepared to lope over to my seat next to Drew and review our game plan for that day's debate tournament.

"When I came in the classroom was already full, and he was just there, sitting in Drew's seat."

"Drew?" Dr. Brasher asks.

"Sorry, her first name is Alice," I say. "But she goes by her middle name. Drew."

"He was sitting in Alice Dunmore's seat?" Dr. Brasher's eyebrows rise.

"Right. We've been best friends since we were both eleven, and I knew her even before that. Drew's dad interviewed my mom for the job at Dow Chemical. Mom still works for him."

Dr. Brasher takes some notes and then flips through some papers. "And Drew took debate with you, right?"

"She was my debate partner," I say. "She wasn't very good, but she usually tried really hard. Brazosport's debate team has always sucked. I'm an anomaly, but there just wasn't much to choose from partner-wise. After an abysmal sophomore year, I convinced Drew to take the class with me and be my partner. She's amazing at research and her writing is decent, but she sucks at speaking, especially in front of people. She freezes up like a mouse facing off with a cobra."

Dr. Brasher rolls his eyes, which doesn't seem very shrinky of him. "Where was Drew that day?"

"I didn't know where she was then, not yet. I just knew someone else was in her seat when I walked into class. But Drew was late a lot, so that didn't really surprise me. Instead of sitting down, I looked at our Coach, Ms. Harris, and asked her-"

"She wasn't upset you were late?"

I exhale heavily. "Dr. Brasher, even for a therapist, you're asking about too many superfluous details. I can't tell you the story if you badger me with pointless questions. Remember, I wasn't late. I'd been at the main office doing announcements and this was our standard deal. Ms. Harris knew that. She didn't think anything of me coming inside after they finished and after everyone else was seated." Dr.

Brasher may mean well, but if he wants my side of the story, I'm going to need to give it without interruptions.

I tap on my lip. "What if I write this down for you? It might be faster and easier. Then after you read what I write, all of it, if you still want to know more or you're confused, we can talk about it."

Dr. Brasher thinks about it for a moment, tapping his desk with his fingers slowly. Then he leans back in his chair and nods his head. "We can try it. It's unconventional but it could work. It might be cathartic for you to put it all down on paper, too. Easier to say some things that way."

He stands up and rummages around in his filing cabinet. He pulls out a large yellow pad, long and lined, like the ones the old-timers use when they're judging debate. Instead of flashing, some of them still flow. I groan. "Don't you have a laptop or something from this century?"

He laughs. "It'll do you some good to get a hand cramp. That's how you know it's time to take a break from writing and reflect on what you're recounting." He hands me the paper pad and an ink pen. Then he walks back to his desk, pulls out a book and starts reading.

"What, right here?" I ask. "You want me to write this down here, while you sit there and read, what book is that?" I squint. *"The Devil Wears Prada?* Are you kidding me?"

He raises his eyebrows. "Isn't this what you wanted? Tell your story, and how did you say it? Stop badgering me with pointless questions."

I frown at him. He might be smarter than I first thought. I look down at the blank paper, so much blank, yellow paper. I guess it is what I wanted. I pick up the pen and begin, well, at the beginning.

———

Mason Montcellier sat in Drew's seat, but somehow, the second I saw him there, it wasn't Drew's seat anymore. It was Mason's. He's that kind of person, the kind who walks in and just takes over, only it doesn't feel like he's taking over. It feels like he was missing before, and he's right where he's supposed to be, wherever he is. He wore a simple red t-shirt and dark blue jeans. His leather shoulder bag sat next to his chair, instead of a backpack like most kids, and a light jacket was draped across it. I almost couldn't bring myself to walk across the room toward him.

His eyes immediately met mine, light and curious. They followed me to my seat, and he smiled when I sat next to him. "I'm Mason," he said. "I'm new."

I sighed in mock relief. "Phew. I'm Lacy," I said. "I was worried. You're in my friend's seat. For a minute, I thought Drew had undergone some major plastic surgery. Welcome to B-port High."

"Thanks," he said. "Well, was the surgery successful?"

"Uh, no," I said, "see, she's not really having surgery. I was making a joke. In fact, Drew's a girl, so that would be some really major surgery." Geez, he was thick. The gorgeous ones always are.

"Drew being a girl kind of messes up my joke, but not totally."

I was so accustomed to no one getting my sense of humor, that I didn't even realize he was flirting at first. Mason raised his eyebrows in that way that cocky guys do, and I realized this time I was the one who missed his joke. Right then, I knew I was a goner.

"What are you doing in speech and debate?" I asked, by way of an answer. "You don't really fit in here, what with your surgically enhanced pectoral muscles, or you know, any muscle definition at all."

"I don't?" Mason looked around the room. My eyes

followed his. I see Kelly Willis, a little on the heavy side, with red curlicue hair, plaid skirt, spiked collar, and black combat boots. Taylor Morris grinned at us, his braces gleaming, almost as brightly as the shiny zits all over his cheeks. We were too far for Mason to realize it, but Taylor also had a pretty bad body odor problem. Off to the side from Taylor, Kim Huynh, pronounced like "win", was digging through piles of printouts from Newsweek, updating the Extemp files last minute. His glasses slid down on his nose twice in ten seconds. Pushing them back up had become a permanent nervous tic, and he did it now, even when they hadn't yet slid down.

My eyes circled back to Mason's. He shook his head slowly. "My mom's going to be so disappointed if I can't cut it in here. She's the one who made me sign up, you know, back at my old school."

"I didn't mean you couldn't cut it," I said. "No need to disappoint good old Mommy just yet. I was only pointing out that you don't really look the part."

"You don't either," he pointed out. "Does your friend Drew look the part?"

Not really, not like the other kids in here anyway. Drew looked a lot like me. Like an endearingly cute regular person, but with a slight gothic vibe. I feel a flash of pre-emptive jealousy, wondering whether Mason will prefer Drew when she finally shows up, but I stamp it down.

"Drew definitely doesn't fit in either. She only joined because I badgered her into it. She's really cute. A little dark and angsty maybe, but she's not a typical honors kid appearance wise."

Neither of us was in Mason's league, though. No one at Brazosport High that I could think of really was, not by a long shot.

Before I could ask about where he came from or why he

was here, Ms. Harris emerged from her little office on the side of the classroom. I have no idea how she managed to get a classroom with it's own private office, although dodgy theories abounded, but she put it to good use. I doubt she'd survive a day here without it, since she's frequently in there drinking. She told us over and over that her thermos was filled with water and lemon juice, 'for her throat.' I may not have had alcohol myself yet, and my mom never drinks, but even I recognize the smell as something stronger than water.

She didn't look too drunk when she shuffled out in her slippers that morning, but she had her insulated cup of 'lemon water' in hand, so it was only a matter of time. That's the other reason we scheduled Varsity speech and debate for first period. It was our best chance of getting something out of good old Ms. Harris before she put her head down on her desk and started snoring. We all made a lot of jokes, but back in her day she swept at state and did well at nationals, too. I kind of feel sorry for her. She hasn't had an easy life.

"We have a new student with us today, class. Mr. Mason Montcellier," she slurred. She made Montcellier sound like Mont-chaleer.

"Actually, it's Mont-sell-ee-ay," Mason said.

Ms. Harris tried, she really did, but after a few failed attempts, Mason gave up on correcting her. I suppressed a chuckle. He'd learn eventually.

She smacked her lips a few times and sighed. "Well ya'll, please welcome him in here and make him feel at home." She turned around in her slippers to shuffle back to her office, but I couldn't let her escape quite yet.

I raised my hand. When she didn't notice, I shouted. "Ms. Harris, have you heard from Drew or her mom?"

She looked confused, like she didn't know who I was

talking about. Drew had been in this class for almost two years now, but I still wouldn't put it past her to not be able to pick Drew out of a line-up.

"Aren't we supposed to leave here in the next few minutes?" I prompted. "She's my partner. I kind of need her or I'll have to forfeit. It's happened before, and today I'd really rather not."

"Oh dear." She put her cup down and patted her enormous, flaming red beehive hair. "If Drew doesn't come, you'll need a substitute partner, won't you?"

"Umm, yeah," I said. "Drew might more closely resemble a warm body that occasionally speaks, but I can't do *team* debate alone." I was the only successful student on our entire debate squad. I managed to pull Drew along with me well enough that we occasionally won. Last year, to everyone's absolute shock, she and I qualified for state. We even won our first two rounds there before going up against the team that eventually won the whole thing. That loss didn't hurt as badly when I saw that Reynolds and Reynolds (yes, you guessed it, a cheesy twin team) took the entire tournament.

"I'll call her mother," Ms. Harris rasped, before she turned and ducked back into her office. I texted Drew again, but she hadn't responded to my text this morning after breakfast either. I was starting to get worried. Drew's mom is a surgeon who works bizarre hours and Drew's a night owl. The combination meant that she was late a lot, but she kept her phone on high volume so messages from me would wake her up. What if she was hurt? I texted her mom and no dots showed up from her either. She was probably in surgery.

I tried not to panic about Drew since this was hardly strange for her, but this tournament was kind of a big deal to me. Every year the same schools, the ones with competent coaches and lots of smart kids, fill the majority of the slots for the state debate tournament. Last year, the qualifying list included one team from B-port for the first time in a long time, my team.

I intended to make a repeat appearance, but in order to qualify I needed twelve points in policy debate. I only had six right now for ending in second place at Alief Taylor, and making it to quarters at Clear Lake. First place at the Katy tournament would net me eight points, which would put me over by two. Of course, if Drew doesn't come with me, it won't help me much anyway. We both needed twelve points to qualify. Assuming nothing was wrong, how could she do this to me?

I cursed under my breath.

"Does your friend do this a lot?" Mason asked. "Leave you hanging?"

I felt a pang of guilt. "Not all the time," I said. "Especially not when she knows something matters to me. But she's got a tendency to forget things and sometimes she sleeps in. I just didn't expect it today."

"You do CX?" Mason asked.

Most people called it policy debate. CX stands for Cross Examination, and it's a nickname used only in debate circles. I assumed Mason signed up for the class under pressure from his mom but didn't know anything about it. Maybe my assumption was wrong. I turned to him, suddenly hopeful. "Have you debated before?"

He smiled. "No. I've observed a few rounds, you know for class at my old school."

Better than nothing, I thought. I forced my best grin. "How'd you like to compete in your first tournament?"

"Shouldn't we wait to see if Drew shows?" he asked.

I nodded my head, "Of course, but if she doesn't, would

you do it? I can do most of the heavy lifting. I can take ones or twos, I don't care."

"Ones talk fast and get a lot of stuff read into the record, right?"

I nodded again. "Right, and the twos sort of explain it and connect the dots." He looked athletic. I thought I'd try a sports metaphor, the only sport I know anything about, and that knowledge came exclusively from playing, rather poorly, on the beach on boring summer days. "It's like in volleyball, the ones set the ball, and the twos spike it over."

"I think I'd do better as a two," he said, "since I'm not an especially fast talker."

I was usually a two, since Drew couldn't see how things connected, much less explain the connections, but I could take over as a one. My diction's good, and I usually planned what we'd run anyway, so that wouldn't change.

"Could you get a field trip form signed quickly? And faxed back to the school?"

Mason laughed, almost bitterly. "My dad's at home, like always, so yeah. I should be able to get that done."

I whisper, "Although Ms. Harris isn't the most observant. You could probably forge one and be just fine, as long as your parents won't be mad if you aren't at home on time today."

"I doubt they'd even notice," he said. "Is it just one day? I thought these things lasted two."

"We have to win today to make it to Saturday. You planning to win?" I smiled.

"Heck yeah. If I do something, I'm in it to win it."

"Then yeah, we'd need to go tomorrow, too." I cocked one eyebrow. "Is that a problem?"

He shook his head. "I just got here so I have no plans. I wasn't even supposed to start classes until Monday, but the truck came early, and my parents were—let's just say I needed to get out of the house. Besides, if I stay at home tomorrow, I'll just be stuck unpacking my room."

He went to Ms. Harris' office and spoke to her. She was actually the most coherent I'd seen her in days, which was good since we were about to leave campus under her direction. She picked up her phone and made a call and a few minutes later, Mason came back and sat down by me.

"Are we good?" I asked.

Mason nodded. "My mom said my dad would come sign the form and bring me some slacks."

I hadn't even thought about clothes. "Hey, that's great." I beamed.

Mason smiled back, but he looked almost nervous. "Don't get too excited. I have no idea what I'm doing, remember?"

I pulled out my laptop and started showing him our files. "The topic this year is renewable energy."

"I knew that," he said. I must have looked surprised, because he said, "I told you I observed a few rounds."

"Okay, well most people are focusing on a particular type of renewable energy they think will solve the crisis, right? Wind, solar, nuclear, etc."

"Which one did you choose?" Mason asked.

I shook my head. "That's the thing. I tried a few, but I didn't like any of them, so I developed something a little different."

I spent the next few minutes going over my new affirmative plan, one that would likely confuse opponents and judges alike because it existed outside the normal framework. Instead of proposing a plan to save America or on the opposing side, tearing it down, my plan was, in either position, to outline an alternative. By promoting humans to look at the world in a different way, we might actually affect the change the policy topic hints at. With my case, I was really trying to change how the future policy leaders looked at the impact of human energy use. It might take a bit for the judge to get what I was saying, forget about the opponents, but once it sank in, their link arguments and Kritiks and DAs should just fall away. It would be so empowering to only have to argue one thing really well, instead of running around like a beheaded chicken with a billion DAs and Kritiks and links and topicality attacks.

Of course, I did prepare a few of those, but for the most part my plan was to focus on our strengths. I'd won the entire tournament at UT's summer camp with a partner from Grapevine, but we used a solar power plan. Which meant not even my old partner Todd would see this coming. I was hoping this plan would get me the points I needed. Drew didn't help me write it, but she knew the hopes I had for it. I was worried about her, but I was getting kind of pissed, too.

I spent the rest of first period explaining the basics of the affirmative and negative positions to Mason, which he picked up quickly. Since it was not only new but also unique and utterly unheard of, I was surprised how quickly he grasped it.

"Hey what's your schedule?" I asked.

"I have Physics next with Broussard. Then History with White, and Calculus with Grigassy, I think."

"You're kidding. I'm in all those classes." I smiled, and he smiled back.

"Great, then maybe you can help me smooth things over with them when I ditch their class on my first day here."

"I think I can swing that. They love me," I say.

"I bet they do."

The bell rang then, startling me. Ms. Harris came out of her office, a big grin on her hot pink lips. "Okay everyone who's going to the tournament needs to grab their things. We're all going down to the buses."

"Is your dad coming soon?" I asked. "We leave in like five minutes."

"He'll be here," Mason said. "You can count on it."

I was pretty nervous, despite Mason's certainty, but sure enough when we got down to the bus, a dark blue Audi was sitting in the parking lot. A tall, handsome man got out, wearing slacks and a polo shirt. I could see where Mason got his looks. His dad had dark hair too, and even though he wore sunglasses, I could tell he had the same nose, and the same light brown skin.

Mason snatched the proffered backpack from his dad's hand, not acting grateful at all, and turned away sharply. His dad stood there dazed for a moment, and then turned and went back to his car. When Mason reached the bus, top of the backpack clutched tightly in his fingers, I asked him, "Is everything okay with you and your dad?"

He nodded, but didn't offer any other explanation. I turned and waved at his dad, who smiled back at me. Then I followed Mason onto the bus and sat down next to him on a big yellow bench. Somehow, with him next to me, the bench didn't seem quite so large. After a moment, the Audi drove off and Mason seemed to breathe a big sigh of relief. The bus sat for a moment while Ms. Harris did heaven knows what. The driver finally closed the doors and the bus rumbled forward slowly. We were starting to pick up speed when I saw her, jogging toward us full tilt. The backpack straps over her shoulders bounced, and her knuckles were white where she clenched her laptop in her hands.

Drew.

Chapter Five

LACY

Drew's dark hair and cheeks flush bright red whenever she's been running, which she pretty much never does. Unless she's being chased, or she's late like today. Her dark hair was pulled up into a high ponytail, with little braids feeding into it on each side. Her eye makeup was just as severe as usual, with thick eyeliner around each eye, turning her blue eyes almost cerulean.

Normally I'd be happy to see her. Normally I'd grin and make some joke about her cutting things close, or ask her what came up this time. Her mom had never texted back, which wasn't so weird, but I'd been worried Drew was sick or hurt.

Once I realized she was fine, I wanted to yell at her and swear. The more I thought about it, the more upset I got. I already had six points with her and we'd been debating together for two years. I really should debate with her for the first time with my new plan, but now Mason and his dad had gone to great lengths to fix her mess last minute, and I didn't know what to do. And since Drew's obviously not sick and had time to do her hair, she'd been up for more than an hour. She should have texted me so I didn't worry. Careless and obnoxious.

The bus doors opened and she came flying up the stairs, her eyes searching for mine. When she saw me, she did a double take. She scowled at Mason and came to a stop in the aisle right in front of me.

"Who's that?" she asked.

I was a teensy bit relieved she didn't seem interested in him at all.

"Hey Drew." I stood up. "Drew Dunmore, this is Mason Montcellier." I intentionally mispronounced Mason's name, saying it the way Coach Harris had.

Mason smiled.

"What's so funny?" Drew asked.

"No," I said, "this is not where you get all defensive and rude. This is where you apologize to me, and maybe you say 'Nice to meet you, Mason.'"

"Nice to meet you." Drew turned to me. "Now, what was so funny?" She dropped her voice. "And who *is* this guy? I don't care about his name at all, no offense."

"None taken," Mason said from behind me. "And I don't really know what I'm doing here, if you really are the elusive Drew. Up until a few moments ago, I was filling in for you."

"What happened this morning?" I asked her. "Why were you late? It better not be what I think."

Drew looked down at the rubber-coated floor of the bus, and bit her lip. "I just slept in, okay, that's all."

I lift one eyebrow. "So you weren't online, gaming until sun-up? Chatting with your little internet friends?"

Drew sighs. "My mom was at work, and I was up late last night... finishing up a paper."

"Finishing your English paper?" I rolled my eyes. "The one you finished and handed in yesterday? This matters to me, Drew, and I figured you knew that." I lowered my voice to a whisper. "How do you think I felt sitting and waiting on you today? You're supposed to be my best friend and you didn't even text to say you were late."

"I made it here in time, didn't I?"

"Not in time, no."

I pointed to the bench next to me and Drew sat down. Her snottiness and Mason's politeness cinched it for me. "Mason, as I'm sure you've already surmised, this is the very late, and very rude Drew. She chronically shows up last minute, but she's usually not so rude when she does." I stare pointedly at Drew's flushed face, then I turn toward Mason again. "You're still filling in for her. She can't stay up half the night before her best friend's big tournament *playing video games*, forget to plug in her phone so that she doesn't see my texts, and then waltz in and think everything's fine because she managed to sprint to the bus as it was driving away."

Mason tried to stand, but he was too big to manage it very well on the inside of the bench. "I'm not trying to cause any problems. I can just head back to class. It's no big deal."

The bus lurched forward and I fell back against Mason, landing forcefully on his lap. His arms wrapped around me. "Whoa there, you okay?"

My heart sprinted faster than Drew was running for the bus moments before. I hoped my face didn't flush like hers had, too.

Drew cleared her throat. "If you've survived your terrifying near death ordeal..."

I snorted. "Obviously I'm fine." I slid off Mason's lap and back into the seat. "But we're on our way to the tournament now, and Ms. Harris already changed the roster to me and Mason." I leaned toward Drew and put my hand on the seat in front of her. "You were late, again. Today of all days, when I'm going to run my new case, the one I've been spending every waking moment on. I had no idea if you were even coming. Sometimes late isn't a big deal. Sometimes it's *too* late." I turned around and looked straight ahead at the back of the seat in front of me. I had no idea then how right I was.

"That was kind of harsh," Mason said.

"She does this all the time," I said. "She used to be the most amazing best friend anyone could have. Heck, she joined debate for me. But a few months back she got addicted to this dumb internet game, and now she stays up all night playing it. Her mom doesn't care, and the only person who even seems to be annoyed about it is me. It's our senior year, and our grades matter, and this matters." I gesture at my debate briefcase. "But she's always running late, and forgetting things. It's part of what makes her a crappy partner, actually. I'm sick of it."

"Out with the old?" Mason raised his eyebrows.

"I don't know," I said. "For all I know you might really suck."

"I doubt it," Mason said. "I'm pretty smart. I can't even think of a time I forgot to plug in my phone."

"Mental note: Mason's memory is unreliable."

He laughed. "I have an excellent memory. Let me rephrase. I've never forgotten to plug in my phone. I'm practically perfect in every way."

"And about as humble as Mary Poppins was, too."

He shook his head. "No, I don't think I've ever been called humble."

By the time we reached Katy, we had run through some possible contingencies on my new case, and I felt like Mason understood it at least as well as Drew did. It helped that I planned to use essentially the same thing for both affirmative and negative. Drew was speaking to me again when we all exited the bus, but she ignored Mason entirely as though he wasn't even present. We walked to the cafeteria in a bunch, finding a clear spot on one of the long, graffiti covered tables. I sat next to Mason, and Drew took a seat on the opposite side of the table. She pointedly never looked at him, as though she forgave me because she was complicit in my decision, but she'd never forgive Mason for being new and helpful. It was better than her being rude to him, I supposed. Or flirting with him. The thought sent a dagger to my heart.

"Should I be worried?" Mason whispered, bobbing his head toward Drew.

"I think you could take her," I said.

"I would never, ever hit a girl." Mason arched one eyebrow. "My dad would kill me, so it wouldn't matter whether I won or not. But that's not what I was asking. I meant, do you think if she ignores me long enough, I might really disappear?"

I shouldn't have laughed, because I love Drew and I knew she was upset, but she was acting like a baby. If she couldn't give Knight Fort a break on the night before our big tournament, then she could suffer the consequences. This time I raised my voice so she could hear me clearly. "You're going to be fine. Her mock displeasure won't make you disappear. She obviously has some issues with managing her disappointment in a constructive manner."

"Obviously."

Drew rolled her eyes so hard I worried they'd get stuck up inside her eye socket.

Coach Harris handed us the list with team match ups. I was surprised to see Katy had already updated our team on the paperwork. We were listed as Shelton-Montcellier. It always made me happy to see my dad's name on paper. My parents were both only children, so they decided to keep their names when they got married. I was the first born, so I took my dad's name, Shelton. Hope got my mom's last name, Vincent.

It's kind of funny, because apparently I look and act just like my mom, and everyone says Hope is just like my dad, so I guess they named us wrong. Hope's stunningly beautiful, so I guess I got the short end of the stick there. At least I got something of my dad's, even it was only his name. Mom's brilliant and everyone says I got her brains, so it's not all bad.

I tried not to feel guilty about Drew when we walked past her on the way to our first round. It wasn't like she had nothing going on. She had Extemporaneous to do, even though she wasn't debating. Her eyes followed me out the room and I tried to hang on to my righteous indignation over her lack of care for me and what mattered in my life. Anger felt better than guilt.

When we reached the room, my stomach fell. I should've recognized the names, but in my defense, there are a lot of Millers out there and he's changed partners again. Todd Miller, my partner from UT's summer camp, looked up at me when we walked in. He looked about the same as he always had. His hair was still parted on the side, with about a bucket of gel holding it in place. His enormous white teeth would have been more at home on a sportscaster, but he flashed me an enormous smile with them, completely un-self-conscious about their size. I wish heartily that I hadn't ever kissed him, but I couldn't change that now.

"Hey, Todd," I said. "This is my new partner, Mason. Mason, meet Todd Miller. We were partners at debate camp in Austin this summer."

Todd crossed the room and held out his pale white

hand. Mason started to hold his out as though Todd meant to shake. I shifted in between them and placed a flash drive in Todd's hand before he noticed. He handed me his with a sideways glance at Mason and I knew he realized my partner was completely green. I tried not to care.

I uploaded their files into my computer so I could follow his arguments without trying to make sense of his unintelligible slurring. Todd took a step over to Mason and held out his hand again with a half smile, this time intending to shake. I shuddered to remember how his hand felt in mine, like a dead fish lying in my palm, cold and clammy and deathly still.

Mason turned back to me and tilted his head to the side questioningly, as if to say, 'what the heck?'

"We won the summer tournament together."

"We expected great things from you after this summer," Todd said. "But so far I'd say Angela and I have a slightly better record."

I frowned. He and Angela hadn't debated together before. Which was his insult, I guess.

Todd and Frank had won almost every tournament they attended in the past four months, using the solar plan Todd and I wrote together. I wonder what happened with them? I wanted to ask, but I didn't want to make him any worse than he was naturally inclined to be, since it would be Mason's first tournament.

"You may be wondering why I'm not with Frank."

I shake my head. "I don't care actually."

Todd went on, undeterred by my feigned lack of inter-est. "We had an undefeated record, after all."

"I think I heard that." I frown.

"We figured we'd help some other people qualify for state since we were already qualified together."

My stomach twisted in knots and I wanted to smack

Todd in his big horse teeth. I should be happy for him. We should be friends. But it was hard to be nice to someone who stole your case after you wrote it and lied to everyone he encountered about it. I wanted to beat him so badly, but with a brand new partner, odds weren't good.

"The thing about records," Mason said with a grin, " is that they're always getting broken."

Todd's mouth dropped open and I barked a laugh. At least Mason didn't seem intimidated. Before Todd could say anything back, the judge walked in, and we all took our seats at our respective tables.

Our judge was tall and almost painfully thin. He wore an expensive suit. He glanced briefly at both teams before he spoke. "My name is Anders Langston. I'm a senior associate at a law firm in town, Fulbright and Jaworski, and I debated in high school at Clear Lake before I went on to debate in college. To give you a little input," he pulled out a large yellow legal pad, "I believe in flowing. I know it's old school now, but there's no better way to follow an argument than here on paper, with little lines connecting the arguments, and if I can't understand you, then you don't get anywhere with me. I won't let you send me all your data files, because I want to listen to how you present the arguments, not spend my time trying to read through your research. I care less about your preparation before the round, and more about how well you can formulate an argument. As far as my paradigm goes, I'd say I'm a games player. I look at this whole thing as an exercise. I expect you to really think, to wow me, and to bring things together cleanly and efficiently. I'm a lawyer in that way, and I want you to lead me like you would a jury."

I nodded. I had flowed for an entire year on paper before figuring out the software that did the same thing. I didn't bother pointing out that you can do it all faster on the laptop, even without flashing the quotes. Old school was okay with me.

"Do you mind spreading?" Todd asked.

"I don't care whether you speak quickly because I understand the desire to get more information out there, and to have a rigorous debate, but I will yell 'clear' if I can't understand what you're saying. I don't give you credit for telling me something if I can't comprehend what you're saying. Sometimes you kids lose sight of the goal. You're supposed to be preparing for the real world. It's good to think fast, but just talking fast for the sake of saying more is pointless."

We all nodded, and I grabbed my iPad and stood up to read our case. Todd was surprised to see me standing up as a one. I'd been a two for years now, and I was a two at camp over the summer with him. I was pretty good at wrapping things up, but I can also talk really fast, more than three hundred words a minute at high clarity. Not that I need to with my case. In fact, although I still had to read quickly, my case was intentionally short enough that the people listening could process what I was saying. I suppressed a smile when Todd leaned over to whisper in Angela's ear. Todd might already have qualified, but he didn't write the case he won with and he hasn't had an original thought in years.

The judge seemed pretty open to my ideas, nodding along whenever I looked up at him. In my experience, there aren't many new ideas in the policy debate realm. When you find a relatively unique one, people either love it or they hate it. I did bring a copy of our old solar panel plan, for when I met a particularly rigid judge, but I'm glad I didn't pull it out for Mr. Langston.

When I finished, Angela asked me my cross-examination questions while Todd prepared for his first constructive round, which would form the crux of their negative attack. Most of Angela's questions dealt with topicality at first, but once she realized we were squarely arguing about how we as debaters could literally impact the future policy with our plan, she dropped that line. Her last question was the only really good one, but I had a response.

"You're saying that your entire plan centers on this one debate round?" Angela asks.

I nod.

"So, and correct me if I'm wrong, you don't have a proposal for the government to enact. Your entire plan is to come to these tournaments, and explain to the humans present that looking at the world as a good that we can consume is what caused this mess? And somehow, that will solve the energy crisis?"

I smiled. "You hit the nail right on the head. I see where you're going. The glamour of passing sweeping legislation about solar panels, for instance, is pretty sexy. But when you get right down to it, we're high school students. We might one day become important, like our judge here already is, or maybe we will become world leaders even, but for today, we have absolutely no say in what happens in the world government. What we do control is how we as students, and others here involved in this activity including our judge, view the world. So unlike all the other plans out there, our plan *actually impacts real world policy*, not some pie in the sky dream of the federal government passing a coherent plan without a million special interest riders."

Angela laughed. "So you expose, what? A few dozen people at most to this notion-"

"I'm sorry to interrupt," I said, "but that's just wrong. I flashed you the plan a few moments before this began, which means every student at Grapevine will have this case in a matter of hours. When you take it back, you'll likely email it to everyone you're friends with in the debate world. They'll upload it to the open evidence project to make sure everyone is ready for this in the future, and voila, massive exposure. Hundreds, if not thousands of people."

"So after just one round, your entire plan is destroyed? You've done all you can do?" Angela smirked.

Mr. Langston called, "Time, but you may answer the question."

"Of course not," I said. "The only thing that will make people study it, consider it, and really change their minds is when we *win*. Round after round, debate after debate. In that regard, my plan gains increasing significance with every single round, and every single win."

I smiled and sat back down. Mason whispered in my ear, "Wow girl, you were really great up there."

"You starting to get the picture?" I asked him.

He nodded.

While Todd outlined his defense, focusing pretty heavily on the traditional stock issues, I watched Mason taking notes. He used a yellow pad since he hadn't brought a laptop, but he kept up pretty well. I handled the cross-examination questions, but I noticed while I did that Mason was preparing for his speech. When I wrapped up my questions, we took three minutes of our eight minutes of preparation time to review what he intended to say. His responses were already pretty well formed.

To say Mason did better than Drew ever had was the understatement of the year. He fumbled around a little bit near the beginning, but once he found his stride, there was no stopping him. He shored up our arguments on topicality, and used an analogy I'd never thought to make, comparing our case to lighting candles across America, while the other cases were like politicians, all talk and no action. I can't remember exactly how he said it, but it made the judge laugh and that's never a bad thing.

Todd managed to confuse Mason on cross, and we took a step or two back, but it was nothing I couldn't repair during my rebuttal. He did have one great comeback, though.

Todd asked him, "If part of your whole point is really that we should value animals as much as or even more than people, does that mean we shouldn't what, shoot a bear if it's attacking us? Wouldn't you?"

Mason got a strange look on his face and said, "For there is no folly of the beast of the earth that is not infinitely outdone by the madness of men."

"What does that even mean?" Todd asked.

"I'm just saying that for every bear that has killed a human, humans have killed a hundred, or maybe a thousand bears. Before we get up in arms about how we can't defend ourselves under this view, think about how much harm humans have done, believing they're the end all, be all in the world."

When he sat down, I asked, "Where did that quote come from?"

Mason shrugged. "It seemed to fit."

"A fan of Melville, huh?"

Mason's head whipped around. "Are you?"

I just smiled. He might have been the hottest guy I knew, and he was shaping up to be the smartest, too. A dangerous combination.

During his rebuttal at the podium, Mason did even better. He slowed down from the pace of everyone else, and really spoke to the judge. He didn't look at his paper more than once. I may never forget his closing line.

"While I may never completely abandon my anthro-pocentric view of the world, after all, I'm a mighty fine man and I appreciate that, studying the idea that the world revolves around other creatures in their spheres, and recognizing that we share this big rock we live on has helped me want to do better myself. It even made me look into the state subsidies for solar, and I plan to talk to my parents about choosing an electric plan that offers a higher percentage of renewable energy for the same price. It's not much, but it's a start. The best way to change our anthropocentric view is by shifting one small thing at a time. I hope you'll join with me and help us turn these candles into an inferno, one that might affect real change here on the planet we live on." He threw a fist in the air and shouted, "Vote affirmative and save the whales!"

I couldn't help it. He was so exuberant and he tried so hard. I laughed. Mr. Langston did, too.

I wasn't surprised half an hour later when I got our copy of the judge's ballot reflecting that we won. He awarded Mason and I both perfect speaker points, an even thirty apiece. Mason and I were both pretty pumped, and Ms. Harris wasn't too drunk yet, so she knew why we were cheering and shouted and jumped around with us. She sat down and went over the notes with us. She even shared a helpful tip I used in the next round. I could only imagine what a great coach she could've been if she'd have been able to kick the drinking habit.

The next team was a pair of novices who shouldn't have even been in the varsity circuit. They started to cry after we finished our counterplan. Mason argued the anti-anthropocentrism case better every time, and I started throwing in a few topicality attacks and a kritik or two that didn't conflict with our counterplan. By the time our last round ended, Drew's mom had come to pick her up and she was already gone. Mason and I advanced to the second day undefeated.

Mason showed up on Saturday morning in an amazing tan colored suit. He brought a laptop with him this time, with the proper software downloaded and prepared. I was surprised when we took first place late Saturday night after a very grueling final round against a team that went to semi-finals in state last year.

Mason was as giddy as a schoolboy when we found out we had won. He had taken off his suit jacket and loosened his tie while we waited. He fiddled with his tie nervously. When the ballot came, awarding us both perfect speaker points again, he tossed me up in the air like I weighed nothing, and then caught me and swung me around. He set me down and I hugged him. I was looking around his shoulder when I saw Drew in the corner of the room. She looked at me with a look I'd never seen from her before, and I thought I'd seen every face Drew had ever made five thousand times. I pulled away from Mason, but before I even took a step toward her, she turned and left.

"Mason, I'll meet you at the awards in a minute. Drew just left, and I want to make sure she's okay."

I took off after her, but by the time I got out of the auditorium, she was already gone. I checked each of the rooms closest to us without luck. When I glanced at my watch, I realized I'd looked for her for almost twenty minutes without success. I was about to give up and head back for the awards when I heard voices. One of the doors to the back parking lot had been propped open and cold air rushed inside.

Drew was sitting next to an idiotic rich kid from our school, one I didn't know very well, but I knew he wasn't on the debate team. He was wearing dark jeans and a Metallica t-shirt, but otherwise I had no idea what Drew might like about him. He had his dark hair all gelled up, and when he glanced up at me, I saw that he had the rich guy smirk down perfectly. They were leaned together, and as I walked up, I remembered where I'd seen him. His friends called this guy Juan, and when I asked Hope why, since he clearly wasn't Hispanic in any way, she told me it was because he always had a joint. Juan, for Mari*juana*.

"Seriously?" I asked. "You stay up all night and show up late. Then you sulk all weekend, and when Mason and I win first place, you bring Juan to the debate tournament? What is wrong with you?"

Drew sat up when she heard me and placed both hands palm down against the tile. "What's wrong with me? I'm supposed to be your best friend. I run a little late, and you replace me?"

I spluttered. "I didn't replace you, I found a last minute sub. But now that you mention it, maybe I should."

Drew scrambled to her feet. Her pinstriped pantsuit was rumpled, but her white shirt and suspenders looked clean, at least. "I changed my entire schedule to be your partner because you had no one else."

I lowered my voice. "I know you did. I'm sorry. I don't want to fight with you. I came out here to see where you went and make sure you were okay. I guess I was just surprised you were out here with Juan." I tossed my head toward him.

"His name's Jack," Drew said. "And he's a friend."

She had been sitting awfully close to him for a friend. "Whatever you say."

"I appreciate you checking on me," Drew said, slumping back down to the ground next to Jack, "but you better get back to your boyfriend. We wouldn't want to make him anxious waiting for you. He might replace you with some random girl he's never talked to before."

I blushed but it was dark, so I doubted anyone could tell. "He's not my boyfriend. And we hadn't just met. He was a new student who had observed several rounds in the past. I tried calling you and texting you, I don't know how many times, before I even talked to him."

Drew exhaled and slumped against Jack's shoulder. "I don't even care, okay? Whatever."

She was making me out to be the villain, and it wasn't fair. She'd actually missed two different tournaments without telling me. I had to just forfeit the first round. And she'd been late too many times to count. "You're always so irresponsible," I said, "and you just expect me to be grateful because you did me this favor. You joined the team. Well, I'm not going to keep doing that. Maybe the reason you suck so badly is because you never even try. If you want to be my partner, you'll have to try harder and actually show up."

Drew's mouth twisted and she lifted one carefully plucked and dramatically shadowed eye sharply. "You're not the only person dealing with stuff, Lacy. You just don't notice anyone but yourself."

Her words stung like a slap in the face and I blinked back tears. I wish I could say I thought about what she said and paid more attention to her life, dug into her problems. I wish I could say I wasn't selfish and I took her words as a cry for help.

But that would be a lie.

I think I was embarrassed and angry and maybe a little guilty for good measure. I don't know what I would have said if my phone hadn't binged right then. But I looked down at the screen in relief and saw a text from my mom.

I'M HERE. YOU COMING? I WANT TO MEET YOUR NEW PARTNER.

I glanced up at Drew, cozied up to the biggest idiot at our school, and a rumored druggie too.

"I want to hear about your life too, but I don't have

time right this very second because I spent the last twenty minutes checking every room in this school to find you." I huffed. "My mom's here because she's hoping to see me get a big old trophy. Something I figured my best friend might want to cheer about. I guess I was wrong."

"We should both be getting that trophy." Drew folded her arms.

"You only signed up for debate because I couldn't find someone better. You hated every round! Just come with me to the awards ceremony, please?" It took every bit of my self-control not to glare at stupid Jack.

She shook her head and her new friend smirked at me.

I threw my hands up in the air. "Fine, you know what, stay here."

In spite of my words, I stared at her for a moment to see if she'd get up and come with me. She didn't. My mom texted again. IT'S STARTING IN FIVE. WHERE ARE YOU?

I turned and walked away, looking back over my shoulder a few times, but never turning around, never apologizing. Drew never even looked up to meet my eye.

By the time I reached the cafeteria, Mason was surrounded. A girl we beat in the semi-finals sat on his right, chatting like they were old friends. On his left, Kelly Willis from our team kept giggling and touching his arm. He caught my eye and gave me a look that pleaded with me.

And if that wasn't enough, he mouthed the words, "Save me."

Of course I promptly walked right past him and sat by my mom, grinning ear to ear.

"Where's Hope?" I asked.

"She's spending the night at Gwen's house. She said

she's very proud of you, but she can't withdraw your teammates."

I raised my eyebrows. "Withdraw?"

My mom laughed. "I think she meant withstand. But it was so classically Hope I decided to quote her exactly."

The corner of my mouth turned up into a half grin. When Hope came to my award ceremonies she was treated sort of like a celebrity, but that much adoration could get a little scary as Mason was learning firsthand. I didn't mention that I was a little relieved. I wasn't ready to have him meet her yet anyway.

"You won sweetheart, right?" my mom asked. "That gives you how many points now?"

I shrugged nonchalantly and said, "Twelve."

"Doesn't that mean you're qualified?" she asked. "You're going to TFA state again this year?"

I shook my head. "I need a *partnership* with twelve. So far, I have fourteen, but six are with Drew and eight are with Mason."

My mom pursed her lips. "I hope you can get another four with Mason then. Or are you going to debate with Drew again?"

I thought about Drew and how hard it was to debate with her, how impossible it was to even talk to her right now. Things were so easy with Mason and so natural. And he had so much raw talent. "I think I'll stick with Mason, but..."

My mom's eyes told me she understood. "Drew must be pretty disappointed. She's never missed an awards ceremony. Where is she now?"

I sighed. If I told my mom Drew had ditched the debate awards to hang out with a spoiled rich drug dealer from school, Mom would call Drew's dad so fast that watching her pull out her phone would give me whiplash. I might be mad at Drew for ditching me and being so rude, but I couldn't bail on her, chew her out, and rat her out in the same day. "She left right after we found out we won."

"She's not taking the bus back?" Mom narrows her eyes at me, clearly combining her engineering analysis capabilities with her motherly intuition to sniff out my weak cover lie.

I wanted to give more details, but I'd learned the hard way that the more I talk, the more she uncovers. I shook my head.

My mom pointed. "Is that Mason right there?"

Mason saw her and waved, like a drowning man lunging for a floatie. When she waved back, he snatched the opportunity to stand up and make his excuses. He walked over to where we were sitting and pulled up a chair on my left side. Before he sat down, he held out his hand. "I'm Mason Montcellier. Nice to meet you."

"I'm Angelica's mom."

He put his hand down in mock confusion. "Wait, who's Angelica?" He turned to me. "I thought your name was Lacy."

My mom tuts. "No, not really. Lacy's only a nickname. Her father wanted us to name her Lacy, and he insisted on calling her that. The nickname kind of stuck. She's always gone by that, but I insist on calling her by her given name. It's so much more elegant, don't you think?"

Mason nodded. "I do. Angelica sounds much more sophisticated."

My mom gave me a pointed look. "See? Someone gets it." She turned back to Mason and practically purred. My mom liked to be right. "Nice to meet you, Mason. I hear you're quite the debater. It's great for my daughter to finally have a partner equal to her in skill."

Mason leaned forward, his elbows on his knees so he

could see my mom around me. "I wouldn't say I'm equal to her skill, but she dragged me along with grace."

The Katy Coach stood up on stage and started to announce the awards. There aren't ever very many kids who have hung around for the final awards ceremony at the end of a long two-day tournament. You're usually cheered on by the other students who are receiving awards. And maybe a handful of kids who came by bus from another city and are consequently too far to drive back home themselves. Tonight was no different, but it felt good, really good, to walk up to the stage and take a big old first place trophy. After the awards had all been handed out, Coach Whitrock surprised me by calling us both back up.

"This doesn't happen often, ladies and gentlemen, but I'm going to invite our first place winners back up to the stage, because we have another award for them. Both of them. As you know, we offer five speaker awards for policy debate. Tonight, whether we dropped the high and low speaker scores or not, two debaters still tied for first place. They just so happen to be teammates. Please hold your applause until the end, in the interest of time, but I'd like to congratulate Mason Montcellier and Lacy Shelton on their first place win. You are tied for best speaker in the policy debate arena."

He handed us two trophies and then said, "I know this is a first and second place trophy, but we didn't anticipate a tie. You two can duke it out when you get to your bus to determine who takes which trophy home."

When we reached the seats next to my mom again, the awards concluded, I tried to give the first place trophy to Mason. "It's your first tournament. You have to take it home."

"It's yours," he said. "You earned it. The only reason I

even had anything to say was because of your hard work crafting the unique plan, and your excellent explanations."

I stood up and shook my head, leaving the trophy on the seat.

"Oh come on," Mason whined. "Just take it."

My mom picked it up. "Well if neither of you want it, I'll take it." She sounded exasperated, but she was smiling.

Before we could argue further, our first judge walked up to us. I had no idea any of the judges who weren't coaches had stuck around. He held his hand out to me and I took it.

"Mr. Langston, right?" I asked.

He nodded before he shook Mason's hand. "I wanted to say congratulations to the two of you. Did I hear the rumors right?"

"What rumors?" I asked.

He stared Mason in the eye. "Was this your first time debating? I saw your very first round?"

Mason grinned. "I was just explaining that Lacy's an excellent teacher."

Mr. Langston whistled. "You better not give up after this tournament. I didn't mention this earlier, but the college I debated for was Yale." He turned so that we could both see his face. "My good friend and former team captain is their recruiter now, and he was lamenting the sorry group of debaters they wound up with this year. He's looking to aggressively recruit some new blood for next year's team. I'd love to send him your information. I bet he'd like to come out and watch the two of you debate, if you're interested."

Uh, heck yeah I was interested. I hastily scribbled down my information and then Mason did, too. After that we had to rush to catch the bus. I could've gone home with my mom, but Mason was riding the bus, and I wasn't ready to say goodbye yet. My mom widened her eyes at me knowingly when I told her my bag was on the bus already.

But also, I wanted to check on Drew. I told my mom she wasn't riding the bus so Mom wouldn't press me about where she was, but I thought she'd be there.

Only when the bus pulled out, she wasn't on it. I texted her. WHERE ARE YOU?

She texted back right away. JACK'S TAKING ME HOME.

I sighed. PLEASE BE SAFE. I DON'T WANT YOU TO DIE WHILE WE'RE FIGHTING.

She texted back. WHATEVER, I'M OVER IT.

I gritted my teeth, but everything I thought to say back seemed like it would just make things worse, so I finally put my phone away.

I fell asleep on Mason's shoulder on the way home. I was horrified when I realized upon waking that I'd drooled. I wiped it away quickly and hoped he didn't notice. If he did, he didn't say anything about it. He just gave me a hug goodnight and headed for his dad's car. I walked to my mom's, thinking I'd never had such a great weekend in my life.

—————

I stand up and pass the pages to Dr. Brasher, massaging my cramping hand as I do. I doubt I've ever physically written that many words in my life. He takes his time reading them, and he doesn't offer me a Chick Lit novel, or an iPad, or anything to look at while he does. I sit down on the chaise lounge while he reads and lean backward, closing my eyes. It's not bad in here when no one is pelting you with questions. My reprieve ends too soon.

"What you wrote was fine, but I don't see any problems

in any of this," he says. "I thought you were starting with the root of the problem. At some point we'll need to talk about why she died, and your perceived role in that."

"You don't see a problem in those pages?" I ask, wondering again at his intelligence.

"You mention Drew briefly, and this Jack person, but other than that, no, I don't see any problems."

I sigh. "I didn't see a problem yet either, Dr. Brasher, and let me tell you, that's how the worst ones creep up. It's the problems you don't see that whack you right between the eyes."

Chapter Six

HOPE

Dear Diary:

It's the second Monday since winter break, which means I got my report card today. This might not sound so great to you, but I'm delighted. Straight Cs, which means not a single D!! My mom won't be as happy as me, but then what's new? We can't all be Lacy.

Sometimes I think they should have named me after my dad instead of her. Lacy got his name, but from what Mom says I'm the one who's just like him. I wish he hadn't died in that car crash. It would've been nice not to be the odd one out in our family all the time. Mom's a genius just like Lacy. With Dad gone, I'm the only dumb one. Half the time I have no idea what they're talking about.

Getting my report card wasn't the only good thing that happened in first period. Today has been completely awesome in every way. I usually hate starting the day with science, but Mr. Archer was out sick and the substitute in Physics just turned on this old movie, *Ferris Bueller's Day Off*. In some crazy twist of luck, my health teacher had a family emergency. I guess that sounds kind of bad as I write it. It wasn't lucky for him obviously, but we ended up watching another old movie, *What About Bob*, which I loved so much. All in all, eligibility across the board, plus the first half of two different old movies instead of boring class equals a great day for me.

I was in an awesome mood already when I walked out to the natatorium. We're pretty lucky for a crappy old school. We have a natatorium right next to our stadium, and it's actually pretty nice. There's a diving area for the team we currently don't have a coach for, and a ten lane Olympic sized pool. We share it with Brazoswood High School and they have a lot of jerks on their team, but that still gives us five practice lanes each day and we have all ten for half an hour or so, until their team arrives by bus.

When I walked in the door to the natatorium, Dave, who had been a big baby since I broke up with him, was yelling at Coach. You said I needed to describe stuff better, and I noticed his nostrils were like really big and his face was all red.

"That teacher is out to get me. It has nothing to do with my work and everything to do with-"

Dave stopped talking when he saw me and grabbed his bag. He stormed past me, glaring the entire time.

The words just shot out of my mouth. "What's your problem?"

He didn't even pause, much less stop to answer me.

As he left, other members of the team began trickling in. I walked over to Coach and asked, "What was that about?"

"Dave's failing English."

I should've felt bad, and I kind of did. That could've been me. I only got a 71 in English. And also, Dave's one of our best swimmers, his sorry performance last week notwithstanding. So that sucked, but I was also kind of relieved. Maybe by the time he got his grades back up, he'd be over his sulking about our break up. We weren't even really together before anyway. We'd just sort of been hanging out a lot, and then that kind of changed to making out. We hadn't had a discussion about it before he started throwing around words like boyfriend at last Wednesday's meet.

"That's too bad," I said.

Coach shrugged. "It means we have a Team Captain position open."

Just then, someone I had been thinking about non-stop strolled through the doors from the boy's changing room. Broad shoulders, dark hair, light eyes, dark skin. My mind went blank.

"Hope?"

I turned back to face Coach Collins. "Yeah?"

He grinned when he said, "Any ideas who might fill that spot?"

I didn't want to, but I felt obligated to defend Dave at least a little. "He goes ineligible for one quarter and you give him the boot? Maybe we could just choose a temporary captain. A substitute until Dave gets his grades up."

Moby grinned. "Did someone say they were looking for a new captain?"

I kept my face serious. I couldn't let him know I had been thinking about him daily. "We might be considering options for a fill-in."

Coach Collins ignored me. "You up for it? Want to be the new co-captain, Moby?"

Moby said, "Hell to the yeah," and then dove into the water. He swam an easy fifty fly while I rolled my eyes and walked to the girls' locker room to change.

"Temporary," I yelled to Coach before I ducked into the locker room.

I barely heard him respond. "We'll see."

I didn't know why I was trying to stand up for Dave, except that it seemed like the right thing to do. Or maybe I want to show Moby that I'm not sold on him so he stays interested. Honestly though, we don't even know anything about Moby, so we had no idea what kind of captain he'd make. Coach shouldn't be so giddy to name him on his first day.

While I changed, I admitted to myself that I was excited. My heart had begun beating faster the second Moby walked in the door. I knew he was coming, but not when he'd show up. I had no idea he'd be here today, or that we'd be working together to train and run the team.

When I went back out for practice, Coach set the team to do a dozen freestyle sprints, but asked Moby and me to come talk to him first.

"I'm going to leave Hope in charge of the sprinters," he said. "Moby, can you take over Dave's job and train the distance swimmers?"

Moby nodded, surprisingly serious now that we were discussing the nitty gritty details. He continued to be focused and stay on track for the rest of practice, but I caught him looking at me several times. Each time he just smiled and shrugged. It occurred to me that I only caught him staring because I was turning to steal a glance at him. He didn't seem super smart, but he'd probably worked out that much. So much for my plan to play hard to get.

Me and my three lanes of sprinters finished first, and I lifted my hand to him as we left the pool. He pulled up at the edge and waved me over, forcing the other swimmers to do kick turns on the far left of the lane.

"Yeah?" I walked over to him, but lifted my eyebrow so he'd know I was annoyed about being summoned.

"Can you wait around until we're done?" he asked. "I wanted to go over some stuff with you."

"Captain stuff?"

He shrugged.

I rolled my eyes. "Fine, I'll hang around a few minutes, but hurry up."

"You can't rush perfection." He winked and dove back in the water.

I went to the changing room and took a quick shower. I figured I had time. And if I ran a comb through my hair and swiped on some mascara before I went out, well, you would've done the same thing Mrs. Littleton, I swear it's true. I saw him the second I came out of the locker room, lounging in a chair by the pool.

"Your tan won't last very long in here," I said.

He sits up straight and looks at my arms pointedly. "You're tan."

"That's because I live on the beach."

"You do?" he asked.

"Yep. My mom works for Dow Chemical. She took the job when I was a baby, because she wanted to live somewhere she could afford a beach house. She said the waves and sun make her happy. Which is kind of funny, because she like never ever gets in the water."

"You live in Surfside, then?"

"Yep." I glanced at the chair next to him, but pointedly didn't sit. "So what did you want?"

"I'm in Surfside, too," he said. "And other pleasantries, blah, blah, blah." He stretches. "Isn't this where you're supposed to welcome me to the team?"

I suppressed a smile and didn't even glance at his perfectly sculpted abs. Well, maybe a little bit, but he didn't notice it. "Welcome to the team."

I checked out the oversized clock on the wall. It was

almost five-thirty, and my mom was a nut about eating at six. Cs might be great in my book, but I didn't want to be late on the same day Mom was going to compare my Cs in basic classes to Lacy's straight As in all AP classes.

I cleared my throat. "I need to get home, okay. My mom expects me for dinner, so let's talk about whatever it is we need to talk about so I can go."

"Geez," he said. "You're kind of a drag, huh? Course, I'd be a drag too if my boyfriend was failing out and had to be replaced."

"He's not my boyfriend. It's debatable whether he ever really was, but we broke up last week."

"Uh oh, lover boy's bitter." He raises one eyebrow. "Should I watch my back?"

"I'm here because you said you wanted to talk to me." I put my hand on my hip. "What do you want?"

"A date, mermaid. I wanted to ask you out."

I wanted to grin ear to ear, but I forced a frown instead. "That's not captain stuff. I waited around because I thought you wanted to talk about the team."

"The team is a team. We can give them sprints, dry land exercises, and work on sculling, but it's not going to make a very big difference. One of the reasons I love swimming is that ultimately it's an individual sport. You don't need to rely on anyone else, and no one can really let you down."

"What about relays?"

He shrugs. "I do one or two relays because Coach always badgers me to pull the other guys along. I can usually yank the whole group into first place, but what I love are my individual events. That's where I shine. I refuse to stress about the rest."

"You aren't upset about leaving Friendswood and coming here? We're smaller and don't have the perfect track record they do."

"It's swimming, not track."

"Funny," I said. "You know what I mean. We don't win as much."

He shrugged. "Like I said, I'm not much of a team player."

"Wow, we're lucky to have you as our new team captain, huh?" I stood up. "I'll see you tomorrow."

"Is that a no to the date, then?"

I arched one eyebrow. "Actually, I didn't answer at all."

He stood up and took a step toward me. "You have dinner with your family tonight I guess, so how about we go out tomorrow?"

I shook my head. "I can't. I go out with my mom and sister for dinner every Tuesday night. It's like, a thing we do."

"I like going out."

"We don't bring other people along."

"Why not?" he asked. "Moms love me, I swear."

"But not sisters?" I asked.

He smirked. "Actually, sisters usually like me too much."

I rolled my eyes. "You don't give up."

"Nope, I don't. So what time tomorrow? Should I come hungry?"

"I'll ask tonight," I said. "That's all I can promise."

He nodded. "I'll take it. Let me know tomorrow. And you'll have to give me an address, too."

"I'll let you know," I said. I wanted to say yes, but there's a way this stuff has to be done or the guys lose interest. Usually I didn't care much, but this time maybe I cared too much, so I had to stick with what always worked.

I started to walk out to the parking lot, and he grabbed his bag and followed me.

"Don't you need to go change?" I asked him.

He pulled a shirt out of his bag, and pulled it over his head. "There. Changed."

Guys are so strange. "Well, thanks for walking me out to the parking lot, I guess."

"Are you going to have to wait for a ride?" he asked.

I shrugged. "I'm not sure. Sometimes my sister finds a ride and leaves me the car, and sometimes she comes back and picks me up."

"What about keys?"

I pulled a key from my bag. "Our car's old. We can make as many copies of the key as we want. We both have one."

By that time, I could see our old blue Thunderbird, battered, but parked in our normal spot. Lacy must've found a ride. "Well, thanks for seeing me here safely, but my chariot awaits."

I fumbled with the key for a second, but eventually I got the lock turned. I opened the heavy door, climbed into the car and tossed my bag over the seat. I closed the door with a noisy thud and waved. Mason just stood there and watched as I got the car started, put it in reverse, and drove away.

It didn't occur to me until I was home that I ought to have asked whether he needed a ride.

As I pulled into the driveway, I saw my mom's face in the window. When I saw her lopsided grin, I breathed a sigh of relief. She waved at me cheerily and I waved back. Mom's not always feeling so hot, but on days when she's smiling, life is brighter. I jogged inside just in time. Mom had dinner on the table, and Lacy was already there, perfect and pristine as always, putting silverware on the table.

"How was practice?" she asked me.

"Good. Great actually." I walked across the family room and ducked into our tiny laundry room. I blobbed my duffel down and went back to be social, as my mom liked to say. I plopped down on the couch with a sigh. I texted a few people on my phone, including my best friend Gwen. She couldn't believe Moby was finally here, and Dave was ineligible.

"What do you want to drink?" Lacy asked.

"Water's fine, but I'll get it myself." I tossed my phone onto the end table and hopped up.

"Dinner's ready." Mom said. "Hope you're hungry."

"Hope is always hungry," Lacy said with a smirk. She was taking an apron off when I went back into the kitchen. That was pretty normal, actually. She probably made most of dinner too. She and my mom were like two peas in a pod, and Lacy wasn't even a suck up. She was just always doing extra stuff without even being asked for no reason other than she wanted to be helpful. She'd like, pick up and wash my clothes and Mom's too. Wipe off the counters. Take out the trash. No wonder Mom loved her more than me.

Honestly, Lacy made me feel like a real slacker sometimes. And kind of like the one person who doesn't belong. Especially when Mom and Lacy would do things together, like making dinner, or working on complicated school projects for Lacy's AP classes.

My class projects are more like, put some baking soda in a dirt volcano, or whatever. Mom and Lacy would always get matching glassy-eyed looks on their faces when I tried to talk to them about my stuff, so I sort of stopped. If only my dad hadn't died, maybe I'd fit in somewhere too.

We all sat down, and my mom repeated the same prayer she always did.

"Lord, bless this house and all of us in it. Keep us safe and bring us all home. Bless Harry to know we love him up in heaven, and bless this food. Thank you, Lord. Amen."

Usually we all scooped our own food, but tonight it was different. Lacy stood up like a waitress at a restaurant, scooping food for me with a dreamy, beamy look. She kept smiling as she handed me the rolls, and then put a pat of butter right on my plate. I couldn't tell if she was like, super happy, or if she could just sense that I had a great day and she wanted it to continue. Sometimes Lacy's like that, just super nice and excited. When Mom passed me the green beans, I scooped my own and then put some on Lacy's plate, too.

"Thanks." Lacy's smile made her eyes kind of squinty.

Her mood was so contagious that I could feel the corners of my own mouth lifting.

"Why are *you* so happy today?" she asked me.

"Why are you?" I lifted one eyebrow.

"You first," she said.

"Okay, I met someone. Someone new."

"New?" Lacy looked down at her plate and fiddled with her napkin. "What happened to Dave? Good looking, talented, funny Dave? I liked him. I thought you liked him."

I drop my fork and it clatters against the edge of my plate. "You hated Dave. You called him an 'over-inflated burp of an ego', and I know that's what you said because I had to think about it for a minute before it made any sense." I pick my fork back up. "Besides, Dave wasn't even my boyfriend, not really."

"Wasn't he?" Mom raised her eyebrows and exchanged a glance with Lacy that made my hand ball my napkin into a wad.

"No. He wasn't." I was sick of everyone asking about it. "But that's over anyway."

"Onward and upward I guess," Lacy said. "Who's the new guy?" She jabbed at her green beans with her fork, quickly turning them into mush. The smile had slid right off her face.

"His name's Moby. He's from Friendswood. He just moved here."

"Moby?" Lacy asked. "You're sure?"

"Umm, I'm pretty sure. He watched me write it on the attendance roll and didn't say a word about it. He's a swimming icon, and we're really lucky to have him." I thought about the enormous whale tail tattooed on his back. I doubt he'd get something like that if he was named Brayden. Plus it was on the lane sign in lights at the meet. "He won like every single race by a mile. He's the guy I told you about on Sunday, who did the entire five hundred freestyle alternating between all four strokes like a medley."

She breathed a sigh of relief. "Oh good. I met someone too, and he's new. I was worried for a minute, because you know, how many new guys can there be in the middle of the year? At the same time."

"There's more than two thousand students at our school and we're like a week into the new semester. There are probably several new guys." I thought about it for a minute. But just to be safe, I said, "Tell me about yours. How'd you meet?"

"He's in all my classes at school. He was my debate partner last weekend. We won the entire tournament."

"Oh man," I said, "what about Drew?"

She huffed. "What about her? I only ended up debating with Mason because she hadn't shown up by the end of first period. She had to sprint to catch the bus at all."

"But she made the bus?"

Lacy nodded, but her nose was all scrunched up and her lips were smooshed together. "She did, but I didn't know she would, and by then Mason's dad had brought him clothes to change into and signed his fieldtrip form."

I shrugged. "Didn't Drew like, drop band to debate with you?"

"She hated band. She was going to drop it anyway. She was only in there to play drums, and now she's starting her own band. Any chance you're fixating on this to distract from your own predicament?"

"I have no idea what you're talking about," I said.

Lacy raised one eyebrow, like she always did. "Dave, the very recent ex, and Moby, the new guy you like? All on swim team together? Are we thinking they're going to be best friends?"

I frowned. "Well Dave's not even on the team right now because as of today, he's ineligible. You on the other hand, are going to see Drew every single day in class so I hope you're right about her not really liking debate."

Lacy sighs. "She skipped school today, but she said she was sick. I'm sure she'll get over it. She could even sign up for band again now, if she wanted to."

"Two weeks into the semester?" My mouth hung open.

"Ms. Harris would sign the form. I know she would."

"But what would she do in band now? Marching season is over and it's our senior year?"

Lacy huffed. "I don't know, okay? The point is, I won first place for the entire TFA tournament. I got eight points toward state. And instead of congratulating me, you're criticizing me."

I took a bite of green beans and tried to avoid making eye contact with her.

Mom glanced from Lacy to me and back again, but didn't speak. Sometimes she wasn't enough of a helicopter mom for my taste.

"You disagree?" Lacy asked.

She was right. I really didn't have much room to talk with how quickly I watched Dave get kicked to the curb, but I did at least convince Coach to make it temporary. I shrugged. "I wasn't there. I don't really know, but I think that sometimes there are things that matter more than winning."

"That's easier to say when you always win." Lacy grinned.

I buttered a roll slowly. "It's hard to be this fabulous, I know."

"Two guys fighting over you won't be very fun if it actually comes to that," Mom said.

"I doubt a fight between Moby and Dave would take too long," I said. "Moby would destroy him. He's a lot bigger."

Lacy poked at her food. Why was she so nervous?

I sliced a piece of chicken and popped it into my mouth. "What's he like, this new kid Mason?" I wouldn't admit it, but I was a little uneasy about us both meeting a new guy in the course of the same week.

"He's tall with dark hair."

That wasn't good.

"He's so smart. He quotes literature and he's eloquent. Funny. And when all the girls at the debate tournament surrounded him, he looked super uncomfortable."

Uncomfortable around girls? Uh. No. And I tried to imagine Moby quoting literature and almost snorted the half chewed chicken out of my nose. His most memorable phrase today was 'hell to the yeah'.

I leaned back in my chair. "That sounds like night and day from my guy. Moby's... well, not a thug, but certainly not an honor student. For one thing, he has an enormous black tattoo that spreads from one shoulder to the next." I held my hands up to show the size. "Does that sound like something your smarty pants would get?"

Lacy raised one eyebrow and shook her head.

Mom cleared her throat. "I agree. I met Mason, and I can't imagine him getting a large back tattoo. I certainly wouldn't describe him as a thug. Speaking of, let's hear some details. Is this tattoo like a skull? Or more like 'I love you, Mom?' Because hearing this guy you're into described as a 'thug' isn't really giving me the warm fuzzies."

I laughed and said, "There aren't any horns or skulls or anything. It's a swimming thing."

She raised one eyebrow and said, "Well, maybe I'd better meet him before you get too serious and he's difficult for me to get rid of. It sounds like he'd be a big body to drag away and bury if it came to that."

I roll my eyes. "Geez Mom, creepy much? He wants to come to ice-cream tomorrow, actually."

"That's perfect," Lacy said. "I'll invite Mason, and it can be our first ever double date." She looked happy, bright and full of excitement. I didn't see her looking like that very often, and I immediately decided to like this Mason, no matter how nerdy he was. I could ignore lines from boring old books if he made Lacy this happy.

Chapter Seven

LACY

Maybe the writing thing was a bad idea. Dr. Brasher practically bombards me with questions the next day, and it's got to be because he spent time on my file. He probably cross-referenced what I wrote against the fact recitation and witness statements in the Court Order. Blech.

"I know you're eager to get your story out," he says, "But before we get started I've got some pointed questions."

"Okay." I sit on the edge of the chaise lounge, hoping maybe I can answer a few things and get out of here early.

"You told me about Mason, and you said it all started there. I don't really see how meeting him led to-"

"To her dying?"

His jaw drops, and I can tell I've surprised him. I'm young, and yes, my life blows right now until the Court decides how to dispose of things, but I'm not a lame brain. I know the ending, I know what he's asking about. It's just not that simple.

I frown. "I guess I don't understand why we aren't talking about the real issue. She's dead and she's never coming back, which leaves me where? That's what you're supposed to decide. Being in limbo really sucks. Hard."

He holds his hand up in the air and closes his eyes.

I groan. "I thought your job was to get me to talk. I tell you where it started and you say that's unrelated. I try to get to the point and you act like I kicked a puppy."

He steeples his fingers again and I want to scream. "Maybe it's better if we keep writing after all. We don't seem to communicate very constructively out loud at the moment. Perhaps this time you can focus on connecting for me how meeting Mason is relevant to your current predicament."

"By 'my predicament', do you mean how I basically killed her?"

His eyes widen again. "Yes, I suppose that's what I'm asking about." Dr. Brasher stares at me for a moment, and stands up to hand me another yellow notepad.

"Seriously?" I shake my head. "I can do this so much faster on a laptop."

He sighs and presses a button on his phone. Melinda's voice blares at us. "Yes, Dr. Brasher. What can I do for you?"

"I need a laptop in here. Do we have an extra one we can spare?"

A few minutes later, she walks in and plops a huge laptop down in front of me. Maybe shrinks don't get paid very much. I wonder whether those two ever talked about the raise. I glance at Melinda, trying to figure out if she's happier, whether I helped.

When Dr. Brasher clears his throat, I remember I have work to do. And even a fossilized laptop is an improvement over a yellow pad of paper and a Bic pen. I turn it so that Dr. Brasher can't look over my shoulder, and then I hunch over the keyboard and get started.

____

I texted Drew a dozen times on Sunday, but unlike Saturday night, she didn't reply. I called her at least five more, and she never picked up. I wasn't too worried. We'd had a fight or two in the past ten years, and Drew sulks like a toddler who can't have her pink sprinkle donut.

On Monday, I had to squelch down some guilty feelings when she didn't come to class, but I texted her and she finally responded.

I'M SICK BUT I'LL BE IN CLASS TOMORROW.

Drew may pitch baby fits, but she had never lied to me before. I believed her.

My concern for Drew mitigated, I kept my word and introduced Mason to his new teachers. They really did all love me, so when I told them how amazing he'd done at the debate tournament, they fell for him right away. I took a make-up Spanish exam during lunch that day and generally got caught up on everything I'd missed on Friday in my other classes.

After school I finished my homework before my mom finished with work. I started to research a few issues with my new debate case a few moments before Mom got home.

"Hey Mom," I said when she came through the door.

Her furrowed brow told me she had a headache so I dropped my voice.

"Long day?"

She shook her head. "Work was fine. My headache didn't start until I was almost home."

"Tylenol?" I asked.

She shook her head. "I took one last week. I'd rather not."

Mom hated taking any drugs for any reason. Her uncle

overdosed on prescription sleeping pills when she was little, so she had a good reason for her reticence.

"Why don't you head for your room and take a little nap. I'll make dinner."

Dinner was way more peaceful when I made it alone anyway. Mom and I are so much alike that we tended to butt heads when left in the same room too long, unless we each had something to do. Sometimes I wished Dad was around, just so I had someone to talk to without being stressed out.

With Mom it was always, "How's school, how are your grades, how are your applications coming?" It felt like the FBI was interviewing me. Really, compared to Hope she should've been impressed with whatever grades I cranked out, but I felt like she always thought I could do just a little better. And at some point she'd always say, "When I was your age..."

On that Monday, Mom only napped for a half an hour. When she re-emerged in the kitchen to lend a hand, she was in one of her rare sunny moods. I had started some oven-roasted chicken, but Mom upgraded things into a big production. I loved when she was happy, so I went right along with it. I helped her put all the finishing touches together, like melting butter on top of the rolls, and sautéing the green beans. She and I made cookies too, oatmeal to be healthy and chocolate chip so they still tasted good.

When the door opened and Hope walked in, Mom's face lit up like a sunrise.

"Sweetheart, welcome home."

It hurt sometimes, to see Mom's joy at seeing her, but I guess Hope reminded her of Dad and I knew she missed him. That's why she got sad so often.

I worried for a minute at dinner, when Hope told us

she'd met someone new, but we do get new students pretty often, especially when Dow is about to start a turnaround, which they were. Plus the guy she met was a swimmer and apparently not very smart. He had a huge tattoo that covered his whole back.

I thought about Mason, the orator I knew, enrolled in all honors classes, not mentioning swimming once, and tried to imagine him with a gigantic tattoo. I guess anyone could surprise you with something like that, but I'd seen his dad. I couldn't imagine Mr. Slacks and Polo Shirt had let his son get a tattoo from shoulder to shoulder. Mason mentioned his mom put him in debate, so it's not like she was likely to be a tattoo artist or flower child. Hope's description of this Moby guy just didn't fit. Plus, anyone who liked Hope wouldn't have even noticed me, much less offered to fill in for a debate tournament. I breathed easier for once, knowing we didn't run in the same circles.

When I finished with the announcements on Tuesday morning, Mason was sitting in Drew's seat again. I looked at him in his long sleeved blue shirt and dark jeans and tried again to imagine him with a huge swimming tattoo covering his back. It was ridiculous. I shook my head and forgot about it.

Or I tried.

When I sat down next to him, I might have leaned toward him and inhaled deeply, checking for telltale signs. Hope always smelled faintly of chlorine. All I could smell was his cologne, but he noticed my sniffing.

His nose scrunched up and he tilted his head. "If you smell something weird, it wasn't me. I swear."

I rolled my eyes. "No, I don't smell anything." And that helped me relax.

When he grinned at me, my stomach flopped like a fish

out of water. If Drew didn't show up soon, I'd start thinking of her seat as Mason's instead.

I texted her. WHERE ARE YOU?

I turned back to face Mason. "I'm a little worried about Drew. It's strange she'd miss two days unless she was really sick."

His eyebrows drew together. "Isn't that exactly why she's gone?"

I shrug. "Maybe. She also might be mad at me. For last weekend."

He frowns. "Crap, is that my fault?"

I shake my head. "You didn't do anything. If anyone's to blame, it's me. I thought she'd get over it, but if she doesn't, that's on me, not you."

Mason's frown indicated he didn't quite believe me. I needed to change the subject. "You getting settled in?" I asked. "What're you up to tonight?"

"Why do you want to know?" He cocked his head sideways. "Got another surprise tournament you need me to go to, this one on a Tuesday?"

"No," I said, "but I thought you might want to come meet my family."

I cringed inwardly at how awkward that sounded. I thought you might want to *meet my family*? Like we're adults getting engaged, or something? What's wrong with me? I needed to fix this. Think brain, think. I need to make this into a joke. Quickly.

"You know," I said, "Maybe after my mom has given you her blessing, we can go pick out china patterns. I favor French Countryside. How about you?"

He grinned. "I already met your mom you know, and I think she liked me. But now that you mention that, I should come clean. You and I are probably doomed."

My heart raced and I forced a smile on my face, even

though I felt like crying. Doomed? Because he has a huge tattoo and loves my sister? Because he thinks debate is dorky and he shouldn't be in this class? Or just because he's one hundred times hotter than me? I told my brain to shut up and forced a smile. "Oh yeah? And why is that?"

Or maybe it was just because I'm so dorky that I ask awkward things like 'do you want to meet my family?' Ugh.

He nodded slowly. "The thing is, I favor American Colonial and I don't just dislike French Countryside. I kind of hate it. I'm not sure there's any way to get around that kind of fundamental disagreement in taste."

I rolled my eyes. "French colonial was a test, obviously. No one likes that many flowers. You're going to have to work way harder before I'd even consider going to pick out china. All I really have planned is a little family trip to get ice cream. My mom loves this place called Jutzy's. It's in Clute, and it's a local hole in the wall. It's like a Mexican store that sells all kind of stuff, but they mix ice cream and fruit in all these weird ways. We go pretty much every Tuesday."

"That sounds fun and I love ice cream, with or without mix-ins. The thing is though, I kind of have to unpack my room. I didn't get anything done over the weekend, and my mom might kill me if I don't finish tonight. Debate ate up the first two days, and chores ate up Sunday. Homework destroyed Monday, so."

"I totally get it. I'm sure you have a ton of stuff to do, just having moved here."

The moment the words left my mouth, I'd started to rethink the whole invite anyway. As much as I'd love to bring a gorgeous guy home and impress Hope and Mom, it might be a bad plan. It wasn't like Mason and I were even dating, much less together. With the rate at which guys fell for my sister, I shouldn't introduce Mason to her until I had him bagged and tagged. Picking out china might even be premature.

"I would totally go if I didn't think my mom would kill me about the unpacking, or you know. The lack thereof." He tilted his head sideways. "Although, maybe if I just throw stuff out of boxes really fast, I could get away. When do you usually go?"

"We eat around six, so if you unpack like Barry Allen or something, here's my number." I wrote my number on a piece of paper and slid it over to him. "Text me and I'll get you directions."

"Okay." He smiled. "I will."

We spent the rest of class looking over a few kritiks I'd been working on that I thought might work with our counterplan. He had a few great suggestions. After class ended, I walked with Mason to Physics and then to History. After that it was technically time for lunch, but I took advantage of Senior open campus to do something I'd been putting off.

I drove out to Drew's house.

I banged on her door. No answer. I banged again, harder this time. "Answer the door, Drew. I'm not going to stop until you do."

"I'm sick," she moaned.

"I'm sick as you," I said. "Of your pathetic excuses. Now open the door, or I'm getting the hide-a-key."

I really didn't want to fish the key out from under their cobwebby hollow rock. Luckily my threat worked, and she opened the front door just before I went for the key. Her hair was sticking up in odd places in the back, and she had a stain on her Green Day t-shirt. She looked weird without her signature eyeliner, too.

"Wow," I said. "You look like... like I imagine the inside

of Ms. Harris' brain looks. Too much Knight Fort does not look good on you."

Drew backed away from the door to let me in and ran one hand through her snarled hair as I walked past her. "Telling me I look awful is rude. I told you I was sick."

"We both know you aren't." When Drew's actually sick, her nose turns bright red and her eyes puff up like dough balls. When she's spending all day staring at a video screen talking to her weird computer friends, her hair gets ratty and her eyes turn pink and streaky. "You've got bloodshot eyes, Drew. I'm not a dummy."

It took almost a full minute for my eyes to adjust after I walked into the family room. All the blinds were shut and the room looked like a mole hole. Blankets slumped in piles on the floor, and messy plates crusted with food clung to every surface, in some cases nearly defying the laws of physics.

"What in the world? You and your mom are total slobs, but this is next level. Even for you."

Drew picked up a pair of sneakers and tossed them down the hall toward her room. Like that made a difference. I didn't roll my eyes, though. She had a right to be mad at me. I hadn't been very loyal.

"I know you're mad and I'm so sorry. I really am. I should've said that earlier."

Drew didn't respond.

"I'm genuinely worried that you're skipping school and staying up all night playing your game instead of coming to yell at me. It's not like you."

Drew shook her head. "I don't want to yell."

"I am sorry, but I'm also surprised you're so mad. You never even liked debate. You whine all the time about how you don't get it, and you don't want to talk about or even go over my ideas for my new case." My voice dropped in volume almost to a whisper. "I thought you might be relieved, actually."

Drew folded her arms over her chest and stuck out her lip. "Debate wasn't so bad. I complained to remind you I quit band for you."

"Okay, but even you have to admit, you kind of suck at it."

"Screw you, too." Crumbs scattered onto the floor when Drew shoved a blanket aside and sank down into the couch.

I couldn't handle being in her house, not when it looked like that, and she wasn't saying much. The only way to make Drew talk when she got like this was to wait her out, so I started cleaning. I picked up discarded plates and bowls from all over the family room and stacked them up. I gathered up dirty clothes and piles of shoes and took them to the laundry room. When I returned, Drew's head rested in her hands.

My heart contracted. Drew had been there for me no matter what. I could get upset at her shortcomings, but I was the one in the wrong here, not her. She deserved more than empty words. She deserved my patience with her forgiveness.

I brushed off the couch and sat next to her. "I'm sorry I said you weren't good. I was trying to be honest, because we've always been straight up with each other. That's the kind of friendship we've always had, and it's a great example of what I love about you. You debated with me for a year and a half just because I needed someone, but you never loved it. I'm not sure if you even really liked it. I'm sorry it hurt your feelings so bad that Mason took your spot. I didn't think you really wanted it, honest."

I had to stop talking then. If I kept quiet, Drew would finally be forced to say something. She still didn't meet my eye, so I thought I'd give her some time to process. I crossed to the kitchen and started to empty the dishwasher so I could reload it. I cleared the counter and I was eyeing her crusty countertop when she finally made a sound. I dropped a spoon and turned toward her.

She huffed. "You dumped me like a hot, moldy potato when he showed up."

"I think it's just hot potato. You drop it because it burns you."

"You know what I mean." Her lower lip trembled.

It was almost verbatim what Hope had accused me of doing. I cringed a little inside. I wonder whether my guilty feelings might have made me defensive, because I was a little less Zen than I wish I'd been.

"You were so late," I said, "that you almost missed the entire tournament. And that wasn't the first time I spent an hour texting you and praying you'd show." Maybe I was in the wrong, but she was partially to blame.

She stood up and started gathering trash off the floor. "I know, and I apologized every time I was late, but I was late a lot. You should have had faith I'd make it eventually."

"You didn't always make it at all." I huffed.

"One time," Drew said. "One time I missed."

A cockroach darted out from under a blanket and zigzagged toward me. Drew screeched.

I whacked it with a pot and waved my arms around at the disgusting mess. "What's going on with you? I should've come over Sunday when you wouldn't answer the phone. I should've come over last night after dinner, but I didn't and I'm sorry. I think we can agree I've been the crappiest friend out of the two of us, but I'm here now, and I'm sorry, and I need to know. This is your second day of school to miss when you're clearly not sick. What's the deal? Is it all because you're mad at me?"

"I'm fine, okay? The house is just a mess because my mom doesn't have time to clean, and I don't like to. The cleaning lady usually comes every week, but she's been sick. Her calling to cancel gave me the idea when I didn't want to go to school."

Drew and her mom always played chicken with the housekeeping, but she was deflecting. "I'm not just asking about the mess. You've been online non-stop lately. It's like you're forgetting you have real live friends. And what's with bringing that spoiled rich druggie to the tournament?"

Drew glared at me. "He's not spoiled rich. His family's broke, actually."

"Then how does he drive that shiny, fancy car, and have all that nice stuff? I hear he throws huge parties. With beer, and those aren't cheap."

"He earns it, okay?"

"A seventeen year old kid earns that kind of money?" I raised my eyebrows. "He *earns* enough to drive a Lexus?"

Drew mumbled something.

"I can't hear you."

"I said he sells stuff, okay?"

My head almost exploded. "Drugs, you mean he sells *drugs?*"

"Dude, you need to chill," Drew said. "Your mom's made you crazy. You guys act like taking a Tylenol is the gateway to cocaine or something."

I bit my lip to keep from screaming at her. "My mom's uncle—"

"I know," Drew said. "Your mom's uncle died of an overdose, blah blah blah. Except I've been thinking about it, and I doubt it was really her uncle. Someone who mattered to your mom died and it had something to do with drugs, that's for sure. I don't think an uncle dying when she was a kid would make her as insane about that as she is. She's turned you guys into a bunch of loons. Normal people take Tylenol and a lot of people try other stuff too. My mom said she smoked pot when she was in high school and it wasn't a big deal."

My jaw dropped. It was like I didn't even know my own best friend anymore. My throat felt like the dentist had been spraying it with that air blower thing. I forced the words out anyway. "Are you getting pot from him?"

"No, you idiot. I haven't tried it. I just don't hate him for doing what he has to do. That's all."

"You don't fault him for selling illegal substances to minors?" My voice sounded shrill. I took a big breath and counted to five. "You think he needs a Lexus? And big parties? Somehow his need for that stuff justifies him getting kids hooked on mind-altering drugs?"

"You need to listen to yourself. You sound like an after school special. And no, I don't think he should sell cocaine, okay? But I think selling pot to some high school kids is no big deal. It's legal in Colorado, and that state hasn't burned down yet."

I didn't even know what to say. I stared at her awkwardly.

"Your mom thinks all drugs are bad. But if she would take some stuff for her head, who knows? She might not miss so much work."

I frowned. "Did your dad say—"

Drew shook her head. "My dad thinks your mom's great. Maybe too great maybe. But the point is, some people don't have everything so easy."

"Excuse me?" I asked. "You think my life is easy?"

"Your mom eats dinner with you every night and she has a solid job. You have a nice house, you're beautiful, you're smart, and you have a car to share with your sister. Yeah, I'd say you have things pretty easy."

"Your mom's a doctor," I practically shout. "Your dad is my mom's boss. You have a nice house, two actually, if you ever spent any time with your dad, and you're smart. If my life is easy, yours is cake."

"It's not about money, you know. All I'm saying is maybe don't judge people you don't even know."

"I do know you, and apparently you think I'm judgmental." I fumed. "For trying to suggest you might not be making good decisions, like skipping school and hanging out with a *drug dealer.* But you don't want to hear that? Well, you know what? I'm sorry I even came here. Maybe I don't actually know you very well." I stepped backward, inching toward the door. I needed to get back to campus before lunch ended anyway.

The blood drained from Drew's face. "Don't leave. You do matter to me, and we are close." Her hands balled into fists at her side.

"You aren't acting like it," I said. "Why aren't you talking to me?" I took a step toward her. "What's really going on?"

"I can't talk to you about it." She sat down on the edge of the sofa, her hands gripping her knees so tightly her knuckles turned white.

I breathed slowly in and out a few times and forced out the words I thought she needed to hear. "If you're doing drugs, you can tell me Drew. I'm your friend, no matter what, even if my mom's a little extreme, okay?"

Her voice was so small when she finally spoke that I wanted to pick her up and hug her. "You may wish you could take that back once you know the truth."

My heart sank at the thought of Drew going to rehab, or being all emaciated and strung out with track marks like the images Mom showed us of where drug use can lead. The Faces of Meth, one website was called. I shook it off and crouched down in front of her. If Drew needed me to listen, I would. She had to know I loved her, no matter what.

"Are we five again? Because I knew you when you were five, and that's the kind of dumb crap you said then. I was there for your parents' divorce. You were there when my mom's migraines were so bad she couldn't get out of bed. I was there when your dad had that big-haired girlfriend you hated. You stuck with me through those awful braces and the librarian glasses."

Drew looked up and met my eyes, hers full to the brim with equal parts unshed tears and heartbreaking uncertainty.

I shook my head. "You were my best friend through all that Drew, and you always will be. If you want me to, I'll dump Mason as a partner, okay?" My heart broke at the thought of passing up my chances at winning state, but I pushed past it. Some things mattered more. "I really didn't mean to make you so sad."

"It's not about debate," she said. "Or even Mason, not really."

"Then what's going on?" I asked. "What did I do?"

She shook her head. "I already said. Not everything is about you."

"I don't think everything is about me." My eyebrow lifted and I wanted to defend myself. Which I realized meant I was making this about me. I spluttered. "Fine, so then what is it?"

"I'm gay, okay?"

My jaw dropped and any thoughts I had shot right out of my brain. Had I misheard her? Did Drew say she was gay? She couldn't be. I'd known her for years. I'd have known, right?

"I think I might have misunderstood you. It sounded like you said you were gay. Like you like girls, not guys."

Muscles worked in Drew's jaw and I realized I'd said the wrong thing.

"I'm sorry. But didn't we spend the past four years talking about every guy we knew and making jokes about who we liked and who liked us?" My voice lifted at the end, making it a question and I knew that was wrong too. I stood up and balled my hands into such tight fists that my nails dug into my palms.

"Did I stutter?" Drew asked. "I said I'm gay. You heard me right. I'm attracted to other girls. Like me."

"I don't know what to say right now," I said. "I didn't see this coming."

"Clearly."

"Why didn't you tell me before?" I asked. "Or did you just realize it?" I thought back on all the sleepovers we'd had in the past ten years. I wasn't sure what to feel about that.

"I don't know how long I've known," Drew said, "but a while. I kept wanting to tell you, but I didn't know what you'd think. I didn't want to lose you as a friend. As my best friend."

As a best friend? Or as more? My eyes widened. Did Drew like me? I swallowed hard and cleared my throat. "Are you telling me this for a specific reason?"

Drew lifted one eyebrow and met my eyes for the first time since saying she liked girls. "What does that mean?"

I couldn't possibly say more dumb, wrong stuff. I figured I may as well get it all out there. "Do you like me?"

Drew tilted her head. "Of course I like you, Lacy."

"I mean like, *love* me, like me?"

Drew rolls her eyes so hard I worry they'll get stuck up

in her cranial cavity. "Uh, just because I like girls doesn't mean I'm in love with you."

Duh. "Then why did you struggle to tell me? I meant what I said earlier. I will love you, no matter what."

She shook her head. "Okay, now it sounds like you're saying even if I murder someone and wind up in jail, even if I sell drugs, even if I am a drug addict, even if I, I don't know, get a face tattoo, you'll still love me. Except those are all bad things. So you're lumping being gay in with all that bad stuff. Like you're such a good person, you'd love me in spite of my being gay. It's offensive, Lacy."

I plopped back on the sofa. "I don't mean it like that, and you know I don't. I'm sorry I'm saying all the wrong things. And I'm relieved you aren't in love with me, okay?" I blinked my eyes a few times. "Wait, you aren't in love with me, but you didn't want to tell me. . ." I turned toward Drew slowly. "Please, please, please tell me you aren't in love with Hope."

Drew belly laughed then, which eased something inside of me.

"Thank goodness," I said. "So why didn't you tell me before? And why are you hanging out with Jack?"

Drew sat down next to me and leaned her head against my shoulder. I thought it should feel weird now that I knew she liked girls, but it just felt like Drew. "Jack got into a fight at school after P.E. last month. Punched a kid in the jaw for calling Porter a rude name."

"And?" I asked.

"The kid called Porter a Fag. I figured I could talk to someone who attacked another kid for making fun of someone for being gay."

"Jack, the drug dealer, defender of gay rights?" I choked back a snort.

Drew shrugged. "I talked to him about it when he got

back from being suspended. He said his sister's gay and he doesn't like people who use words like that. He was the first person I told."

I meant to speak loud and clear, but my words came out as a whisper. "Why didn't you tell me as soon as you knew?"

Drew patted my hand. "I kept telling myself that maybe one day you'd wake up and realize I was gay, like you knew I didn't like debate, like you knew I was never, ever going to wear high waisted jeans or those floral rompers. You knew me better than anyone. Surely you'd see it, and then I wouldn't have to tell you. I'd set timeframes for myself. Tell her by Halloween, Drew. Tell her by Christmas. Only, when they got close, I got too scared. You're my best friend in the world, and what if you didn't like me once you knew? I couldn't tell anyone else without you knowing. And if you told me it wasn't okay." Her voice shook along with her shoulders.

"Drew—"

She sat up. "No, I need to explain. It's not your fault, and I handled this all wrong. I need to tell you why."

"Okay," I said. "Go ahead."

She licked her chapped lips. "When that stupid, muscle bound thug showed up, and you ditched me for him in like ten seconds, I don't know. I felt all shaky and weird, and jealous even though I don't care about you like that. It was like I was being replaced in your life and I hadn't even told you the truth. I was jealous of him, but not because I wanted to like kiss you or something." Her grimace felt a little unflattering.

"So I'm gross, then?"

She chuckles. "You're such a girl. No, you're fine, but what I'm saying is, I overreacted about Mason because I was already worried the truth about me would drive us apart. I can't lose my best friend."

"You will never lose me." I glanced at my watch and realized I was going to be late. "I've got to get back Drew, and you need to get your cute gay butt into class tomorrow. No more excuses."

I stood up to go, and Drew nodded. "I'll be there."

One word Drew used earlier got stuck in my head and I couldn't leave without asking her about it.

"Hey, so thug, really?" She used the word to describe Mason in an offhand way. It was the same word Hope used to describe the guy she liked. The guy she had just met, who we knew couldn't be the same person. Who had to be someone different because otherwise I would die a little bit inside.

"What?" Drew asked. "What are you talking about?"

"Why did you say Mason was a muscle bound 'thug'?"

"Are you really asking me about him right now? I don't know, he's enormous. What does it matter?"

"Never mind." This was not the time for me to grill her about her opinion on Mason, clearly.

"I'll be honest about this much," Drew said. "I don't like him. He's more like Hope's kind of guy than yours."

The words stuck with me like they were jackets from popcorn kernels lodged between my teeth. No matter how I tried, I couldn't quite eliminate them.

The drive back to school took forever. I felt drained when I walked into Calculus. I liked Mason, more than I'd ever liked anyone, but now with Drew's revelation and her description of Mason, I didn't know what to think. I wasn't even sure what Mason wanted, other than to unpack his bedroom, apparently.

He sat right next to me in Calculus, in Drew's seat again. I wondered what would happen tomorrow when Drew returned. I didn't have much to say and I guess

Mason noticed. After Calculus but before we parted paths, he said, "Hey is everything okay?"

"Oh, sure. It's fine. I'll see you tomorrow."

"Maybe tonight," he said with a smile. "I'll call you if I can convince my parents that I've made enough progress."

I smiled back, but it felt forced. I didn't know what to do about Drew, and I couldn't help thinking that maybe I had dodged a bullet with Mason. What was I thinking, introducing him to Hope? It's been like this since the day she was born. I'm not a moron. I can see myself in the mirror. I'm thin, and I have thick, dark hair. But it's wavy, and sort of unruly. It's usually pulled back into a messy bun because I don't have time to do anything with it. I have light grayish blue eyes, and they're not bad. I have really pale skin that never tans, but I'm relatively attractive.

Until you stand me next to Hope. Then I look like a Midge doll next to Barbie. Like a Kia next to a BMW. Like the moon next to the sun. No one could even see me when she was around.

Eclipsed. That's the word for what happens when Hope steps into a room I'm in.

She was born with a shock of almost white hair. It frames her face perfectly at all times. Except when she pulled it back into a ponytail, which never got frizzy. Her eyes looked enormous in her flawless face. They're bright, almost indigo, and so big she almost looks like an anime heroine. Despite that impossible coloring, her skin darkens to golden as soon as she steps outside. She walks outside for three minutes and tans to a deep bronze, not kidding.

I haven't even mentioned the important parts. She's stacked. She's got legs that go on for miles, and she's got this toned swimmer's body that leaves boys aged ten to one hundred drooling. She can't remember a grocery list when you send her to the store, but you forget you're annoyed when she smiles, apologizes and hands you a Snickers. Her name fits her pretty well, better than mine does me, but I think my parents missed the mark. She's bright and bubbly and full of light, always happy. They should have named her Joy, or maybe Radiance.

Anyhow, I was actually okay with Mason having plans by the time I got home and finished my homework. I decided not to invite him to anything that involved Hope until he was solidly my boyfriend and couldn't wriggle free. Maybe not even then. It's not that I don't love Hope because I do, but I've just seen too many guys become captivated by her, almost against their will.

Actually that's one thing I could say for Drew now that I knew she, you know, liked girls. She'd known Hope for as long as she'd known me, and she only ever paid attention to me. I think that's why I liked Drew so much in the first place. We went to get ice cream with Drew and her parents once, before they got divorced. I picked mint chocolate chip and Hope picked cotton candy, only when she took a bite, she hated it. She insisted we switch. Drew threw a fit. She said it was totally unfair that I would lose my ice cream because Hope chose poorly. My mom ended up buying Hope another one, and I kept mine.

Later, Drew told me my mom spoiled Hope. It was the first time I'd been able to put into words how I felt about the way Mom treated her.

Drew was the first person I knew who seemed immune to my little sister, like Hope emanated some kind of irresistible hormone and Drew's nose was broken.

I had just put a frozen pizza in the oven for dinner when Hope came bounding up the stairs on the front porch. "Hey," I yelled through the screen door. "Welcome home."

"Hey to you, too! I've got to get ready." She breezed upstairs to her room. "Be back in a minute."

I guess that answered my next question. I was going to meet Moby.

I flopped down to read while I waited for my mom to get home and for the pizza to be done. I was re-reading *The Scarlett Letter*. I had to read it for school the first time and I enjoyed it, but sometimes I reread the classics for fun. If a book was okay the first time around, it's always way better when I don't have to think about it and analyze it and generally ruin it just for a grade. I was feeling pretty bad for poor Pearl, who no one ever seemed to think about, when the doorbell rang.

I hopped up and walked over to see who it could be. I hoped Mom hadn't ordered a pizza on her way home, or we'd be eating reheated cheese and bread mush for days. I like pizza, but I hate leftovers of any kind. When I opened the door, Mason was standing there.

His jaw dropped when he saw me.

Mine did, too. "Uh, what are you doing here? I thought you were going to text if you could make it."

He shook his head, and opened his mouth. Then he closed it. After a few seconds, he opened it again. "Do- Do you live here?"

"Hey Moby, you found it," Hope called from behind me.

I know, I know. I was an idiot. I'm sure you had already figured it out by this point Dr. Brasher, but I was completely shocked. I felt like someone had slapped me in the face for the second time in one day. I peered around Mason to see a blue Audi parked in our driveway. His dad's car.

He was here for a date, only it wasn't with me. He was here for Hope. Eclipsed again.

"You have a huge tattoo?" I felt like an idiot asking that,

but it was the first thing that came to mind, and I always say whatever pops into my head, I guess.

Mason looked at me, his brows drawn together.

"I'm sorry." Hope blushed as she bounded down the stairs. "I told them about your whale tail."

"No, she didn't actually." I stepped back from the door until my legs hit the sofa. "You didn't mention it was a whale tail, but let me guess. It says Moby somewhere near it."

Mason nodded.

"For Moby Dick," I said.

"Language, Lacy," Hope said, making big eyes at me. She turned back to Mason and grinned. "Sorry, she's usually super polite."

"Oh Hope, shut up. It's the title of a book by Herman Melville." I felt sick again. I should've faked sick today. I wanted a do over. "Dick is a common nickname for Richard." I sat down on the sofa with a giant whomp. "Now that I think about it, that's probably another reason he got the tattoo. It's funny."

And suddenly I got it. How someone like him could have a huge tattoo. Hope's swimming demigod and my novice debater are the same amazing guy, a modern day warrior poet. And he was here to take my perfect, eye-candy sister out on a date, which is why he told me he needed to pack his room. Obviously a lie. I should probably be flattered he didn't just tell me he had a date. He'd only make up a fake excuse if part of him wanted to keep me as an option, but of course he didn't text me. Because what guy in his right mind would cancel a date with Scarlett Johansson for Anna Kendrick?

"Are you hungry?" Hope asked Mason. "Lacy made pizza. It's probably ready by now."

"Actually, I'm feeling kind of lousy," I said, stealing a

page from Drew's playbook, eight hours too late. "I should go pack some things in my room." I arched one eyebrow at Mason.

"What?" Hope said. "Pack for what?"

I shrugged. "Not sure. I probably need to pack for something, though."

Hope looked at me like I was losing my mind. "But we have ice-cream tonight. Jutzy's. You have to come."

"I think Moby will enjoy a little one on one time with you." I met Mason's eyes and dared him to say something. He didn't. Coward.

I wasn't going to let him off that easy. "Sorry, Hope. I know you don't like taking the pizza out, but I bet Richard can help you with that. I bet he's great at taking things out of places, like unpacking boxes, or pulling pizzas out of ovens."

Hope shakes her head. "No, his name is easy. It's not Richard, it's MOBY."

"Right," I said. "My mistake, sorry Moby." I met Mason's eyes and he winced.

"She must really be sick, because she's so smart usually, I swear. I can barely deal with it."

I rolled my eyes. "I'm going to my room."

I ducked out before Hope could say anything else. I closed my door a little too hard. My phone buzzed and I looked down at Mom's group text message to me and Hope. STUCK AT WORK LATE. GO WITHOUT ME. SORRY!

I hadn't even thought about it, but Mom met Mason at the tournament. She'd have known Moby was Mason the second she clapped eyes on him, but now it'll fall to Mason to tell Hope himself about the whole mess.

When I thought about it, though, there wasn't much to tell from his end. He knew me and he had classes with me, but what had we done, really? He hadn't kissed me, or even so much as held my hand. He hadn't asked me out either. I asked him, and he told me he was busy.

Because he had already asked Hope out.

I felt like crying. Instead, I shoved my headphones into my iPod, turned on some angry music and texted Drew. YOU BETTER BE AT SCHOOL TOMORROW.

I SAID I WOULD.

I texted again. ALSO, UPDATE. MASON IS DATING HOPE.

She texted back immediately, just like I knew she would.

I DON'T KNOW IF HE'S A BIGGER JERK OR A BIGGER IDIOT. TOSSUP. SEE YOU TOMORROW.

Chapter Eight

HOPE

Dear Diary:

Today was even better than yesterday, until it wasn't. Oh man, I don't even know where to start. I guess at the beginning. School was school. I didn't learn anything, but I didn't really blow anything either.

Today at lunch I saw Moby. He waved at me and I gestured for him to come over. He set a loaded tray down on the table next to me and sat down.

"Hey there," I said. "Didn't see you here yesterday."

"I had some homework to catch up on."

"On your first day?" I thought it was a weird comment at the time, but his explanation made sense.

"It's the middle of the school year. I'm playing catch up in lots of stuff."

"Too bad we don't have any classes together," I said. "Maybe I could help you." I doubted it, actually, but since we don't have any together, he didn't have to know that either.

"We should get together and study. That would be fun."

Studying fun? Was he nuts? Maybe it was code for making out. "Sure. What classes do you have?"

Before he could answer, my friends descended.

"Who's this?" Annie asked.

Before I could answer, my best friend Gwen said, "He's the new swimmer who just moved here. Moby, right?"

When he nodded, Gwen winked at me. She'd been teasing me about him being imaginary, but now she'd seen him, she got it.

He fit right in. The other guys hassled him a little bit, and the girls badgered him, but he slid right into my normal group of friends so perfectly it was like he'd been here forever. The only time I worried was when Dave slammed his tray down at the end of the table. I thought he was going to say something at first, but he didn't. He just glared. By the end of lunch, Moby still hadn't asked me about going for ice cream tonight, which bugged me, but I figured he was trying to play it cool.

After lunch, I went to two more boring classes. I survived until swim team. Coach caught everyone before we changed into swimsuits. We all groaned together. We were doing dry-land exercises today before we swam.

After doing a hundred push-ups, a dozen pull-ups, and more sit-ups than I could count, coach made us run two miles. Then, finally, after the torture was done, he sent us to change into our suits.

"I hate dry-land work," I moaned.

"I like it." Moby looked way too good sweaty.

"Of course you do." I rolled my eyes.

"What does that mean?"

"I mean you're too perfect for your own good." I headed for the girls' locker room, but then I turned back. "Did you change your mind about tonight? Or did you still want to come over later?"

His eyes flew wide, as if I'd surprised him.

"I thought you said it was a family thing."

"So you did change your mind." I leaned against the door. Yesterday he was pestering the crap out of me about coming, but then today he didn't seem to care one way or another. It stung. Maybe I was playing it a little too cool.

"No, not at all, but I didn't want to pressure you into it, plus I've got a ton of unpacking to do."

"I don't bend under pressure." I took a step into the dressing room, but turned back and said, "I talked to my family. They'd like to meet you."

He looked shocked for some reason, almost like he'd seen a ghost. "What's your last name, Hope?"

I scrunched my nose. "What does that matter?"

"I just realized I didn't know it."

"It's Vincent."

His whole face relaxed. "Okay, good."

"Why do I feel like I just passed some kind of bizarre test?"

He shrugged. "No idea. Go change. We can talk about tonight after practice."

It was weird, but guys are weird, so I got over it. We swam for an hour or so, and then I went to the changing room to shower. By the time I got out, Moby was waiting again, in the same chair.

"So are you coming over later, or what?" I asked, annoyed.

"If you're sure, then yeah. But if you'd rather do something another night, that's fine too. I get too pushy sometimes."

I missed the pushy Moby, the one who was pursuing me, but I dropped it. "No, tonight's good. How about six? We always get pizza, so you can have some, and then we'll go out to get dessert."

"Okay," he said. "Text me your address?"

He told me his number and I saved it in my phone, then I texted him my address.

"See you later?" I asked.

"Absolutely," he said. He grinned, but this time, instead of walking me to my car, he headed for the guys' locker room. I walked out to my car a little deflated.

By the time I got home, I was excited again. I rushed upstairs to get ready. I only had thirty minutes, so I had to hurry. I pulled out my blow dryer and diffuser and went to work. I was just touching up a few places with the curling iron when I heard the door.

I ran down, but Lacy had already answered it.

"Hey, Moby, you found it," I said.

He looked dazed, like someone had smacked him on the nose. He didn't even look up at me.

"You have a huge tattoo?" Lacy asked.

Moby looked at her, clearly confused. Trust Lacy to lead with the weirdest, most unrelated thing ever when meeting someone new. Now it looks like I've been talking about him non-stop like some stupid fangirl. I blushed. "I'm sorry. I told them about your whale tail."

"No," Lacy said, moving away from him like an insane person until she bumped into the couch. "You didn't mention it was a whale tail, but let me guess. It says Moby somewhere near it."

I'm shocked. How could she possibly know that? My sister is Sherlock friggin Holmes.

"For Moby Dick," she said next.

"Language Lacy," I said. Geez, what was wrong with her? "Sorry, she's usually super polite." It would serve her right if I called her boyfriend an a-hole when he arrived.

"Oh Hope, shut up. It's the title of a book by Herman Melville," she said, rudely. I wanted to sink into the stairs, and Moby didn't look like he felt much better than me. I love Lacy, but I swear she can be such a freak sometimes. "Dick is short for Richard," she said, right before she collapsed on the sofa. "Now that I think about it, that's probably another reason he got the tattoo. It's funny."

What was funny? I was so lost. I looked at Moby and he looked upset. I should've let him put this off. We hadn't had a single normal date yet, and I was already subjecting him to my sister's weird mood swings and bizarre book jokes. Not a great idea. I looked at my huge, pink, Baby-G watch, hoping our mom would be home soon.

"Are you hungry?" I asked Moby, hoping to distract him. "Lacy made pizza. It's probably ready by now."

He nodded, and I was in the process of leading him into the kitchen when Lacy said, "Actually, I'm feeling kind of lousy. I should go pack some things in my room."

Pack in her room? "What?" I asked. "Pack for what?"

Lacy shrugged. "Not sure. I probably need to pack for something, though."

Uh. Okay. Lacy's weirdness aside, I breathed a sigh of relief she was going to leave. Not that Lacy being sick was lucky, but you know, with the way she was acting, it was lucky for me. The night was shaping up to be a disaster so far. Maybe with Lacy gone I could salvage it.

"That's kind of weird," I said, going for a convincing amount of fake disappointment without really encouraging her. "And we have ice-cream tonight. You have to come." Please don't. Please, please, don't.

"I think Moby will enjoy a little one-on-one time with you," she said as she stepped toward the staircase.

I tried my hardest not to smile. I swear I loved Lacy, but she was being a nut. Bad first date mojo. I had taken two steps into the kitchen, Moby following me awkwardly, when Lacy started talking again. Geez, she was a diva. How many last little comments would she make before she left?

"Sorry, Hope. I know you don't like taking the pizza out, but I bet Richard can help you with that. I bet he's really fast at taking things out of places, like unpacking boxes, or pulling pizzas out of ovens."

What was her problem? I shook my head. "No, his name is MOBY."

"Right," she said. "My mistake, sorry Moby."

Moby even flinched when she said his name. She could not leave the room fast enough. I needed to explain that Lacy was kind of weird. I didn't want him to think I was a troll too. "She must really be sick, because she's actually so smart usually."

Lacy rolled her eyes. "I'm going to my room."

She could not leave soon enough for me.

"Sorry she was acting so weird," I said when she shut her door.

"She's not usually like that?" he asked.

"She's always a little odd, like quoting old books, and making strange jokes that normal people don't get. She always talks really fast, probably because of her debate thing, but she's not usually so awkward. I think what happened is, she was going to ask a guy to come tonight, too. It's kind of sad, because obviously this guy she likes didn't want to come. It probably wouldn't have been a big deal, except of course you're here for me, so that just rubs her face in it."

Moby suddenly started coughing. I patted his back, but it didn't seem to help much. A minute later, he stopped, just as the beeper started going off on the oven. "Oh, the pizza's ready, I bet."

Moby smirked at me, and held out a hand for the oven mitt. "That's usually what the timer means, yes."

"Smart-aleck." I grabbed the cardboard container and flipped it over so we'd have somewhere for the pizza when it came out. "I hate this part. Lacy's right. It's just, I burned my hand a year or so ago taking the pizza out, so I always try to find someone else do it."

Moby used two spatulas and slid the hot pizza onto the cardboard perfectly. "She was right. You're a natural. Maybe you should come around more often." I pursed my lips just so, and he grinned back. I was recovering well.

I sliced the pizza and set it on plates in front of us just before I got a text from my mom. STUCK AT WORK LATE. GO WITHOUT ME. SORRY!

I turned my phone to show Moby and I smiled. This was perfect. I'd miscalculated, inviting him to a family thing on our first date, but now we could go out without my mom or sister. Once we got out, he'd get his stride back and everything would be fine.

Moby started eating the pizza before it had cooled at all. He looked funny chewing around the boiling sauce, trying to keep from burning his mouth. I giggled.

He smiled back at me, but he still looked sort of uncomfortable, like something was wrong.

I blew on my slice. "Is everything okay?"

"Do you remember asking me earlier what classes I have?"

"Sure." I shrugged. "I was just being polite though. I don't really care. Actually, I'm not the kind of person who studies a lot."

"Why not?"

"Why not?" I repeated, trying to think of a reason that didn't make me sound like an idiot. I leaned back in my chair. "Because I don't like school. It's something I do so I can swim. I figured you, of all people, would get that."

Mason finished chewing a bite, and then he swallowed.

"Sure, I love to swim. Obviously, right? But, I don't know. I like school too. I like English, history, and physics. Biology. Even Calculus isn't so bad."

"You're in calculus?" He was making no sense. I didn't know anyone other than Lacy and maybe her weird friend Drew, who actually liked school. "What do you like about it?"

"I guess I like the certainty. In physics, you learn all these principles, things about the world that help you make sense of it. In history, you learn about all the crazy things people did, and what happened when they did them." He set his pizza down and started gesturing. Something about it knotted up my stomach. It was like he was a whole new person I'd never seen, even though I'd been thinking about Moby for days.

"Take Napoleon, for instance. He's one of my favorite men from history. A little short man who was essentially a nobody, and he practically conquered the entire world. He wasn't even French, and his family wasn't rich or anything. He didn't have much going for him, but he joined the military and he worked hard. Why did he work so hard? Was it because he was short? It can't be that simple, because millions and millions of super short people throughout history accomplished nothing. Something about him must have yearned for greatness. I feel like that sometimes, like there are too many things I want to do. I know I can't do them all, but I want to, and it keeps me going, trying harder, pushing."

Yearning for greatness? What in the world was he talking about? He sounded like... well, if I had to pick one person he sounded like, it would be Lacy. I put both palms down on the table. "What are we talking about here? Because this is a strange conversation and I feel like I'm missing something."

"I'm in another class, too." Moby looked down at his empty plate and back up at my face. "I'm in speech and debate. With Lacy."

The pieces suddenly fell together, a little too fast. My head began spinning. "That's why you wanted to know my last name. You were wondering...whether Lacy... because she asked you to come, too."

I closed my eyes, but I still felt dizzy. In fact, I felt like I was going to puke, or hyperventilate, or both. "Wait, so you're Mason?"

He nodded. "My name is Mason Montcellier."

"But your back, your tattoo," I said, confused. "If your name is," I halted, and then forced out the word, "Mason, then why did you get a tattoo that says Moby?"

"You thought I tattooed my actual name on my back, like a football jersey, but with my first name?" He raised his eyebrows. "Or like a 'Please say Welcome to' nametag?" His eyebrows scrunched together and his eyes looked like Mr. Cooper's when I didn't understand a math problem.

"It's for Moby Dick like Lacy thought," he said. "I'd just won at state last year, and my team was pumped. I wanted to do something to commemorate it. It seemed like a good idea at the time. Then the nickname just stuck, probably because Mason and Moby both start with an M." He shrugged. "Since you're captain, I figured you'd seen the roll."

"It updates every six weeks. I just wrote in Moby for attendance." My head was pounding and I couldn't deal with him anymore. "Maybe you better go."

He stood up. "That's probably a good idea."

I walked him to the door, and when he left he turned back, like he was going to say something, only he didn't. I don't think either of us knew what to say or do next. The situation was too strange. I felt terrible for being so idiotic with Lacy.

I went back inside and cleaned up the kitchen, then I forced myself to walk up the stairs and down the hall to Lacy's room. I stood outside for a moment before I got up the nerve to tap on her door.

Nothing.

I tapped louder. When she still didn't answer, I opened the door. "Lacy?"

She was sitting on her bed with her eyes closed and headphones in her ears. I wanted to rush over to her and hug her now that I knew why she was being such a nut job. She was hurt, because Moby, er, Mason picked me, and not her. I stopped myself from rushing forward, because I didn't know how she felt. Hugging her might make it worse. I watched her for a minute or two, leaning back against the headboard like she was sleeping, but there was no way she was asleep at six forty-five at night. Without even eating dinner. She obviously wasn't really sick, either.

"I know you're awake," I said.

She opened her eyes. "I am."

"Can you take your headphones out?"

"Yes," she said. But she didn't.

"Funny," I said. "Will you take your headphones out? I think we need to talk."

She looked at me for a moment without speaking, but she finally took them out. "What did you want to say exactly?" She stared at me. "I'm guessing you aren't here to apologize to me?"

I spluttered. "I do feel sorry for you, but what exactly should I apologize for?"

"Oh, I don't know. Taking everything. Always and forever."

"Umm, excuse me, what have I ever *taken* from you?"

Geez, what a drama queen. I knew she'd be upset, but she wanted me to apologize? For what? "You're the one who should apologize. You were acting like an idiot out there."

"I may be the ugly one, but I've never been the idiot."

"You aren't ugly," I said automatically, because I'm a good sister. Then her words sank in. "Wait, you think I'm an idiot?" It was like she dropped a tank on my chest. I could barely breathe. I don't try hard at school, and I never loved reading and stuff. Compared to her I'm average, I always thought. Did she really think I was stupid?

I stood there staring for long enough that she finally spoke. "I'm sorry, Hope. I never should have said that. You're very smart about things you care about. I just. This wouldn't have happened if- I mean, you haven't heard of Moby Dick, Hope? How are you seventeen years old and a state ranked swimmer, and you don't realize that a whale tail with the word Moby over it is a reference to Herman Melville?"

I wanted to cry. I wanted to curl into a ball while tears ran down my cheeks. My sister, my genius sister, thought I was a moron. And, of course, she was right. She was always right. I was just so dumb I never realized it.

Which made me angry. I wanted to hurt her. I wanted her to feel like I did, but I couldn't bring myself to say anything too awful. "I'm sorry if I spend my time doing things, instead of just reading about doing them," I said. "But I met him first, you know."

"How do you figure?" she asked. "I met him on his first day here in one of my nerdy classes, and then he came with me to a tournament. One we won together after debating ten rounds, I might add."

"I met him last Thursday when he was still on the Friendswood swim team. He's the reason I dumped Dave."

"Oh, so Mason's a land claim? You saw him first, so you have claim to him, and you won't let go?"

"I have no idea what you're talking about, Lacy. You sound like a crazy person again." I hated when she talked like that, but what really made me mad is that Moby sounded just like her. The thought made me feel yucky, and I was a little meaner than I should have been. "Moby, er, Mason I guess, won first place in the five hundred freestyle and the two hundred freestyle at the state swim meet last year. He's on his way to the Olympics. You really think you two have more in common than we do?"

"I didn't expect you to get it, Hope. I knew, once I realized who he was, that you'd be all upset and tell me why he's not right for me. I knew you'd take him, like you always take every single thing I have or want."

I put my hands on my hips. "What are you talking about? What have I ever taken from you?"

She sighed heavily. "Blinky."

I blinked a few times at that one. "I'm sorry, are you talking about your old pacifier?"

Her eyes flashed. "Yep. You asked."

"Okay, but you were done with it."

"I wasn't," she said, "but you wanted it, so too bad for Lacy, because she's almost three years old, so she can suck it. Or, you know, not suck it. As the case may be."

"Okay, anything you can think of that I've taken in, oh, I don't know, like the last decade?"

Lacy held up her hand. She held up her pointer finger. "When I was four you took my bun bun." She held up her middle finger. "When I was five, you took my bed, because you liked it more. The next week you insisted we change rooms too, but you hated my curtains so I kept those." She held up her ring finger. "But you wanted recent so let's just do the last month. At Christmas, you fell in love with my new sneakers and said you needed to borrow them for a run. I haven't seen them since." She held up her pinkie. "But in case those concrete examples aren't making sense, how about the last week, when I saw you borrow my paper on Scarlett Letter off the computer downstairs, and my pink lip gloss went missing, and my frizz smoother magically moved from my bathroom to yours. Is that enough? I could go on, if you need me to."

"You never seemed to care about any of that stuff," I said. She really didn't. I swear, I don't recall her ever complaining that we share stuff.

"I didn't care, not that much," she said. "Because I love you. But I care this time."

"I can't believe you think I'm taking Moby from you. I met him first." I frowned, but then I remembered him talking about Napoleon and I wondered if the timing meant much.

She shook her head. "I know he was probably already gone the minute you met, okay? I'm not dumb. You can't even help yourself, and I know you didn't take him on purpose, but it hurts more this time."

"Why?" I asked. "I really like him. I had no idea you were interested in Moby. I thought you liked someone else."

"You have a new guy every month, but once you date him, I never can." Lacy sounded so bitter.

I hadn't realized how much it bothered her that I had boyfriends when she didn't. "Excuse me for being popular."

"I figured you might come up here and apologize for once," she said, "and I don't know, at least offer to take a step back, even if Mason would never pick me over you. I thought you might toss me a scrap."

"A scrap? You think Moby's a scrap? He's probably the only guy I've ever really been into," I said.

Lacy pursed her lips. "Me too."

"Oh please, you've got an entire class full of nerds. He can't be the first guy you've ever liked."

Lacy choked. "Mason and I have every class together. He's the most talented natural speaker I've ever heard. He reads all the time *for fun*, just like me, and he quotes boring old books, just like me. He might be a little more athletic than I am-"

I snorted.

"But that doesn't mean we aren't a good match. Face it, Hope, he's as much a nerd as he is a swimmer."

I thought about what she was saying and recalled that she thought I was an idiot. She probably thought I wasn't good enough for him. Like somehow reading and math were more important than truly excelling at a sport. I didn't know how to defend myself in this stupid fight, but I thought of another response. It was over the top and I shouldn't have said it, but I was tired of being attacked, and feeling guilty. "I don't think that's why you're a bad match."

"So you do think Mason won't want to date me."

"I don't think it, I know it. He didn't ask you out, did he? He asked me." When I saw her broken face, it twisted my heart, but I was still so angry that it felt good. She thought I was an idiot, and greedy, and I was a bad sister. She had clearly thought it for years, and now I'd met someone really great, and he liked me too, and she thought I wasn't good enough for him just because he was smart. Instead of telling her I was sorry, instead of asking her to forgive me like I should have, I turned on my heel and ran down the hall to my room.

Then I picked up this dumb book. And now I just feel worse, writing this all out. I should go back now and tell her I'm sorry. I should tell her that I'll forget about Moby. I should tell her she can have him, but I just, I don't know, I can't do it. I know I ought to, but I don't want to. I want Moby too much, and I'm still too mad. Lacy doesn't deserve to be rewarded for making me feel like a spoiled brat and a moron. I'm a better fit for him than she is. She'll figure it out eventually, even if it takes her a little while.

In fact, if I know one thing, it's that no matter what her problem is, Lacy eventually gets over it. Always.

Oh, I just heard the door. I should go talk to Mom. BRB.

Okay, I'm back. I talked to Mom, but not about any of this. I told her Lacy wasn't feeling great, which I think is true. Then my best friend, Gwen, called. She's the captain of the track team, and we've been friends for ten years. I knew she'd understand, so I told her all about the nightmare tonight and she was completely outraged on my behalf.

"She called you an idiot? Is she kidding? She can't even have a normal conversation."

"I know," I said. "Books aren't everything. Plus, she thought she had dibs on him since she met him first. Except, I actually met him first. I dumped Dave after I met him last week."

"Poor Dave," Gwen said. "He hates Mob- er, Mason. I had no idea Dave even liked you so much."

I sighed. "Was he like this when you were together? I didn't realize we were even officially dating. I think he pays me more attention now than he did when we were together."

Gwen moaned. "He did that same crap to me. Actually, he got a little scary for a while before you convinced him to join swim team. I was kind of glad when he decided he liked you so he'd leave me alone."

"Are you serious?" I asked.

"He's harmless, but he has a temper. I guess you don't

have to worry, not with Moby around." Gwen laughed. "Too bad he doesn't have a brother for me."

"Or for Lacy," I said.

After we hung up, I tried to feel good about the fact that Moby had asked me out and not Lacy, but the more I thought about our conversation, the more uneasy I got. I hoped Gwen was right, and I really would have Moby around, but I was starting to wonder whether I'd just paid a really steep price for something I didn't even have.

Chapter Nine

LACY

I'm sick of telling my story. I didn't mind at first, but now I don't want to talk-or write-about it anymore.

"Lacy?" Dr. Brasher says. "You've been sitting there for ten minutes without touching the keys. Maybe you'd like to give talking a go."

"This laptop is ancient. I'd rather use a typewriter."

"Are you sure that's the problem? You did fine on it yesterday." Dr. Brasher folds his hands under his chin again. It's freaking annoying. For a shrink, he sure has some things to work on himself. Like not irritating his patients so badly they can't think straight.

"Look, doc, the thing is, I really feel like you can see what happened next at this point. You don't need me to spell it all out for you, do you?"

He shakes his head. "I don't need you to spell it out for me, no."

I stand up, relieved, and stretch my legs. "Phew. I did not want to have to spend another day hunched over that stone age hunk of metal."

Dr. Brasher points at the laptop. "I don't need you to

spell it out for me, but I do need you to spell it out for you."

"What?" I groan and pace back and forth. "You're kidding, right?"

"You're operating under some kind of mistaken belief that we're here for me, or for the Court, or for your mother, or your sister, or the principal, or your friend Drew, or anyone else on the planet. None of those are correct. We're here for you, Lacy. This is your life and you're floundering. You've undergone a substantial trauma, a life-changing event. You can't continue on exactly in the same way, and people are worried, understandably worried-"

"I wish it was none of your business what I did with my life. Why do you think you can make it any better?" I start for the door. I don't care what the Court wants. I don't care what Dr. Brasher wants. I'm sick of giving things up for Hope. I'm sick of poking at memories that make me want to curl up and cry. It hurts too much.

"Lacy," he says, and I realize he's right behind me.

I mean to yell, but the words come out as a whisper instead for some reason. "Nothing can bring her back."

I spin around and it's not until I'm facing him that I realize I'm already crying. Big, messy tears roll down my face.

I hiccup and his eyes soften.

I shake my head and step back a few inches. "If it all stopped there, a little fight with Drew, a spat with Hope, my mom stuck at work, things would still be fine. She'd be here to tell me I'm an idiot. She'd be here for me to cry to. This next part, this is where it all goes wrong, like really wrong," I say. "I can't do it. I don't want to talk about it anymore."

"That's how you know you need to," he says.

His hand reaches out for my arm and I let him lead me

gently back to the enormous relic he keeps calling a laptop. I stare at the screen for a moment before I have any idea what to write. But then it comes to me and my fingers fly over the keys. When I force myself to think about it, every single ugly moment looms in front of me, crystal clear.

———

My phone rang. Early. I rubbed my eyes and looked at the number. Unknown. I didn't see my mom last night, and now I'm worried maybe she didn't make it back. What if she crashed her car on the way, or it's her plant calling, or worse, a hospital? My mom usually works in research, but sometimes she has to go down and supervise stuff on the plant floor. What if there was some kind of awful spill or something?

"Hello?" I asked, my voice scratchy.

"Miss Shelton?"

"Yeah?" I cleared my throat, trying to sound alert. "This is Miss Shelton."

"I'm sorry for calling so early, but I was concerned I might miss you if I waited. I've called your coach several times and never heard back from her, so I thought I'd give you a ring. I'm only calling so early because I'm assuming you can't answer your phone at school."

"Who is this?" I asked.

"Oh, I apologize for being so rude," he said, "This is Mr. Langston, your first judge from the Katy tournament."

"Oh." I sat up straight in bed, wide awake and relieved it wasn't about Mom. "Great. What can I do for you?"

"I know it's short notice at this point, but I was wondering whether you were attending the Clear Creek tournament this weekend."

I wracked my brain. Where was Clear Creek? Was it

close? It sounded familiar. I'd waited too long to reply though and I had to say something.

"I'm sorry," I said, "I don't think we are. I can talk to my Coach, though. I don't know why she wasn't answering her phone, but maybe we can sign up late."

"The friend I told you about is in town on some other business, and I thought I might persuade him to extend his trip and come see you and your partner Mason debate for a few rounds."

"Oh," I said, "well, I'll talk to my coach today and let you know."

"Great," he said. "Please do call or text me back and let me know."

"I will. Thanks for calling." I wanted to scream with excitement when I hung up, but it was 6:45 a.m., so I settled for a little jumping up and down instead.

When I finally emerged from my room, Hope was already gone. She had driven to school in our car, alone. I saw my mom sitting at the kitchen table and couldn't help whining a little. I sat down, put my hands on the table and plonked my face down on them. "Hope took the car. How am I supposed to get to school, huh?"

"I'll take you on my way to work," my mom said. "No big deal. You better hurry, or we'll both be late."

I grumbled, but I ate a quick bowl of cereal, ran a brush through my hair, and twisted it back into its normal knot. Then I grabbed my backpack. "I'm ready."

"Don't you need a lunch?" My mom looked concerned. "I don't know what's going on with you two girls. Hope didn't say, but I can tell something's off kilter. Feel like talking about it?"

I sighed. "Mason and Moby are the same person, Mom, and told Hope he'd come hang out with her, and told me he was busy."

She closed her eyes. She didn't say anything for a moment. "Well that's lousy. I'm sorry, Lacy."

She was sorry for me because she knew, just like I did, which of us any sane guy would pick. Sometimes it really sucked to be the smart one. Why couldn't I have gotten boobs instead of brains? I'd have been fine with a healthy mixture of looks and smarts, even. She can keep her chest, but maybe give me her perfect legs, and a little athletic ability. Luminous eyes and flawless skin. I forced myself to stop picking at the zit on my chin.

"It's not fair, Mom. She has loads and loads of guys, anyone she wants. Why can't she leave just this one guy alone?"

"I don't think that's entirely fair," my mom said.

"Why?" I smear some peanut butter on a piece of bread. "Because she met him first? You think they're fated to be some kind of epic love story? Oh, please. Epic for Hope happens twelve times a year."

My mom laughed. "No, I don't think they're Elizabeth Bennett and Mr. Darcy."

"If they are fated, it's more like Pocahontas and John Smith."

My mom frowned. "Who's Pocahontas in this scenario?"

I smeared the jam and smashed the two pieces of bread together then shoved it into a baggie. "I'm not talking about race or looks. I'm saying they may as well not speak the same language. Mom, she doesn't get half of the things he says. He's smart, like really smart. He's in all honors classes."

Mom frowned. "Your sister's bright, you know. She hasn't applied herself much, but she could. Maybe he'll be good for her. And don't forget, he's also a swimmer, and from what Hope told me, an amazing one." Mom stood up.

"The thing is, I would be happy for him to date either of my daughters from what I've heard, but I don't particularly appreciate the fact that he's driving a wedge between you."

"Mom, you've never paid any attention to it, but that wedge has been there for a while."

She narrowed her eyes at me. "You two are best friends. You always have been."

I choked. "Back in preschool maybe. Now I barely even see her. We share no classes, and we both do activities that take up a lot of time. And they aren't the same."

"You still spend all summer together."

"We're both outside, but I'm cowering under an umbrella reading while she sunbathes and tries to shake off all the guys hanging on her every move."

My mom rolled her eyes. "Don't be so melodramatic. You played volleyball together almost every day."

She's right. We did. I'd set, and she'd spike.

"And you share clothes all the time, and we watch movies together every Friday. And we get ice cream together every week. You have more in common than you're acknowledging."

"If you call her taking anything nice I have sharing, that's true," I say. "But whenever only one of us can have something, it's always her and never me."

My mom put her hand against my chin. "You feel that way, because she's the baby. The baby is always a little more spoiled, but sweetheart, I did her the disservice here, not you. You know how to handle anything. She doesn't handle setbacks or disappointment nearly as well as you do, and life is just a long series of disappointment. How you react determines the path you chart."

I slumped in my chair. "Great. I'm glad to hear you've prepared me to handle it well when I'm the complete failure you expect me to be."

She shook her head. "You know that when one door closes, there's always a window open. You've never resented helping your sister, who doesn't have nearly the grit and tenacity you do, or quite the same mental acuity if we're being brutally honest. And now this boy has come along and he's creating problems. If this continues, I swear I'm going to take him out."

Her determined stare made me smile. "So are you planning to poison him, or turn the dogs on him?"

She laughed. "I knew I should've gotten some dogs. Think it's too late now?"

I shoved my lunch into my backpack and sank into a kitchen chair. "I don't know what to do."

She put her hand on my head. "I know sweetheart, and I'm supposed to have the answers." She stroked my head over and over, but said nothing. Finally, she sighed. "The worst part about being a mom is when your kids get so old you can't just fix their problems anymore. If Hope took your Cheerios, I'd just get you more. When she wanted your stuffed animal, I'd find you another. When she wanted to play on the playground and you wanted to read, we'd go to the playground, but I'd bring you a book. But this one is beyond me. I'm really sorry, but I think you and Hope are going to have to work this out without my help."

It might have helped if Mom had ever bothered to teach Hope to get her own stuff and stop taking mine, instead of getting me a new toy or cereal bowl every time. I didn't mention that. Instead, I stuck out my lip. "I hope we can work it out too, but I thought about something this morning. Last night I assumed Mason asked Hope out, or maybe that when I asked him, he made up an excuse because he didn't like me, and then she asked and he said yes. But there's another possibility. Maybe Mason didn't ask Hope out. If she invited him over, she would have done it before I did, and he already had plans when I asked him. Maybe he came over for her because he'd already agreed to do it. Maybe he does like me, and if he does, I'm not backing down. If Mason likes me, I don't care whether it hurts her feelings. I'm sick of letting Hope have whatever she wants. I don't want a new bowl of Cheerios this time."

"Hope's like your dad," Mom said, a note of quiet warning in her voice. "She's a force of nature. I'm worried that if you don't step back and she gets what she wants anyway, you might hate her forever."

This time, I was not going to hand it over without a fight. "I might anyway."

My mom sat down next to me then and handed me the car keys.

"Mom?" I asked. "What's wrong?"

She held one hand up to her temple. "I have a migraine. I'm going to call in sick to work."

I felt guilty then, really guilty. I knew why she had a migraine. This time it wasn't missing dad or lack of sleep from a late night at the plant. This time, her head hurt because of me. "I'm sorry."

She held up her hand. "I can't talk anymore right now, sweetheart, I'm sorry. I wish I didn't get these, but would you mind calling in for me? I'm going to head for my room." She set her phone on the table and shuffled back down the hall to her bedroom.

I called Drew's dad and he wasn't surprised. My mom would have been his boss if she wasn't always calling in sick. He'd told me that often enough. But as it was, we were lucky he was understanding enough that she still had a paycheck. I drove to school and parked my mom's new-ish Honda in the back of the parking lot. I barely made it to the front desk in time for announcements. Any other kid would've been counted late. I guess I should've been grateful to be me, but I didn't feel particularly blessed.

I raced to first period that day, eager to ask Ms. Harris about going to the tournament that weekend in Clear Lake. Sometimes if they have enough space, you can sign up late. When I walked in the door, I made a beeline for Ms. Harris's office. She was in a great mood that morning. Her bizarre, much younger boyfriend had just bought her a brand new Mustang and she wanted to show it off. After I dutifully oohed and aahed at the photos, and followed her over to the window so she could point it out for me in the parking lot, she called Clear Lake, and they agreed to add our team to the roster. I was over the moon.

Until I looked back into the classroom and saw Drew in her normal seat and Mason sitting in mine. Uh, awkward.

I walked over and grabbed a plastic chair from the back of the room by the extemporaneous files. I dragged it up behind them. "Sooo," I dragged out the word. "How are you guys?"

They didn't look at each other. Drew wore her typical type of clothing, a black dress and boots, with her signature eyeliner and dark sparkles smeared over each eyelid. Mason wore jeans and a polo shirt that clung to his chest. Drew sat with her arms crossed, glaring at him, and I kind of agreed with her, even though I had no real reason to fault him. The more I thought about it, the less I could really think of that he'd done wrong.

"How could you not have known they were sisters?" Drew asked. It was a question I wondered about too. When I wasn't blaming myself for not realizing Moby and Mason were the same. A tattoo? That was my evidence? Maybe I'm the idiotic one and the plain one.

Mason shoved his chair back so there was some space

between them. "They don't look much alike," Mason said, addressing Drew.

"Umm, same smile, same eyes."

Mason huffed. "I suspected it at one point, okay? But then I asked Hope, and she said her last name was Vincent! How do they have different last names?"

Drew sighed. "I guess that's a little weird. Lacy has her dad's last name, and Hope has their mom's. Neither of their parents wanted to give up their name and they thought hyphenation was too problematic. What if Lacy gets married some day and her spouse wants to keep his or her name, and she wants both of hers. Their kid could end up being named Ferdinand Vincent-Shelton-Snuffle-up-a-gus."

Mason raised one eyebrow at Drew. "His or her?"

Drew shook her head. "Never mind."

I rolled my eyes. "I'm glad you're back, Drew."

"Me too. Someone needs to insulate you from the emanation of testosterone. I hear he's a real Moby Dick."

She was on a roll, and it felt good to smile.

Mason glared at her. "I don't emanate testosterone."

"No one asked you, Arnold Schwarzenegger. California may be fooled by your shiny muscles, but here in Texas we don't consider someone who flirts with two sisters and doesn't even realize he's doing it very smart."

"Honestly, other than their smiles, they look and sound nothing alike." Mason looked funny pouting.

He should have been annoying me, but I found everything he did too cute. Maybe Drew was right. She texted me this morning telling me I needed to maintain a distance of ten feet from him to keep my head clear.

"You already pointed that out," I said. "So, are you saying that if we weren't sisters, it would be fine that you were flirting with both of us?" I raised one eyebrow.

"Yes, that's exactly what I'm saying. It's not like I did

anything with either of you." Mason looked shifty and jumpy. I'd never seen him look so uncomfortable, not even before his first round of debate. "I asked Hope if she wanted to hang out, but that was before you invited me over."

I was right and wrong. He asked her, but that did happen first, before I invited him.

Even so. "You asked her out," I said flatly. It was basically the same thing Hope had told me. Which meant she was right. He hadn't asked me on a date, but he had asked her.

"She's easier," he said. "I don't have to think with her."

Drew's eyes lifted almost to her hairline and she whistled long and low. "Dude, that was the wrong thing to say."

"You want someone who doesn't make you think? You know what?" I said, "I don't care. I don't care what you do, actually. If you want to date my sister because you heard she's 'easy', that's not really any of my business." I sat down on the chair and looked Mason in the eye. "But I got a call this morning from Mr. Langston. He's bringing his friend to a tournament in Clear Lake this weekend, which is only about half an hour away. Ms. Harris got us on the roster, and I need you to come, to get us both into Yale. I know you like easy things, so that may not be your jam, but I think Ivy League sounds good."

Mason looked poleaxed. He was utterly quiet for a moment.

Drew glanced from Mason to me and back again. "This is where you say, 'sure, Lacy, I'll totally come. After all, I stole this spot from your best friend who kind of sucked anyway, so I'd be a real whale of a jerk if I didn't go help you get into Yale.' Man, I had no idea I'd get so many burns out of one tattoo." When he didn't reply, she poked Mason's arm like you might poke a cadaver. "Why aren't you repeating after me? I gave you the script this time, man." Drew turned to me and tilted her head. "You ditched me to debate with this guy? Really?"

"I can't go. I have a swim meet this weekend." Mason shifted on his seat. "It's a big one, and there's a recruiter from University of Texas coming to see me. It's a qualifying meet for state."

"And swimming matters more than debate," I said bitterly. "That makes sense. I bet it's easier, right?"

"You've got to be kidding me." Drew shook her head.

"Look, it's not about easier, or whatever. I didn't mean it like that." Mason stood up and then sat back down. "I don't see why I can't do both."

"Are we talking about swimming and debate right now?" Drew raised her eyebrows. "Because I hope we are, and if so, you can't be in two places at once." She looked at me and mock whispered. "Really? I'm understanding his interest in Hope, honestly."

A part of me bristled at her for dissing my sister. But more of me was angry so I kept quiet.

Mason glared at her. "I mean I know I can't do them on the same weekend obviously, but I want to do swimming and debate. Lacy, you said the next tournament was Lamar next weekend. I can go to that one. We have a swim meet, but I already told Coach I can't make it. I'm not trying to be flaky, but I just can't go this weekend on such short notice. I already committed to go to the Cypress Woods Invitational."

"It's Yale," I said. "I didn't pick this, Mason. Or wait, maybe you prefer for me to call you Moby now?"

He rolled his eyes. "My name is Mason. That's like a whole swimming thing, okay."

"Which I obviously can't understand, right? I just can't comprehend what it means to work hard, to be talented, or to achieve excellence, not when you add water." I huffed. "You never even mentioned swimming you know, not once. And I sniffed for chlorine and didn't smell any."

Mason's eyes light up and he smirks. "So that's what you were doing."

"Shut up," I say. "You don't get to make this a big joke. It's my life and my future on the line."

Mason nods. "I know it is, but the thing is, I just, it's like there are these two parts of who I am, and they don't entirely line up. My mom wants me to debate, but she said swimming takes priority and my dad, he says focusing on one thing is a mistake. He played for the Astros for twelve years, and then last month they terminated his contract because they found someone better. That's why we moved here, where my mom's parents have a vacation home we can live in for free, and my mom got a job working as a nurse. Focusing on swimming may be myopic or whatever, but I can't just quit either. It's part of who I am." He sat back down and clenched his hands into fists. "I don't know if that makes sense to you, but it's the truth."

"Being a debater is who you are, too," I said. "I've never seen someone with more natural talent."

"Why can't I do both? Call Langston back and just tell him we can't do Clear Lake. Tell him to bring his buddy to Lamar."

I groaned. "Lamar's a joke. I signed up because it should be easy to get another six points there. It's the smallest TFA qualifying meet because everyone good goes to Alief Kerr that weekend instead, okay?"

Mason threw his hands in the air. "Then let's go to Alief Kerr! Geez, what's with you? Nothing makes you happy. I told you I can go next weekend, but that's still not good enough. I'm not the one trying to change things last minute."

Drew leaned over and whispered in my ear. "Umm, the whole class is watching, including Ms. Harris who didn't notice an entire semester of half the class playing Dungeons and Dragons last year. They brought wooden swords sometimes. And played with them. Maybe we continue this later?"

"Fine," I said. "Go to your swim meet, but Drew and I are going to Clear Lake."

Drew's eyes went wide and darted back and forth between Mason and me, but she didn't say anything.

Mason shrugged. "Do what you've got to do."

"I always do. I don't always pick whatever's easiest."

"Okay." Drew poked me. "You two crazy kids sure are fun, but Lacy and I need to get ready for this weekend's tournament. Mason, why don't you help Kim update the Impromptu files back there?" She pointed toward the back corner of the room.

Kim sat up straighter and waved at Mason, who sighed and moved over to the back to dig into the photocopied articles. I slumped down into my seat, worn out. It was about the worst time for Drew to pester me, and she usually could sense that, but not that morning. She cleared her throat first, then she tapped the table with a pen, and eventually she poked my arm.

"What?" I said. "Can't I have a minute to process all this? I'm sorry I said we were going this weekend without asking you. We don't have to, okay?"

She turned her laptop screen toward me. "This weekend is fine. I was being an overly sensitive idiot yesterday and I should've trusted you way before. You've always been my best friend, and you're a good best friend. But none of that was why I'm poking you."

Drew tapped on her laptop screen. The webpage for the open evidence project was pulled up. It's a website where debaters upload their work and everyone can use the stuff they've come up with. If you can't afford a summer camp, it's a good place to get your first case. Sometimes I find decent links there, or the rudiments of a new kritik.

"Hmm, well, while I appreciate your concern, I don't think we're that desperate. You went to Baylor and I went to UT. If we decide to scrap my weird case, we can always pull from our summer cases."

"It may come to that," Drew said without taking the computer back.

"What?" I glanced down at the file she opened. My jaw dropped. "It's a counterplan to my plan. It's based on Singer's slightly more moralistic anti-anthropocentrism, one that doesn't equate humans to a blade of grass." I cursed. "Look! It incorporates an analysis of Zimmerman's critique of Heidegger for his failure to condemn Treblinka."

I felt like crying.

"What are you going to do?" Drew asked. "I don't totally understand what that says, but it doesn't look good."

"This is Todd," I said. "I know it is. He's still pissed I beat him last weekend, so he spent the past few days on this. I can't take my plan to Clear Lake until I figure out how to counter this. We only have tonight and tomorrow to get this done."

Drew arched one eyebrow. "Umm, you're saying we, but I don't even really understand your plan, much less this attack on it. I think you meant to say that *you* only have tonight and tomorrow."

I sighed. She was right. She wasn't going to be able to help me.

"Or, and I'm just throwing this out there to help you, not because I don't want to go, you could back out of Clear Lake. It's not like Ms. Harris has even sent the check in yet."

I glared at Mason, who kept glancing our way. "I'm not backing out of Clear Lake."

"Fine, but you know we have our Chaucer projects due Monday. And that Calculus test."

"I know," I said. "I know all that. It's going to be fine."

Drew's perfectly plucked eyebrows went up, but she didn't say anything else.

"It's Yale, Drew. Yale."

"You have a pretty good chance of getting in on your own, you know, even without debate." When I ignored her, Drew said, "Not if you get Fs in calculus and English, though."

"Helpful, thanks." I should be hearing back from them on early admissions in the next few weeks, but being Valedictorian was not as impressive at Brazosport as it is at other, bigger and more impressive schools. Support from the debate director could be just the thing I need to be one of the few accepted.

"Unlike you, neither of my parents went to Yale," I reminded her. "I have zero family members contributing to their alumni fund, and no legacy of Sheltons, or Vincents for that matter, attending. I need something else. I can feel it."

I spent the rest of class reading through Todd's freaking counterplan, the one he had posted online to ensure every single idiot debater from here to Dallas had a copy. The problem was, it was good. If I was being honest, it was probably better than my original plan. I couldn't see a way around his criticism. His is only a critique though, not a real plan, so I couldn't take his and turn it into anything I could use. It was like a parasite—it needed my plan to survive.

With Drew actually present at school, Mason got stuck sitting in any empty seat he could find in physics and history. I tried not to look at him, but I couldn't help it. Every time I did, he was looking back at me. The first time or two he tried to smile, but he quit when I kept turning away. In calculus we had started the week out as partners, and Ms. Grigassy said we couldn't switch. Drew reluctantly went to work with Ewelina Vaijahovski. She had been my arch nemesis for years, trailing me by a fraction of a grade point since freshman year. At this point, unless one of us screwed up, I had her beat.

"I'm not sure this one's right," Mason pointed. "I think the derivative is actually-"

"How about you just work on these and I'll do these," I said. "It's probably easier that way."

"Knock it off, Lacy. Seriously."

I looked up at him, and my heart stuttered when I saw his gorgeous face, all earnest and sad. I started the day wanting to fight for him, but somehow, knowing he asked Hope out, and hearing him say she was easier, I don't know. It knocked the wind out of my chest and I just, I couldn't. I didn't even want to fight Hope anymore.

"Here's the thing Mason. I've never been in this exact situation, but you can't understand what a nightmare it is to me. Hope's always been athletic and pretty, much prettier than, well, everyone." I felt my throat closing off. I couldn't tell him she's the pretty one because I couldn't bring myself to say I'm ugly compared to her in case he hasn't already noticed, but it's true. If I wasn't honest, I'd have looked stupid. "She's the pretty one, okay, the one everyone wants to hang out with, and the one everyone wants to take to the beach. I'm the one who people ask to help them with their homework. And now I meet this guy I really like, a guy who's perfect for me, and get this, he's hot. Like, really, unbelievably hot." I looked away, focusing on the chalkboard. "He could star in a movie or something and he likes me. He debates, and he's smart and he's going to try and finish unpacking really fast so he can come spend time with me, maybe."

I took a deep breath and forced myself to look at him. "But then it turns out, he didn't rush packing. He might not even have had to unpack at all. The thing is, he made that up, because he'd already asked out my sister, the one who everyone loves more than me. The one I can't compete with, and I never could. And he has a lot in common with her, too."

I knew I should stop, but I couldn't seem to do it. "I have two options, right? Be pathetic and try and beat my sister in her perfect little kingdom, or you know, just give up and watch the inevitable unfold." I paused, and then whispered, "I'm many things, but so far I've never been pathetic. I really don't want to start."

Mason put his hand on mine. "You're not pathetic. You're the opposite of pathetic." Which is exactly what he would say to a pathetic person, because he'd feel bad for her.

I pulled my hand away. "I'm choosing option B. I'm not a moron, I know how this will go down, but I don't want to watch it, okay? Now you can take Hope to the beach, and out to get pizza and everywhere you go, heads will turn right and left and people will sigh and clap because you're just soooo perfect for each other. Just don't rub my nose in it."

"It's not like that," Mason said. "I like Hope, but–"

"If you like Hope, then it is like that." I looked down at the math problems. "Please do those, and I'll do mine. I don't need a partner, and I think this working together crap is pointless. Go to your super important invitational swim meet and leave me alone."

"What about next weekend at Lamar?"

I exhaled loudly. "What happened to the smart guy I knew yesterday?" I shoved my books into my bag and stood up. "I don't even know if I have a case to run anymore, but I'm certainly not asking for your help with my problems. I'll be fine with Drew, okay? You can make it to the swim meet you were going to bail on." I walked up to the front of the room, told Mrs. Grigassy I was feeling sick and marched down the hall to eat lunch in the library.

Drew showed up a few minutes later. "You okay?"

I smiled bitterly in response, and went back to trying to wade through Dombrowski's stupid analysis of Zimmerman and Heidegger. Geez, who are these people that have nothing else to do other than pick at the philosophical ramblings of these long dead pontificators? This is where our funding for education is going? It's a rat hole, a complete waste. I slammed my laptop shut and squished my eyes with the palms of my hands. My brain hurt from trying to make sense out of that utter rubbish.

One of the best things about Drew was how she always knew, just knew, when to leave me alone, and when to make me talk. When I spun out, she sat next to me, quietly eating her almond butter sandwich while I fumed, and read, and fumed some more. By the time lunch was done, I felt a little better.

She and I walked to Spanish in silence until right outside of the classroom. "Did you want me to come over today and help with anything?"

I shook my head. "It's nice of you to ask, but you never really understood the point of the counterplan, anyway, not really."

She didn't disagree. "I can come over for moral support, if that's what you need."

"It's okay. I'll focus on that tonight and tomorrow.

There's always Sunday to work on Chaucer, study for calculus, and catch up on my reading for history."

Señora Diaz announced we would be having a test on Monday in Spanish. We only had a few weeks until the Advanced Placement tests and we were behind schedule. I added one more thing to my list for Sunday, and tried (unsuccessfully) not to stress about it.

I didn't notice that Ms. Harris was too happy to be, well, Ms. Harris. I didn't notice Hope's ex was being annoying, or that she was hurting about our fight, or that my mom was sick again. I didn't notice that Drew was pasting on a happy face and supporting me when she still felt isolated and misunderstood by nearly everyone in her life. I didn't think about anyone but myself.

See, when you're drowning, at first you think you'll be fine if you just hold your breath a little longer and kick a little harder. By the time you realize there's a problem, you're too far down and you don't have any time left. I didn't notice any of the stuff I should have, because I was too busy drowning myself.

Chapter Ten

HOPE

Dear Diary:

What a sh- er, what a bad few days. I haven't written because I've been so busy, and I'm sorry if you can't read this, but I'm writing it on the bus ride home from the Cypress Woods Invitational. It's the first time I've had a chance to write in days and I need two more entries by Monday.

I'm getting ahead of myself.

To get ready for the meet, Coach insisted on extra practice time, like over an hour a day. After finding out that Moby... Mason... I don't even know what to call him... was the guy Lacy liked, I wasn't sure how to act around him. He wasn't sure what to say around me, either. I swore to Lacy that I didn't care what she wanted and I wouldn't back down, but I kind of did.

On Wednesday, Moby came and sat with us at our lunch table, but he sat two people away from me and didn't say more than a few words. He was already in the water when I got to the natatorium. He kept the distance swimmers busy, and he was underwater every minute. When I went to change, he was still swimming, but by the time I finished, he was already gone. I had been hoping he'd be waiting for me, like he was before.

Even though he had asked me out, I started to wonder whether he really liked Lacy more than me.

Things were bad with her. When I came home late on Wednesday, dinner was still on the table, but only my mom came out to talk with me while I ate. "When is she going to get over it?" I asked Mom.

"She's hurt," she said.

"So am I." I stabbed the cold, mushy broccoli with my fork and pushed it around. I hated broccoli, which Lacy knew. She was kind of mean.

"It's not the same." My mom reached over and tucked a strand of hair behind my ear.

"How is it not the same? We both liked the same guy. I think he liked us both and was trying to figure things out, but now, Mom, he's being really weird. No one knows what to do and this whole thing just sucks."

My mom was quiet for a moment, but just after I stuffed my mouth with chicken, she said, "What do you want to do?"

Chewing and swallowing gave me time to think. "I want things to go back to how they were with Moby. And I want Lacy to calm down about it and realize he's not right for her. Then I would get what I want and Lacy wouldn't be mad anymore. There are a zillion dorky, smart guys out there. Everything would be normal again."

My mom's face looks pained for some reason. "Is he actually wrong for her?"

I dropped my fork and it clattered on the table. "Are you kidding? Mom, you haven't seen him swim, so I guess I'll let that one go, but he's like, Olympic caliber. Lacy doesn't even get in the water. And I won't go into what they'd look like together."

"Lacy's a beautiful girl," my mom said. "It's taken her some time to grow into her looks because they're unique, but she's coming into them now. Her face is striking, Hope."

I knew that. Of course I knew Lacy was cute. I picked my fork back up. "I know she's pretty. That's not what I meant. I'm sure any guy, including Moby, would be lucky to have her. I'm just saying that you're a little biased because the only time you met him they were debating. But that's like a passing thing. He's been swimming since he was a kid. He's not going to quit doing it. It's kind of consuming. And Olympic swimmers don't have time for anything else."

My mom looked at me like she always did when I was missing something. I wanted to scream. "What?"

"The Olympics are a one time kind of thing. They come, they pass and you have to keep living after they're over."

"Umm, some swimmers can do several rounds. Wait, are you saying Lacy's a better fit for him than me?"

My mom shook her head. "I wish he'd never moved here, if you want to know what I'm really thinking. I wish neither of my beautiful girls had ever laid eyes on him. But since you have, I try to focus on what is true, and the truth is that people change over time. They aren't just one thing and they stay like that forever. Some people love running and blow a knee and can't do it anymore. Maybe they take up knitting or showing dogs. Other people weigh four hundred pounds and love to eat candy, but then they have a cardiac episode and they lose a ton of weight and take up cycling. Life is like a river, and we're floating down it. We can paddle our boat, but we're shifted by the current."

"Mom, you sound like a guidance counselor."

Mom shrugged. "I've been compared to worse things. All I'm telling you is that I don't think your solution is quite fair. You're suggesting you get exactly what you want and Lacy gets nothing, but comes to terms with it gracefully."

For some reason my mom almost looked guilty, like she thought what I wanted was her fault.

"Well, Drew agrees with me," I said. "I ran into her in the hall the today. I asked her what she thought about Moby and Lacy. She thought they'd be terrible together."

Mom raised one eyebrow. "You sure that's what she said?"

"She looked disgusted," I said. "Drew is Lacy's best friend. Wouldn't she know if they were a bad match?"

"She might, if she wasn't dealing with other stuff."

"What does that mean?" I asked.

Mom frowned. "That's not my explanation to make. And maybe I'm wrong. I don't know anything for sure. But I don't think it's up to Drew, or me, or anyone else. You need to talk to Angelica about this. I'm not going to be happy about anything to do with this Montcellier kid until you and your sister are alright again."

"Why is it my job to fix things?" I stuck out my lip.

My mom stood up then, startling me. I shoved back so fast that I almost fell off my chair.

Her voice was stern, like Principal Skinner this time, not the guidance counselor. "You're missing the point, Hope. You have such tunnel vision when it comes to swimming. And you don't see Angelica, not really. She's always been another person in your life who lets you have whatever you want. You've never even thought about what she wants, because you never had to care. That's not fair, and it's given you an inaccurate view of what Angelica's like. She could appreciate Mason's accomplishments as much as you could, and she's teaching him something new. Something he liked and he was very good at."

I stood up and pushed my chair back under the table. "Are you saying I should just bow out and let them, what? Be together?" The whole thing made my chest tighten and my hands shake. "I don't bow out. I don't give up on anything, it's not who I am."

"Your father never backed down from a fight either," my mom said. "It's one of the things I loved about him. No, I'm not asking you to give up, because I know you can't. It's the reason you're such a fierce competitor. It's why you're such a talented swimmer."

"Then what do you want me to do?" I asked.

"I'm not telling you what to do. You're old enough you need to figure that out yourself. But love shouldn't be a fight my darling, and you're turning it into one. You're focused on the wrong person. This isn't about Mason, or Moby, or whoever he is. This is about you and Angelica. You shouldn't be at odds with her, you should be loving her. Anyone, anything that splits the two of you up is a cancer, and I will treat it as such."

The idea of my mom attacking, well, anyone really, made me laugh.

"This isn't funny, Hope. You're my family, and you're the only thing I really care about. I'd quit my job and burn down the house and kill someone if I had to, to help you and Angelica."

"Oh, Mom, stop being such a diva. It'll be fine eventually."

My mom pointed at Lacy's room. "Your sister is holed up in her room, trying to figure out how to fix some big problem I can't even comprehend for her tournament this weekend. She's alone with it because Mason has a swim meet. Instead of telling her how much that sucks and at least being there for her emotionally, you're over here complaining to me about how awkward things are for you. You didn't even know she had a tournament this weekend, one where a recruiter from Yale is coming to watch her debate. Did you?"

I know my mom meant to point out how I'm a calloused jerk, and show me it's all my fault. The thing is, all I heard her say was that Lacy was smarter than me, and her problems were bigger and more important. Lacy was doing stuff that even my brainy Mom can't understand. I should be fixing the problem I made by what? Being alive and having the face and hair God gave me? It's all so monstrously unfair.

Mom was on Lacy's side? Fine. I didn't care. I put on my swimsuit and flip-flops and walked down to the beach. Listening to the waves always made me feel better.

The next morning I got up before either of the two mopey book nerds in my family and went for a jog. I left for school while Lacy was still in the shower. Let her take the bus. That day, Mason didn't even sit with me. He waved to some guy from one of his classes and sat at a table with a bunch of nerds. At least Lacy wasn't there. She was probably hiding in the library as usual. Some of my anger faded then, sliding into something that felt a lot like guilt. I used to try and get Lacy out of the library and into the cafeteria, where she'd be interacting with real humans. Now she's in there because of me, kind of.

The rest of Thursday was essentially a repeat of Wednesday. Mason ignored me, and Lacy holed up in her room. Mom barely said two words to me. She was in one of her moods, and just kept flipping the channels on the television. I decided to go for another run on the beach. I only went a mile that morning since I had to get ready for school. I grabbed my shoes and headed out the front door, and no one even noticed.

I could get shot. I could twist my ankle and get washed away by the tide. I could get bitten by, like, a sea snake, and die, and they wouldn't even notice.

My phone buzzed. I pulled it out. It was Dave.

I knew I should ignore it. He'd been texting me over and over since I dumped him, but no one else was paying me any attention, so I texted him back and told him I was running. At least if I died, someone would know where to look for my body.

When I saw him standing on the corner a few minutes later, I almost fell over. "What are you doing here?" I asked.

He smiled. He had a nice smile, a little crooked, with lots of shiny, straight teeth. "I was out jogging, too."

He didn't look sweaty, but maybe he had just started. It wasn't hot either, so that made sense. He fell into step next to me.

"You always ran better than me," I said.

He grinned. "It was about the only thing I did better than you."

"You're a good swimmer too. We've missed you."

"The whole team? Or anyone in particular?" he asked.

"Me," I said. "I've missed you."

Well, to be honest, I'd only missed the attention from him. I was feeling a little attention starved lately, with Moby ignoring me, my sister sulking, and my mom taking her side.

"I have a test tomorrow," he said. "If I get a B on it, it'll bring my D up to a C, and I can come back."

I smiled at him. I was kind of glad. Maybe a little competition would help Moby step it up. In my experience, not much brought out a guy's A-game faster than jealousy.

When I finally got home, Mom was in bed, but Lacy's light was still on. After my shower, when I was about to go to bed at eleven o'clock, I could still see her light. I swear, sometimes I wonder whether she's a vampire. She's pale as the dead and she never sleeps. If I didn't see her eating ice cream and pizza all the time, I'd be checking the back of the fridge for blood bags.

On Friday morning, my legs were sore from my double jog the day before. I slid into my flip-flops and grabbed a bagel. I decided to take it to the beach to eat, so I didn't get stuck talking to Mom or Lacy.

"Mind if I join you?" Dave's voice startled me. He lives on the beach, too, but almost a mile down from us.

"No," I said. "Go ahead."

He handed me a coffee. "I couldn't sleep and got up early. I figured I may as well bring you a coffee."

A chill ran down my spine. He never did that when we were dating. "Uh, were you just like, hanging out by my house?"

I looked down at the coffee, but I wasn't sure if I wanted to drink it anymore.

"That makes it sound weird. I was enjoying the waves, and I've missed you. That's all. After I ran into you last night, I thought maybe you'd like some coffee. I was on my way to your house when I saw you."

I wasn't sure what to say and he was staring, so I finally took a sip. He sat a little too close to me, so I stood up. "Well, I guess I better head to school."

"Need a ride?" he asked.

I shook my head. "Dave, we aren't getting back together. You know that, right?"

He choked on his coffee. "I'm not crazy. But we can be friends, right?"

I shrugged. "Yeah, I guess so."

"Coach told me you fought for me when he made Moby

the new captain. He said Moby doesn't care if I take over once I'm eligible, so maybe we'll be working together again soon."

Something about the way he looked at me made me uncomfortable, but I couldn't tell what it was. "Sure, that's good." It was true. I had fought for him. Why was Moby bowing out, though?

"Will you be at the meet this weekend?"

He shook his head. "Nah, I won't get my score by then, but next weekend, I hope I will be."

I sort of hoped he failed his test, but I felt bad thinking that. "Well, I better go."

"You don't want a ride?" he asked. "You and your sister share a car, right?"

"Nah, she's been riding with my mom. I'm cool."

"Okay." He walked off, but when I glanced back, he was looking at me.

That day, Dave sat right next to me at lunch, and Mason sat at the end of the table, talking to Annie and Vivian almost the entire time. I had no idea how he was getting to practice before me at the end of the day, but there he was again, already swimming when I got there. This time I kept the sprint team's practice short to keep us from being too tired for the meet tomorrow. I changed into clothes so fast that I caught Mason on the way to his car. He was still wearing his swimsuit, with a parka thrown on over it.

"Hey stranger," I said, determined to return things to normal.

"Hope." He stopped walking until I caught up. "You ready for tomorrow?"

"Of course," I said. "You?"

He shrugged, staring at the asphalt. "I guess so."

"Are you ever going to look at me again?"

He turned surprised eyes toward me. "I look at you. What do you mean?"

I put my hand on his chest and leaned close. "You aren't *looking* at me anymore."

He cleared his throat. "It's weird now."

"It doesn't have to be."

His eyebrows drew together.

I felt like screaming in frustration when he didn't flirt back, or even smile. "Look, Lacy always makes everything so dramatic, okay? It's not like you did anything wrong. She thought you liked her. You didn't know she was my sister, so it's no big deal if you were flirting, right? She'll get over it."

Mason stepped back then. "She was right, Hope. I do like her."

Oh. I didn't expect that. "Well, I'm really happy for you two, then." I thought about Lacy's closed door. Was Mason in there last night? Was she laughing at me this whole time? Were they both? My nostrils flared and tears sprang to my eyes, hot and fast. I spun away from him, and started walking toward my car.

Mason caught up with me before I reached it and grabbed my arm. "Lacy's not even talking to me, okay. It's not like there's anything going on. I completely ruined everything."

I yank my arm away. "If you liked her, then why did you ask me out?" A memory surfaced of him trying to wiggle out of our date. I shoved it away.

"I liked you both at first. Is that a crime? I was new here and I had no idea you were sisters, Hope. I met this girl who was an amazing swimmer. She was funny, flipping me off to get my attention, and she had this loser boyfriend it was fun to piss off. Then suddenly she doesn't have a boyfriend anymore and she's interested in me. She would understand swimming, and she would be there with me at swim meets. I don't know, it made sense."

I smiled. "It still makes sense."

"It does." He nodded. "What doesn't make sense is that I met your sister. And she's amazing, too. She's smart and she keeps me on my toes, and... you don't want to hear this, but look, what I'm trying to say is, I liked her a lot, and I liked debating with her. It was my very first time to ever do it and I liked it as much as I like swimming. I liked who I was when I was standing up there, arguing points against geniuses and being judged for my brains, not my backstroke. I didn't think I was doing anything wrong flirting with both of you, or even taking you both out. I figured I had time to work out who I wanted to really pursue."

"Play the field," I said.

"Yes!"

"It's what we're supposed to do," I said, "right? We're teenagers, after all." What a load of crap. But I didn't want to go back to having these weird, stilted exchanges anymore, so I didn't say any of what I was thinking.

"Look, Hope, I want to be your friend. I want us to be team captains, and I want to get to know you too. But I can't, I'm not sure it's a great idea-"

"You can't date me."

He sighed. "Right. It would be weird, too weird, right? Plus, it would hurt Lacy."

Screw Lacy. It was already hurting me. "Right, it would and we don't want that."

"Okay, so." He held out his hand as if to shake mine. As though we were like, striking a business deal or something. "Friends."

Uh, no. I leaned forward and hugged him instead. "Friends." He felt so amazing to hug that I held on a little too long. He was just so big and so warm.

He pulled away first and I mentally cursed my dumb arms. "Okay, so I'll see you tomorrow, then?"

"Tomorrow."

I had the entire house to myself Friday night. Mom had texted to tell me she was at Clear Lake for Lacy's tournament. I watched some television, ate a few Oreos, packed my bag for tomorrow, and then looked at the clock. Seven thirty.

I texted Gwen. Her date was going great, which was awesome, but I was so terribly bored. And I felt like a loser. When there was a knock on the door, I practically ran to see who it was.

Dave was smiling his crooked smile when I opened the door. Mason had just told me we were friends. He wasn't even flirting. And did I already mention that I was super bored?

That's why I invited Dave in for a movie. The movie kind of sucked, but we weren't paying much attention to it anyway. I had forgotten what a great kisser Dave was. Someone hot and funny and talented liked me. I sent him home around ten, since my mom and Lacy could be back anytime, and I didn't want them to see him. Okay, fine, I was hiding him.

When I woke up Saturday, Lacy and Mom were already on their way out the door. Lacy looked amazing in a dark blue suit, and I took a good look at her. I realized Mom was right. She had impossibly high cheekbones and stormy grayish blue eyes. She was almost bony she was so thin, but she had a lovely face and a willowy, super model look. I felt like the Pillsbury Dough Boy by comparison.

"Oh, hey," Lacy said when she saw me.

"Hey yourself," I said, feeling strange still sporting my bed head and bunny pajamas while she actually had makeup on. "How'd your meet go yesterday?"

"They call it a tournament for debate," she said, "not a meet. But it went okay, I guess. Drew and I are still debating today." She grabbed her laptop bag.

Mom pulled me in for a hug and then kissed my forehead. "There are eggs in the fridge. I boiled some for you, and I made you a smoothie to put in the cooler for the middle of the meet."

"Thanks, Mom. Good luck Lacy," I said. "Tell Drew I said hello."

"I will. And good luck to you at your meet today. I'm sure you'll destroy all those other schools."

I smiled. "Hey, you remembered it was a big meet."

"Yep, an invitational." She ducked her head and followed Mom out the door.

I put the boiled eggs and smoothie in a little ice-chest and made some scrambled eggs for breakfast. Then I grabbed my bag and headed for the school parking lot. I was one of the last people to arrive. Moby was sitting near the front of the bus. I slid onto the bench next to him. "Want to go over the roster?"

"It's too late to change it since everything is seated."

"I know," I said, "but just to make sure everyone knows their events."

He shrugged. "Sure. It can't hurt."

It was amazing how much he loosened up on the bus ride. The less I flirted, the more normal he got. By the time we reached Cypress Woods, he was smiling and so was I. It felt good.

We warmed up in the same lane, and when he lapped me, I grabbed his foot. Instead of kicking me off and continuing on his way, he looked back at me and smiled. My heart executed a perfect flip turn.

The rest of the meet went as well as it could possibly have gone. I thought we might struggle without Dave for the men's medley relay, but Adam really stepped up and came in with a time almost as good as Dave's in backstroke. He even managed to take third overall in the hundred back. With Adam stepping up, and Moby getting first in every single event he swam, we had a chance.

A tall, blonde recruiter came to talk to Moby after the medley relay. I was standing just behind him, so I heard it all. "I was worried about you when I heard you'd moved in the middle of the season," the man said. "It's hard to switch teams and not lose momentum."

Moby smiled. "Momentum is just mass and velocity. I have a lot of mass. A little thing like a move won't impact my velocity."

"Smart too, huh? Well, University of Texas is very interested if you can repeat that medley performance. You wouldn't have to worry about a thing with us. We prioritize for our athletes, and we're the best place you could be to prepare for the Olympics. They're only a little more than two years away, so it's time to be thinking about them already."

Moby nodded. "I know sir, and I really appreciate your interest."

"I'll be watching." He turned to walk away.

"Wait," Moby said. "Mr. Deville, there's another swimmer you should be watching as well."

"Oh?"

Moby slung his arm around me. "Miss Vincent here is the best swimmer at this meet."

"Other than you."

Moby grinned. "Sure, other than me."

"I'll keep my eye out," Mr. Deville said. "We're always interested in recruiting good talent, and I take your recommendation seriously."

After he walked off, Moby dropped his arm.

"That was nice," I said. "Thanks."

"He'd have noticed anyway," he said. "You're an amazing swimmer." He looked at the board. "I'm up. Good luck on your fifty free, if I don't see you before then."

He headed for the pool to do a few warm up laps before his individual medley and I couldn't take my eyes off his retreating back. I was definitely not sad to watch him go.

He won, of course. First place in the individual medley, and then he pulled our team to first in the relay. No one else could even touch him.

When it came time for my fifty free, I felt shaky and nervous. I always did, but this was worse. I saw Mr. Deville watching and I thought my heart might explode. I hadn't given much thought to college. Lacy had been working frantically on her applications since the Fall, but I hadn't started yet. I figured I might take a class or two at Brazosport College next year, if I felt like it. I hadn't even considered a school like University of Texas. Austin seemed so far away.

It probably happened because I was so nervous, but I hit the water weird and my goggles rolled back. I spit them out and yanked them down to my neck, but I'm sure it cost me. Every hundredth of a second matters in the fifty. I still managed to get second place. I hoped Moby hadn't been watching, but I knew Mr. Deville was.

I did better in the hundred fly. My goggles stayed on, and I ignored the butterflies in my stomach and focused on my form. I got first place and Mr. Deville was smiling at me when I climbed out of the pool. Moby congratulated me when he saw me in the cool down pool.

"Nicely done, Ms. Vincent."

"Thanks, Mr. Moby."

He quirked one eyebrow. "Do you know my last name?"

I did. I just wasn't sure how to pronounce it. "It's on the event roster, duh."

"Then say it."

"Montcellier," I said. I pronounced it, "Mont-shell-yer." His face told me that was wrong. Which was his own stupid fault for having such a ridiculous name.

"Well, Mr. Deville told me he's very interested in talking to you." Moby smiled. "Pretty exciting."

"Yeah, it is."

"Would you like to go to UT?" he asked.

"Of course."

"Where were you planning to go?" he asked.

I shrugged. "I'm not sure. I hadn't thought much about it."

His head turned slightly, like he hadn't heard me, maybe. Then they started calling for his heat.

"Good luck," I said.

"Thanks."

He swam the entire five hundred free as a medley, just like last time, and that cocky jerk still beat everyone else by over ten seconds. It really wasn't fair. I sat there watching him, his body moving like a perfectly oiled machine, and I knew he was wrong for Lacy. How could she ever understand this? She never even came to my meets. She always had debate tournaments.

I glanced up at the stands. Not many people came to watch swim meets, actually. The stands were pretty sparse, even at a huge meet like this. Except when I looked up there, familiar blue grey eyes met mine. Lacy sat at the very top of the bleachers. She was still wearing her blue suit skirt, but she had taken her jacket off. Her pearls, ivory silk shirt and high heels looked so out of place I almost laughed. She must've been melting. They kept it about ten degrees warmer in natatoriums than any normal building because of all the wet bodies getting in and out of pools. I should've waved to her, but she just smiled at me, so I smiled back.

"Where's Mom?" I yelled.

She tapped her head with her finger. "Headache," she mouthed back to me.

I didn't bother asking her how her meet went. If she had won her heat, she wouldn't be here. Not this early. No point in making her say it out loud. Annie came up with a goggle malfunction then, and after that Coach needed me to help him record our points. We were doing so well, I could hardly believe it.

When Moby won, I figured she'd come down and congratulate him, but she didn't. I looked back up at the bleachers, and I didn't see her there. Had she left?

I didn't see Lacy again until it happened, I swear. I thought she had gone home. But after the final relay, when Moby's team took first, and Adam's team took third, Coach Collins and I calculated the points. We did it separately to make sure neither of us missed anything. We're both total crap with math. We came up with the same thing every time. I guess I shouldn't have been too surprised. Moby got first in two individual events and two relays. I got first in two relays and one individual event. Second in another. Adam did pretty well, and so did Vivian, second and third in their races.

Still, Moby was shocked when he climbed out of the cool down pool and I told him we had scored third place overall.

"You're kidding," he said. "No way!" He tossed me up in the air, and then swung me around. I couldn't help myself. Before he put me down, I leaned in and kissed him full on the mouth. I know I shouldn't have, and he pulled back and set me down right away, but it was too late. His mouth had tasted so good. All warm and minty, with just a hint of chlorine.

"Sorry," I said.

He wasn't even looking at me. Where else would he be looking? I followed his gaze up until I saw her. Her hair was pulled back, and her ivory blouse clung to her, but this time, all I could see was the expression on her face.

Misery.

Lacy was running down the steps so fast I was worried she'd twist her ankle, but she lived in heels and moved well in them.

Moby took off after her. I tried to stop him. "Moby, wait."

He turned back to me. "Hope, my name is Mason, not Moby. Mason. Try to remember that."

Then he was gone.

I should've been happy. We hadn't come in third in any big invitational ever. There was a recruiter interested in me from the University of Texas, and I'd just kissed Moby. But when I watched him leave this time, I wasn't happy at all.

I glanced back up into the stands and I realized Lacy and I weren't the only ones who were upset. Dave was glaring at me from the bleachers on the other side. I hadn't even realized he was here.

Basically, Saturday was a terrible, miserable, awful day.

Chapter Eleven

LACY

Dr. Brasher is ready for me today when I reach his office. He has a little table set up, and the laptop is sitting on top of it, plugged in, with Word pulled up on the screen.

"Wow, you're prepared."

He nods. "It's unorthodox, but this is working for us. You're opening up, and you're doing it in your own way. I think we're almost done."

Thank gosh for that. I'm not sure how much more I have to say. I look at the blank page. It reminds me of a flow chart. I really wish I could just do one round, even observing. I could use a good clean flow right now, so clear, so uncomplicated.

Instead, I force myself to write the bad parts. The parts I want to pretend never happened.

———

By the time I reached the tournament Friday morning, I hadn't slept in days. It wasn't a good way to start a tournament where I wanted to impress a Yale recruiter. Of course, neither was having my coach arrested for grand theft auto.

Seriously. Check the records. You can't make this stuff up. Remember her fancy (did I say fancy? I meant crazy) boyfriend who bought her the mustang? Well, he didn't so much buy it, as take an extended test drive. Except, he told her he bought it for her, and she's such a head case that she believed him. For the past few days she'd been driving around a brand new, stolen mustang, thinking that her young boyfriend loved her enough to buy her a fancy car. Our bus was just pulling up to the curb when the police car showed up. Lights, sirens, handcuffs, the works.

Ms. Harris is lucky they didn't do a breathalyzer on her before they hauled her away. Then the school would probably have had to fire her on top of everything else. As it was, she got out the next day when they discovered her boyfriend was the real culprit and Ms. Harris was just your ordinary dupe. None of that helped us on Friday morning. In retrospect, it might have been better if we'd just thrown in the towel.

Instead, Drew and I both called our parents. All we really needed was a sponsor, any adult sponsor. Drew's mom had a surgery that couldn't be rescheduled, and her dad had some kind of plant emergency. My mom got every other Friday off, and after I called her, she convinced a friend to switch Fridays with her. I don't know how she still got Fridays off with the number of sick days she used for her migraines, but she did. I wasn't even surprised, because Mom always came through in a crisis.

Mom was on her way back to the school to be our chaperone and fill-in coach when the Vice Principal showed up. Before we could leave for the tournament, Vice Principal Fayton had to come search all of our bags for drugs. Apparently drug use was getting more and more prevalent at our school. For me though, it was just a nuisance.

"What's with the random drug searches?" I asked, while Mrs. Fayton searched my bag. "Be careful with that." I snatch my laptop from her. "It has my case on it."

She frowned. "Youth today think drugs are a joke. They're not."

"I don't think it's a joke." I widened my eyes at Drew, feeling a little validated for my position, even if Drew thought I was a loser for it.

We made it to the tournament just in time for our first round, but we had to run to get there. I was huffing and puffing when we met our judge, and Drew's cheeks were bright red. Not an auspicious start.

"We're affirmative," Drew whispered. "What am I supposed to read?"

I handed her a copy of the wind power plan I had modified at the last minute.

"Not solar?" She didn't even ask about the anthropocentrism case. Wise move. I had read every scrap of analysis and back and forth discussion frantically, but hadn't come up with a solution to the counter plan.

"I won't give Todd the satisfaction."

"Is he even here?" Drew asked.

I shake my head. "I don't think so, but his school is. He'd hear."

"Can't have that." Drew rolled her eyes.

"Oh, shut up."

We managed to win our first round, barely. We won our second much easier, falling back into the groove we used to have. I spent all our prep time getting Drew ready for her speeches and I passed her short cards with prepped answers for cross-examination, so whenever a question I expected came up, she had an answer. She floundered through the others.

Right after the second round, I got a text from good old Mr. Langston. HAROLD HAD A FAMILY EMERGENCY. HE FLEW HOME EARLY. SORRY TO MISS YOU. ALIEF KERR NEXT WEEK?

I was crushed. I'd gotten into a fight with Mason, badgered Ms. Harris into signing us up, and then made my mom trade days at work and drive out to Clear Lake. All for nothing. And now, I had to decide whether to go to Lamar and get an easy few points next week so I could get to state, or whether to go to the harder meet to try and impress Mr. Langston's friend.

It did give me another week to figure out a solution on my case, and maybe if Mr. Langston's friend sees me debating with Drew, Harold would see that I can basically carry any team on my own. Besides, Drew and I were doing well. Maybe we'd get the points we needed to qualify this weekend.

YES, I texted back.

SEE YOU THERE. He replied.

I didn't bother to tell him I'd be with a different partner. I worried he might change his mind if he knew.

After that, things went downhill. We lost our next round, but managed to win round four and qualify to return on Saturday morning. That night I slept almost eight hours for the first time since Tuesday. It felt amazing. The next morning, we managed to win our first round and make it to Quarters. We lost in Semis, which was okay. We got another two points, bringing me up to eight with Drew, same as I already had with Mason. I tried not to think about him, but it didn't work very well. It was hard not to compare debating with him to today's miserable mess.

When we washed out, I looked at my watch. I could tell

Mom was tired, but I felt strangely peaceful. We listened to music on the drive from Clear Lake back home, and dropped Drew off in Lake Jackson on our way.

"How are you doing, kid?" my mom asked me once we were alone. "Holding up okay?"

"I'm fine," I said. I was surprised to realize I meant it.

"I've been worried about you." My mom's hands were at ten and two exactly. I thought about her life for a moment. She called in a favor to spend her day off judging at a debate tournament last minute. She never dated. She never went out. She was always there for me, and she tried to help her two very different daughters navigate school, activities and relationships.

I didn't thank her enough.

"I'm fine, Mom. I'm figuring things out. I'm sorry I've been so hard to live with lately."

"You say it like the bad parts are past." She turned and smiled at me and the world felt a little lighter.

I shrugged. "I guess maybe they are. For the past few days, ever since I found out Mason likes Hope, I guess I felt like I couldn't survive without him. Today Drew and I did okay, scored a few points, and I realized, I'll be okay." I looked down at my hands. That sounded pretty silly, a declaration that I'd survive my crush liking someone else. "When Hope called me a drama queen it ticked me off, but maybe she's right."

She shook her head. "Not at all. I felt that way after your father."

I sighed. "That's not helping. You were married to him and had two kids. Plus, he died. I barely know Mason, and I know that. I guess since I really liked him, and I knew he liked Hope, that somehow I conflated the two. If he liked Hope, he was choosing her, and I punished him by saying he couldn't debate with me either. And that made me think

I couldn't win without him. Now that I've gone to a tournament on my own again, I realize I can do it, whatever needs to be done. Even if he and Hope get married and have kids, I'll just move on, you know, and keep kicking."

My mom smiled at me. "I'm glad to hear that, but I wasn't comparing this to when your father died. Your dad, well, he and I had some rocky roads. Things between us weren't perfect and sometimes I felt like I couldn't breathe. We broke up once, I dumped him actually, and I didn't think I'd survive it."

"I didn't know that." Actually I knew almost nothing about my mom and dad, I realized. "On Wednesday, when Mason said he wasn't going to come with me this weekend, maybe in part because the Yale recruiter was coming, I felt like my world was falling apart. After what we had done at Katy, the idea of debating with anyone else filled me with a sick kind of despair."

Mom smiled but it looked sad for some reason. "I know exactly what you mean."

"Plus, I didn't tell you this before, but there was some weirdness with Drew, too. I wasn't sure if I'd even have her as an option anymore."

"Because you switched to Mason at the last tournament?"

"Uh, sort of."

My mom cocks one eyebrow. "Or did she finally tell you?"

"Tell me what?" I asked.

"That she's gay?"

I coughed. And then I coughed some more. When I could finally speak, I said, "How did you know?"

Mom tilted her head. "I pay attention to little things."

"I really do worry too much about my stuff and not enough about other people," I said.

"You're wonderful," my mom said, a dreamy smile on her face as she drove down the road.

"Nuh uh. Not really. I need to be more like you."

"How's she doing?"

I shook my head, not that she could see it. "I don't know, really. She hasn't brought it up again. I'm kind of letting her lead the whole thing. I don't think she's come out to anyone but me yet."

"Her mother doesn't know? Or her dad?"

I shrugged. "No idea."

"Maybe you should ask," Mom said.

I should have. I was so selfish. I cringed a little, ashamed at being such a poor friend.

"I'm proud of you," my mom said.

"Why?" I asked. "I'm screwing everything up."

"Sometimes the best thing we can do is keep trying. And your heart is in the right place. It always has been."

I need to fix things with Hope, though. I didn't have any perspective before. "I want to go to Hope's meet," I said suddenly.

"We're almost home." My mom sounded dismayed.

"I can drive myself," I said.

"It's an hour and a half away."

I didn't care. I needed to talk to Hope, and tell her I didn't care whether she dated Mason. I just wanted us to be us again. A family.

I dropped off my mom so she could lay down. She put her arm on mine before I left. "Drive safely, please. I couldn't bear it if something happened to you."

"Mom, you're being weird. I'll be fine." Dad died in a car crash, so Mom was always kind of odd about us driving. "I'll drive like a grandma, I swear."

She looked down at the floor. "I don't think I could go on if I lost either of you girls like I lost your father."

I turned toward the wall before I rolled my eyes so my mom wouldn't see. "I know. I'll be careful."

I had plenty of time to think on the way to the swim meet, and something hit me. I'd been flogging my poor brain relentlessly, and maybe what I needed all along was some peace, some time to think. I couldn't use Todd's plan alone, but I could combine his and mine. If I incorporated the parts of his counterplan that worked, I could shove them into the place of the objectionable parts of mine. I could merge them into one proposal that was entirely mine, but would address Zimmerman's criticisms of Heidegger in the first place. And I'd be able to use the counter plans popping up on the open data project as further evidence that I was solving for the issue.

It was brilliant, and I hadn't felt this happy in a long time.

I arrived at the Cypress Woods Invitational meet just in time to see my sister swim the hundred fly. Seeing her body moving so beautifully, it had always made me envious before now, but today I saw it for the miracle it was. I would look like a seagull plonked in a fish tank out there, but Hope flowed through the water like a dolphin or, I admitted begrudgingly, maybe a mermaid. Every part of her body did just what it was supposed to. It was awe-inspiring.

I watched her interact with Mason when she got out, becoming more certain every moment that I was right. I knew from her attitude this week that she wasn't involved with Mason. She was around the house all the time, stomping and yelling, slamming doors. She was as upset as I was, and I knew it. She might have told me she wouldn't pull back from him for me, but obviously she had.

Then I watched Mason swim. That's when I really got it, the reason he couldn't bail on this swim meet. He was a wonderful debater. He spoke so clearly, so eloquently, that he got perfect speaker points in every round. He had such a quick mind it was hard to believe he was real. But I was as good as him, and there were others even better than we were.

When he got in the water, it was like he belonged there. He made it look even easier, even more natural than Hope did. I saw what she saw, his beauty, his grace, and I saw a whole future unfold before my eyes. They would both go to the Olympics, they'd get married under five multicolored rings and they'd give their beautiful babies a handful of gold medals for teething toys.

I was ready to tell Hope to date him, and I would go down and do it today. Hope waited for my blessing, unwilling to date him until she knew her sister would be okay. She always took what she wanted from me, but not this time. She'd grown up. She cared about me after all, and I felt even better about what I came to do. I could make peace with Hope and give her my blessing.

Telling her it was okay would be hard, but it was the right decision. It felt like, somehow, seeing him here, every bit as at home among these jocks, every bit as comfortable in the water as on land, I understood him better, I saw who he really was. Trying to choose one side of himself was tearing him in two, and I wouldn't be part of that.

I'd never thought much about God. Mom never read us the Bible or anything. She always prayed over our meals, but she never took us to church. But that day, sitting in those bleachers, I had this overwhelming sense that there must be a God, for something so perfect as Mason in the water to exist. At the same time, I wondered what kind of God would create someone so perfect for me, and so perfect for my sister and then throw him between us.

I looked up at the roof of the natatorium. "You couldn't

have split that zygote? Seriously. Throw me a bone here. I'd even have taken a little brother."

When Mason won his race by a wide margin, I climbed down from the bleachers and went to cool off outside for a moment. On my way out, I noticed Dave was sitting way up high, like I had been. I waved at him, and he waved back. I wasn't sure why he wasn't swimming, but he seemed happy enough to watch. He was better looking than I remembered, and I could see why Hope liked him. He was nothing to Mason of course, but he had classic looks that reminded me of Hope's a little bit.

When I went back inside, Hope was just winning a relay. She looked so happy and so free. I wanted to be able to sit front and center and cheer her on. I wanted to fix this rift between us.

I figured when this ended, I could give her a ride and we could talk. I'd tell her I was sorry, and say that she could date Mason. I'd promise not to get upset, and I'd just try to stay away when they were together so I didn't have to see them, you know, making out. At first, anyway.

I rehearsed my speech a time or two, polishing a few parts, but keeping to the same general ideas. Then I watched as Mason won another relay. He really was amazing. I'd need to stop looking at him in a swimsuit, or I'd have trouble keeping my resolve. I watched Hope instead. She was hunched over some kind of paper, and then talking to her Coach with a big smile.

A moment later, she ran down the concrete, a big no-no I thought, and yelled something to Mason. Then it felt like time slowed down somehow. Mason grabbed Hope, tossed her up in the air and spun her around, just as he had with me at the tournament we won. I could still feel his arms around me, and I could feel the excitement. I saw that same thing reflected in his face, but directed toward Hope and something inside of me broke. Then Hope leaned down and kissed him. In front of her teammates, her peers, even her Coach.

My stomach roiled, my resolve to accept this wavered and I leaned over and puked. Even over all the other noise, I could still hear the splat when my vomit finally hit the pavement a dozen feet down. I wiped my mouth on someone's towel, sorry random person. I stood up to go, and I locked eyes briefly with Dave. He looked as sick as I did and I actually felt sorry for him.

When I started down the stairs, something about the motion in that moment must have drawn his attention, because Mason's eyes locked on mine and I knew I couldn't cover up my feelings. Not nearly well enough, so I looked away and ran. I shot down those stairs faster than I ever had in my life. There should be some kind of athletic event where you fly down stairs in high heels. I'd have won that day. I was out the door and to my car in a flash. I got in and started driving. I refused to think, not at all, until I reached Drew's house. I knew I shouldn't go there, that I shouldn't bother her with this, but I couldn't bear to go home. What if Mason and Hope came back there after their win to celebrate, or to go hang out on the beach? No. I couldn't.

I should've thought about how Dave was feeling, but I didn't think about that either.

Drew was confused when she answered the door, but she waved me in without hesitation and patted my back when I cried. She really was the best friend in the world. When I was finally cried out, I curled up on her couch and went to sleep.

When I woke up, it was almost ten at night. I swore.

"Why didn't you wake me up?"

"Lacy, you may not believe this, but humans need to sleep. It's about this thing called an REM cycle."

I stood up and rubbed my eyes. "I'm serious. I need to read Chaucer and then write a paper on it. I need to study for calculus, and Spanish. I need to finish my reading for history. That doesn't even include all the stuff I'm supposed to be doing to prepare for the AP tests I have coming up. Plus, I think I figured out how to fix our case, and I need to get to work on that too. I only have thirty hours until the paper's due, and I have to take both tests. I don't have time for sleep."

"Calm down," she said.

"Why aren't you more panicked?" I asked.

She sighed. "While you were freaking out over debate stuff last week, I read Chaucer and wrote my paper. I've been studying for Spanish, and all I need to do tomorrow is history and math. I'm not trying to kill myself at the age of eighteen."

I scowled. "Where's your mom, anyway? How come she didn't wake me up?"

Drew's dad left her mom years ago because her mom worked too much. Now her dad lived in a little house on the bay and spent all his free time fishing, and her mom still worked too much. Drew didn't seem to mind the setup much.

"Mom's working a twenty-four hour shift. She'll be back in the morning."

I sighed. "Well, thanks for being here for me, but I need to get going."

"Study here for a while. You can use my books." She tossed her copy of The Canterbury Tales at me. She didn't even ask why I was crying or what was wrong. I didn't offer up any reasons.

I sat back down on the sofa and started reading. When I almost dozed off around eleven, I stood up and walked in a big circle around the surprisingly clean family room.

"What's wrong?" she asked.

"I'm falling asleep!"

"I'm telling you, you slept about four hours just now, which is not enough. It was only a partial catch up for the past week of sleep deprivation."

"So what, I should just give up? Who cares if I completely fail my tests, or if I don't hand in my paper?"

Drew smirked. "Ewelina would be giddy."

I scowled. "That is not funny."

"Too bad you don't suffer from ADHD," Drew said.

"What does that mean?" I asked.

"My mom has a prescription she uses on her twenty-four hour shifts sometimes. She had to convince another doc she suffered from adult ADHD to get it. It's called Desoxyn. It's basically speed." Drew grinned. "She said she couldn't sleep when she's on it if she wanted to."

Drew's mom, a doctor, abused prescription drugs? "Wow, that's terrible."

"Is it, though? It's regulated, controlled, the right dosage, and it helps her not kill people when she has to work. I'd say that's a good thing."

"You are morally ambiguous," I said. "Clearly."

Drew raised one eyebrow. "Because I think my mom can take a prescription? I think your mom broke your brain."

Speaking of moms, I thought about how my mom suggested I talk to Drew.

"Hey does your mom know?"

Drew sat up straighter and picked at invisible lint on her pajama pants. "Know what?"

"Does she know you're gay?"

Drew frowned. "I don't know."

"So you haven't told her?" I asked. "Like you hadn't told me?"

Drew kicked at the coffee table. "No. I haven't."

"Why not?" I asked. "Your mom's pretty cool. I think she'd be okay with it."

Drew's eyes look down at the floor and her shoulders slump. "She calls gay women lesbos and makes a lot of jokes about how they don't know how to wear makeup and look like men."

When Drew said that, I remembered. It was true.

"She doesn't know about you, though. And she loves you. I'm sure she'd stop."

"I can't tell her right now, okay?"

I put my hand on her knee. "It's fine, seriously. But if you want me around when you tell her, just say the word. What about your dad?"

"He knows," Drew said, "or at least he suspects. He's said some weird things, like when I get married one day, my future spouse, he, *or she,* might want a beach wedding, but he'd totally be willing to hold the ceremony on his house overlooking the bay. That kind of stuff. The kind of stuff you don't say unless you know."

I pulled her close. It must be really hard to always be listening to little things people you care about say or watching what they do, just to try and figure out whether they will love you, the real you. "I'm sorry. I wish I'd noticed before you had to tell me."

"It's fine." Drew's eyes are teary when she finally pulls away.

After that, Drew worked on her history reading while I started on Chaucer. The second time I dozed off, the sound of Drew's snores woke me. I slapped at my face a few times, but I could feel my eyelids, slowly closing, inexorably moving downward.

I couldn't sleep. I had to catch up on too many things. I only had tonight and tomorrow.

I probably shouldn't write this in here, but maybe honesty will count for something. I thought about what Drew said. My mom was crazy, and prescription drugs were fine. Useful, even. My mom was a little irrational.

I paced back and forth a few times, trying to wake up, and I walked right past Drew's medicine cabinet. I knew where it was because I'd gotten throat lozenges there before. I'm not proud of this, but around three a.m. I found the bottle of Desoxyn written to Drew's mom. There were only three pills inside.

I put the bottle away and slammed the cabinet shut. I knew the sound would wake up Drew, but it didn't. I went back to work, but when I nodded off again, this time waking up to the timer I set on my phone in case I dozed off, I crossed back to that cabinet without thinking. I pulled out a single pill, a white oval with little blue speckles. Before I could think about the litany of reasons I shouldn't use it, I popped it into my mouth and swallowed it.

Within fifteen minutes, the world became startlingly clear. I was jittery, sure, but my exhaustion evaporated. I finished The Canterbury Tales and wrote my paper faster than I imagined possible. It felt like my mind was running a mile a minute. That little pill was literally the best thing I'd ever taken.

When I saw the time, five a.m., I shut down my laptop and tiptoed out of Drew's house. It wasn't like my mom would care. I was fairly sure she'd passed out before I reached Hope's meet. But Drew's mom should be home soon, so I knew I had better clear out. I tried not to think about how awesome it would be to have two more magic pills, solely in case of emergency. I put the bottle back, but then it occurred to me. Drew's mom might notice one was missing if I left it there. It might be better if she thought she had misplaced the bottle. Besides, it wasn't like there were a lot left. Two pills, that was it.

I took it with me.

I knew my mom might be upset that I came home so late, but I was not expecting to see anyone else sneaking into my house just after five a.m. Hope looked as surprised as me when I pulled up in Mom's car. Coming home at this hour after a huge win at a swim meet? After kissing Mason? I had a pretty good idea where she'd been, and I didn't like it any more than my mom would.

Chapter Twelve

HOPE

Dear Diary:

I'm beginning to think that the only person who cares about my thoughts is you, Ms. Littleton. Mom certainly doesn't and Lacy isn't speaking to me. Moby, er, Mason has obviously written me off. I'm not usually someone who feels sorry for myself, which might be because my life is usually pretty great, but I screwed things up big this time, and I don't even know what to do about it. I even managed to piss Dave off, sweet old dopey Dave.

I think last time I wrote in here, I was saying that Mason left to chase after Lacy. In case you're not very savvy with relationships, when you kiss a guy, it's a very bad sign if he goes running off after someone else.

A few minutes later Moby came back, but without Lacy. We were all loading up on the bus to head back home when I saw him.

"Hey Coach," he said, not even looking at me, "is it okay if I go home with my mom?"

"Sure," Coach Collins said.

"I thought you might want to talk about the plan of attack for our next meet," I said. "We have a few swimmers who are only a few points shy of qualifying for state."

Mason shrugged. "We can talk about that Monday. Or you can talk to Coach and fill me in. I heard Dave may be coming back. If he is, I'm fine for him to take over, too. Either way."

Just like that, without saying anything else to me, he left. I was furious, but also kind of embarrassed. I'm not used to feeling foolish about boys.

The bus took forever to get back to B-port, and I was sick of the day by the time I reached my car. Dave texted while I was headed home. I SAW YOU. CONGRATU-LATIONS.

I pulled over on the side of the road. That was too cryptic to ignore. YOU SAW ME WHERE?

He texted back. AT THE MEET.

My stomach dropped. I've been telling Dave we aren't back together and I meant it, but if he was there, he saw the stupid kiss. Could anyone else in the world have possibly been there to make it more of a mess? I didn't know what to say. I knew he had to be mad.

WE AREN'T TOGETHER, I texted him.

I didn't know if I was talking about me and Dave, or me and Moby. Both were true.

When I got home, I saw a car parked in front of my house. Mason's car. I pulled into the driveway and cut the engine. I noticed another car behind me. It was Dave's. I panicked, but he idled in front of my house for a moment before speeding off.

Once my heartbeat slowed down, I got out of my car and stood up, finally as prepared as I could be to see Mason and Lacy together. Why else would he be here? When he couldn't catch her at the meet, he left with his mom and beat me here.

When I reached the porch, I heard some voices and stopped. It had been a warm day, pretty common on the coast in Texas, even in January. The window was open. I could hear snatches of conversation. I crept closer, my ear turned toward the window.

"The thing is," my mom said, "you have to choose, Mason. I want to like you, and I know you don't know them very well yet, but you've got to pick one or the other soon. Or neither would be fine, too." She paused. "I can't take the back and forth, and neither can my girls. You understand, I'm sure."

With a deep voice I loved to listen to, Mason said, "If they weren't sisters, I could just date both of them. Take Hope out a few times and Lacy too, but I feel awful knowing they aren't getting along."

"You have to pick one."

"It's hard to choose between them. You're their mother. Surely you can see why."

"I know that. It's difficult when you're young. So many decisions are thrown at you and the world wants you to choose, and you do, but you have so little knowledge of what your choices will lead you toward, or how that will alter who you become."

"Yeah, I guess."

Mom laughed. "I'm waxing nostalgic, but Mason, even if you don't know them well, if I told you both of them were drowning, you'd save one of them first."

"Lacy," he said immediately, "because there's no way Hope would ever drown."

Mom laughed again. "I see why they like you. Bad analogy, I guess, but if you had to choose one of them right now, who would it be?"

Mason sighed. "Lacy, probably. She's so smart, and I

could talk to her forever. When we were debating, I felt like I was growing, becoming better than I am now. She challenges me, but Hope is so much easier to be around. She's funny and kind, she laughs at all my jokes and she's always happy to see me. She's less complicated. And if I'm being honest, she's less angry."

If he had any idea how angry I was right now, he might take that back. I was simple? I'd show him simple.

My mom clucked. "My two girls are very different, and Mason, you're a good guy, I think. You could probably make either one of them happy. I'm not saying this because I favor one girl over the other. I adore both my girls. Hope is so much like her father. She's so free and delightful. She's always been the center of attention, and she demands a lot of time and effort in her own way, but it's part of her charm. She is simpler to understand than Lacy."

"You get it, then."

"I do, maybe more than you know. Did either girl tell you about their father?"

Mason didn't speak, but I was assuming he shook his head. I knew I hadn't spoken a word about Dad.

"In case you don't know this, we aren't divorced. He's dead. We got together when we were both quite young, and Harry was quite the womanizer. He had dozens of girlfriends, and they all knew he liked loads of women. He was totally honest, but the world's best flirt."

"I could see that," Mason said.

"I liked him, but I wasn't going to put up with any of that nonsense, and when I told him, he dropped them all, just like that. I was worried when we met that he might cheat on me one day. If that was our worst problem, I think he'd still be here."

I couldn't breathe. Mom had never said a word about any of this to me.

"But he got into drugs, Mason. First pot, then cocaine. Ironically, we did better when he was on cocaine than when he was using pot. He got a lot more done." She laughed but it sounded pained. "I found out after we were already engaged. I would've broken things off, maybe, but I was already pregnant with Angelica, and I knew I couldn't do it alone. After Angelica was born, named because she was an angel for him, he tried to turn it all around. He swore he'd do it for her. He did too, for a few months, but he relapsed. It was just after his relapse I found out I was pregnant with Hope. By the time she was born, he had things back under control. We named her Hope, because she was literally a new Hope for our family. She looked so much like him."

It was quiet, and I realized my mom was crying. She was telling Mason about this, stuff she'd never even told her daughters. I couldn't stand it anymore. I opened the front door.

"Seriously, Mom? You didn't think I might need to know any of this?"

She jumped off the kitchen chair she'd been sitting in. "Hope."

Mason's eyes flew wide. "Hope, we didn't know you were here."

"You don't say."

"What have you heard?" my mom asked.

"Oh, I've heard enough to ask why you lied about Dad for so long."

"I was waiting until you were old enough to understand. I wanted you girls to love your Dad, and think good things about him. If you knew, you might think you were doomed. And I didn't want you to think of him as a druggie."

I sunk down on the sofa, and she came to sit next to me. "After you were born, I lost my job and your dad couldn't get a decent one, not with his recent history, so I went to apply for government assistance. It was too much for him. He relapsed, but this time, he graduated they called it. To heroin. He took too much. We still don't know whether that was on purpose. When I realized it I called 911, but it was too late."

"Oh man," Mason said.

I had almost forgotten he was there and I jumped.

"I'm so sorry about that."

My mom took my hand. "We're okay now. This happened a long time ago, but that's why we don't take anything at our house. When I get a migraine, I sometimes take a Tylenol or two Ibuprofen, or sometimes I don't, but then I go to my room and ride it out. We don't take anything stronger than that, not ever. It's just better that way. We'd all be better off if most of the drugs we rely on had never been created."

"Maybe not insulin," Mason said.

Mom glared at him.

"Wow," I said. "You think just teaching us not to take anything stronger than a Tylenol was the way to go?"

My mom's face crumpled. "I didn't get a handbook, you know. I've always just done the best I could."

She looked so broken, that I felt bad about questioning her.

Mason stood up. "Maybe I should go."

I glanced back at him. "Yeah, maybe you should." When he stood up, so did I. "But maybe I can help with your 'difficult decision-making.' I'm no longer interested." My heart kind of cried when I said it, but I was so sick of the drama. They could say I was simple, or easy, or an idiot, but I had a happy life before, and now I hated it. I was done with all of the back and forth, the not knowing, and most of all, I was done being mad at Lacy.

"Thanks for coming by Mason, and telling me about

what happened at the meet. I'll call Lacy, and I won't go to bed until she comes home."

My mom sounded better. When she stood up to show Mason to the door, I walked over with her. Before Mason walked down the porch steps, she said, "Even with everything that happened, I wouldn't change a single thing about my life. I loved Harry and I love my girls. Nothing of worth is ever easy, but that's why it's valuable. That's why you fight for it."

I felt betrayed. My mom basically just told Mason all our family baggage, stuff she'd never told me, and then she told him anything good is hard. And we all know that compared to me, Lacy is complicated. I felt a tear roll down my cheek and ran to my room before anyone else saw it.

It wasn't until I reached my own bed that I realized something. My dad's a druggie who either overdosed, or committed suicide, and I've been told my whole life I'm just like him.

My phone buzzed and it was a text message.

From Dave. I FORGIVE YOU.

He forgave me? I wanted to say I didn't do anything wrong, but maybe I did. Maybe I shouldn't have made out with him last night if I liked Moby. Maybe I should have backed off of Moby when my sister who never ever wants anything expressed an interest. I definitely should have when I learned it was reciprocated.

I thought about how good it felt to make out with Dave last night. Yes. I need something easy, I thought. Instead of replying to his text, I snuck out and jogged the mile down to Dave's house. He was just as happy to see me as I knew he would be. When I woke up with a start, I was on the couch in Dave's movie room. I snuck, or is it sneaked? I can't ever remember. Anyhow, my movement woke Dave up, and he insisted on driving me back home.

Imagine my surprise when I saw my sister pull up in my mom's car while I was in the process of sneaking back in myself! My genius sister, the complicated one, the one who I just realized was stunningly beautiful. The one Mason probably found after his conversation with Mom and took back home to his place. I had made all these promises to myself, to let go, to give her my blessing, but seeing her looking so perfect, sneaking home just like me, I hated her in that moment, more than I had ever hated anyone.

I couldn't handle her, not then. Not sneaking home like this, with my hair in a messy snarl, my swimming bag slung over my shoulder, my parka pulled around me. It didn't help that she looked amazing. She still wore her pencil skirt and ivory blouse. It wasn't even rumpled. Her hair was still twisted up, almost like she hadn't slept on it at all. Her makeup looked flawless, and her eyes seemed completely awake.

I got inside before her and locked the door behind me, but apparently she was fast too. I hadn't even set my bag in the laundry room before she had unlocked it and was inside the door.

"Shh," I whispered when she shut the door and flipped the lock. "Don't wake up Mom."

"Duh," she whispered back. "I know."

"Where were you?" I needed to know if she came home, got a text from Mason or something, and went over to his place. I knew I was scowling, but I couldn't help it.

"I could ask you the same thing, but I don't want to know the answer," she said.

Since she didn't want to know, she wasn't at Mason's. Good. Probably just did a sleepover with Drew. Boring. And typical.

"Look," she said. "I've been thinking and I'm sorry. I've

really screwed this all up, and I should've been a better sister. We shouldn't have let a guy get between us."

She was trying to fix things. Of course she was, because Lacy was always right. I wanted to, I really did, but I was too angry, my mom's words still ringing in my ears, and I was so tired.

I hated that she apologized first. It might sound crazy, but it just pissed me off more. I could hear the tally in my head. She was smarter, she was harder working, she was complicated, and interesting, and worth it. Oh yeah, and she forgave faster, too. Instead of breaking down, and crying like half of me wanted to, I just said, "Whatever."

"Don't be like that." When she frowned at me, she'd never looked more like Mom. The parent who wasn't an addict. The one who was always there for us, the one everyone on earth would pick as the best parent, and the one who told Mason that Lacy was his best option.

"Like what?"

She just looked at me expectantly, so I turned to head for my room. She grabbed my shoulder and tried to turn me back to talk to her. I was too tired, and sick of hearing how great she was. I certainly didn't want to deal with her showing me how amazing she was by being fake humble.

"Let go of me. You're always telling me what to do and acting all superior." I pulled away and shoved her back into the entryway. Unfortunately she dropped her bag and her laptop fell out, clattering on the floor loudly. We both froze, expecting our mom to come down the hall any second. When she didn't, we both breathed a big sigh of relief. Lacy leaned over and picked up her laptop, and then she set it on the table. When she opened it and the screen lit up, I breathed a sigh of relief. We could not afford a new laptop.

She grabbed the strap on her bag without looking and

pulled it up, but it was twisted, and the contents of the bag spilled all over the floor, spinning out in every direction. Lacy's eyes followed a weird little brown bottle with a white lid as it rolled across the floor of the family room and came to a stop in front of the sofa.

A pale white hand shot out from the sofa and grabbed it.

Mom's hand.

This wasn't good.

"Lacy," my mom said in a deceptively calm voice. "What is this?"

"It's nothing." She sprinted across the room and tried to take the bottle from our mom. Mom yanked her hand back and squinted to read the words on the bottle in the low light.

"This is a prescription for Dr. Priscilla Dunmore. Why do you have it?"

"She gave it to me." Lacy grabbed for the bottle, but Mom sat up and pulled it out of her reach.

"Do you know what Desoxyn is, or what it's used for?"

Lacy didn't say a word.

"Judging from your face, that's a yes. I'm going to call Dr. Dunmore now, at 5:15 a.m., and explain that somehow a bottle of her prescription medication ended up in your things and we are so very sorry for the mix-up."

Lacy groaned then. "No, Mom, you can't tell her that. Look I need that, okay."

My mom stood up then, and I'd never seen her look so fierce. "You do not need this young woman. If I ever hear of you taking something like this, much less stealing it, you will not survive the fury that will rain down on you. Do you understand me?"

Lacy nodded.

"Now go to your room, right now."

Lacy grabbed her laptop and began walking.

Mom whirled around. "Wait. Give me your cell phone." She held her hand out.

Lacy opened her mouth to say something and then stopped. She pulled her phone from her bag and handed it over.

Mom still wasn't done. "You won't come out of that room, except for meals and school. No ice cream. No boys. No parties, and no best friends. You will not do anything but eat, sleep, and go to school. Are we clear?"

Lacy didn't bother asking how long her punishment would last, but she couldn't quite help herself from clarifying one thing. "But this weekend? I can still go to Alief Kerr, right?"

My sister is such a nerd.

My mom looked confused. "I thought it was Lamar?" She shook her head. "You know what? I don't care. I'll let you go if you give me a solemn promise." She leaned down and put one hand under Lacy's chin. "A vow."

"Anything," Lacy said.

"You vow to me you will never again take any kind of drugs. Prescription or not. Lacy, never again."

"Prescription drugs? I can't take something a doctor tells me to take? So what, are we Amish? Seventh Day Adventists?"

"I mean it," Mom said. "Unless I direct you to take something, you don't take it."

Lacy rolled her eyes and sighed dramatically. "I promise."

"Fine. We'll talk about the details tomorrow, but the debate tournament is still fine."

Lacy opened her mouth, thought better of it, and shut it with a click. Then she went to her room. I walked to my room too, and I felt a little better. Sure, maybe Mom thought Lacy was more "complicated" than me, but after tonight, I had the feeling Mom might appreciate simplicity.

Chapter Thirteen

LACY

I ask Dr. Brasher for a little privacy this time. I'm sick of typing away in his office while he reads a book, and periodically circles the room to look over my shoulder.

"Can't you stick me in a room you don't need somewhere? I'll take a closet, even. It's not like it would be for very long. I'm almost done, right?"

"It certainly feels that way," he says. "I happen to know the Alief Kerr tournament took place two weeks ago."

I nod. "Yes, it did. So if you could just let me write for a little bit, maybe I can finish today and you can get your afternoons back."

He buzzes his secretary and finds me a little room. It's too large to be a closet, but not by much. Still, I'll take it.

———

My mom found out about the speed, which really sucked because she took it all. Plus, she overreacted, clearly. I almost never saw Dr. Dunmore, so it would probably be awkward when I saw her again. But I was more worried about Drew. She had used her mom's medicine as an example. She hadn't meant for me to actually use any.

I stole from my best friend. And now she and her mom know about it.

I tried to shake off my guilt, and the sick feeling in my stomach and focus on what was actually going on in my life right this moment. Thanks to that one little pill I took, I stayed up the rest of Saturday night, and all day Sunday before I got tired. It gave me plenty of time to study for Spanish, finish my calculus work and study for that test. I even worked on my case. It wasn't done, but it was close. Much closer. And I got a full night's sleep Sunday and woke up completely refreshed on Monday morning.

Drew was right. Mom was a little unfair about the nature and benefit of pharma. If she wasn't so mad at me, I'd ask her about her uncle, and try and find out what really happened. I actually wondered whether maybe she had a brother or someone who died that she didn't want to talk about, so she made up this uncle story instead. Certainly my Nana wasn't going to contradict her story from the nursing home. She could barely remember our names.

Monday was another story. Mason was frustrating, so frustrating.

"Lacy, I need to talk to you."

"I don't want to talk to you Mason. Not now. Not later. Not ever."

"Why not?"

I scowled at him. "I think you can figure that one out, actually." I spun on one heel toward him. "But really it comes down to this. I'm sick of all the drama and the easiest way for me to get my life back to normal is to try and love my sister and cut out the unknown quantity."

"It's not like that," Mason said. "If you'd just give me two minutes, I could explain."

"Explain why you kissed my sister in front of the whole swim team?" I asked. "You're only sorry now because I saw you, and you don't need to be. Because I know that I shouldn't be upset, because we were never together. I'm not an idiot. I know that I have no right to be mad, but I'm a girl. We have a carte blanche on being unreasonably upset. Or did you want to give me more details? Maybe you guys have picked out names for your children and you wanted some input? I don't know, but either way, Mason, I don't care. I'm over it."

He looked hurt, but he walked back to sit with Kim again and work on the hopelessly boring Extemporaneous files no one cared about. I still noticed him looking at me pretty often, but I tried to ignore it. I talked to Ms. Harris, now that she was back at work. I asked her if she could switch our plans from Lamar to Alief Kerr this weekend. She just handed me the phone. I pretended to be her, and surprisingly it worked. I even forged her name on a check from our school for the tournament fee. I wondered why I hadn't thought to do this years ago. My signature looked much better than hers, and I was a way better coach than she was, excepting the few sober days a year we got of actual instruction. I went back to my seat, feeling proud of myself.

Right up until I saw my best friend's face. Drew was late and when she did show up, she pursed her lips and scowled at me. "You stole those pills."

"So I take it your mom was mad?" I forced a grin to try and lighten her mood.

"Don't pull that crap with me. You think you can just smile at me and I'll forgive you, but this was a big deal, Lacy. After years of lecturing me, and insisting you never even took a Tylenol, and then you stole from us. From my mom." She shook her head. "That's messed up."

She was right. It was a big deal, and what I did was, well, it was inexcusable. I glance at the ground, embarrassed. "Was your mom really ticked off?"

She shrugged. "At you? No."

"What? Why not?"

She sat down and mumbled so quietly, I could barely understand her. "I told her I gave them to you. I figured if she got mad at you, she'd never let us hang out again. I was furious, but not so dumb I'd give up my best friend forever. I told her I suggested it, which I kind of did, and she yelled. A lot. She did get over it eventually. She told me she could lose her license, and we could lose our house. Blah blah. It's fine. And I don't see her that much so even though I'm grounded for a month, it's not like she can really enforce it much. She did take my phone, though. And pulled the plug on Knight Fort. For the entire month."

"Geez, I'm sorry Drew. I lost my phone, but Mom's letting me go to Alief Kerr."

"Yeah, your mom called and bam, lost the phone first thing. But my mom, nerd that she is, said I can still go to the debate tournament this weekend too."

"Yeah, the second after Mom found them, her hand was out for my phone. I figured since the bottle only had a few pills, if I took it, your mom might think she'd lost the bottle."

"That probably would've worked if your mom hadn't called her. And, next time you're going to steal something, maybe it would be better if you did notify me. Just so I'll have time to come up with a better lie when I take the heat for you."

Drew really was awesome. I didn't tell her enough how lucky I was to have her in my life. "Thank you. Honestly."

She shrugged her shoulders and looked at the floor. "You're like the only person I love who I can really talk to."

I thought about that. She'd told two people about being gay, and I was one of them. And I just completely tossed her into boiling water. I was a horrible friend.

"I'll make it up to you, I swear," I said.

"You don't even need to. That's what being a friend is. As long as you stop doing stupid crap. You're going to stop doing dumb stuff soon, right? Cuz I can't take a lot more."

I laughed then, and Drew laughed with me. Laughing felt good. Really good.

The rest of the day sucked. Tests in every class, a paper to hand in, and a new paper due on Friday, but since we were leaving for the tournament, I had to turn it in on Thursday. Even though Drew and I studied through lunch, I wasn't sure how well I did on the Spanish test. I tried not to obsess, because at least it was all over. I figured I'd go home, watch an episode or two of television, and work on polishing up my new case. I'd have all night tomorrow to work on the changes I'd need to make it work as a counter plan. Then I'd have Wednesday to write my paper, and Thursday night to study for next week's physics and English tests. Other than the pain I felt every single time I saw Mason, and my discomfort in being mean to him, I was doing pretty good.

Until I grabbed the mail that afternoon and saw a letter from Yale. I slid my fingers under the seal, slicing open my index finger. My hands shook, and I sucked on the bloody one. I gulped one big breath in, then another, and I yanked the letter out.

Dear Applicant, it said, then blah blah, many worthy students applying, esteemed university with a long history, but limited space, blah blah, wish me the best.

Yale rejected me.

I dropped the letter on the ground and stumbled over to the sofa.

I really wanted to work on my case, but I just couldn't. I shouldn't have been so upset. It wasn't like this was my first rejection letter. I'd gotten one from Brown, and another from Dartmouth. I'd also been accepted to Duke, Stanford and Princeton.

None of them were Yale.

Every time I looked at my case, or thought about debate at all, I felt like crying. I tried to watch some television, like I'd planned to do before I checked the mailbox, but I couldn't focus enough to understand what was going on. I pulled out C.S. Lewis instead and read *The Screwtape Letters* in a single sitting. It was so interesting, I almost forgot about Yale. Almost. I did feel pretty guilty the whole time. I wondered whether I might have a devil assigned to me, and if he or she was doing some kind of happy dance when I stole those pills. And when I called Hope dumb. And when I let my mom down. I hadn't been getting much right lately.

I heard Mom rummaging around in the kitchen and I knew I ought to go help her out, but I didn't want to tell her about my letter. Thankfully I'd had the insight to pick it up and bring it to my room. Plus, I knew she was mad at me. All I wanted to do was moan and groan and generally feel sorry for myself. I snuck next door to my mom's room and grabbed the home phone. I took it to my room and dialed Drew's home number from memory. I was glad she'd had the same phone number for ten years.

"Hello?" Her voice sounded wary, like she was expecting a telemarketer. She obviously didn't have caller ID. Or maybe she didn't recognize my home phone number anymore. We'd had cell phones since fifth grade. One of the joys of having single moms.

"It's me," I said. "They think we can't communicate without our phones. But look at us, going old school."

"So, did you get your paper done?"

"I haven't even started, but I did read the book for it." I don't know what to say exactly. I want to blurt it out. I didn't get into Yale. But I can't quite make myself do it.

"What did you pick?" Drew asked.

We made small talk for another few minutes before she got tired of waiting for me to get to the point.

"Why are you risking your mom's extreme wrath by calling me?"

"I guess I wanted to complain to someone."

"Well, you've called the right number. I have an honorary degree in complaints and general dissatisfaction. I'll be sure to let you know if any part of your whine is insufficiently entitled or unclear in any way."

"I got another rejection letter today."

She knew right away what school would bum me out this bad. Drew swore. "Oh man, those people at Yale are morons. I swear, Lacy. I wish I knew someone there to call and yell at them. My mom probably does, but I'm not sure she's quite as in my corner right this moment as usual."

"Eh, I'm just a little bummed, is all."

"Want to sneak out and come smoke a joint with me?"

I was pretty sure she was kidding. "Very funny."

"I know a guy," she said. "Jack. Remember?"

"I guess I can't even tell you how stupid that sounds?"

"Nope," Drew said. "Your high horse is now imprisoned in the stables. Hypocrites don't ride."

I snorted into the phone. "Cute."

"I try. But seriously Lacy, I know everything seems crappy lately, but things will look up soon. I can feel it."

I smiled as I hung up, because I had no idea how wrong she was.

I went into the kitchen and ate dinner with Mom. As bad as things were with Hope, I kind of wished she was there as a buffer. I didn't want to endure a meal with Mom alone, seeing as how she was still mad at me. But I figured the more friendly I acted, the shorter my sentence was likely to be.

"Good meatloaf, Mom."

"I bought it," she said. "Boston Market. I was too upset to think about cooking."

I glanced around. She had disposed of all the evidence. The food was all on plates, as though she had made it. I wondered if she'd ever bought food and passed it off as something she made before now.

"What's wrong with you? Just depressed about being grounded?" she asked.

My mom knew how much I wanted to go to Yale. I hadn't said anything because I really didn't want to talk about it, but telling her I got rejected should be good for at least a little pity. Maybe even enough to get my phone back.

"No, it's more than just being justifiably grounded. I got a letter today."

"Oh?" she asked.

"Yeah," I said. "From Yale."

I didn't say anything else. My mom got it. She stood up and walked around the table, and then she pulled me up into a hug.

"I'm sorry, honey, so sorry. I know how much you wanted to get in there."

I tried to act nonchalant, like it was no big deal, but I could feel my eyes filling with tears. "It's fine." The tears spilled over, and suddenly my attempt at pity became a real meltdown. My mom pulled me down onto her lap, even though I'm way too big to be sitting on her like a baby. I may be eighteen years old, but it still helped to have her stroke my hair and tell me everything was going to be alright.

"I know the past week has been hard. I know as the year wraps up, you feel like you have too much to do, and not enough time. I understand that feeling, believe me, as a single mom, I really do. But it's important you know that you can never resort to chemicals when things are hard. There's a reason your body acts tired. It's because you need sleep." She turned my face so we were eye to eye. "It stinks you didn't get in to Yale, but there are other schools that are just as good. You can't let the pressure you put on yourself take over. I have to be able to trust you. Do you understand?"

I nodded.

"I can't handle it, Angelica. I just can't. Do you hear me?"

"I do, Mom. I promise."

"I believe you. Don't make me a fool. I can't handle losing you, okay?"

Losing me because I took some speed? I suppressed an eye roll. Obviously she wasn't going to get over her thing in a day, so I leaned forward and hugged her, then pulled back and sat in my own chair. "Mom, you're acting crazy. I took one pill so I could study and write a paper. I'm not about to die. I swear. Everything is fine, and I've got it under control."

"I am choosing to trust you," she said. "I'll give you your phone back on Friday morning, mostly because I don't want you at a tournament with no way to reach me, but I'm willing to ease up on the grounding next week, if you convince me I have nothing to worry about."

"You don't," I said. "I swear."

I went back to my room and wrote my paper on *The Screwtape Letters*. I had a few insights of my own on how it would feel to encourage the worst in someone. I'd completely botched everything up with Hope. I brainstormed ways to get things back on track, like writing her an apology on a poster using candy bars, buying her a vat of ice-cream and eating it with her, holding hands and singing Kum-Ba-Ya and braiding each other's hair, but all of those would require us to communicate and I still had no idea what to say. The serenity I found seemed to have shattered into a million pieces when I saw she and Mason went right ahead, knowing it would upset me.

When she came home late that night, I ran out of my room. I figured I could talk to her while she ate, but she breezed past the kitchen and headed straight up the stairs. I grabbed her arm just before she ducked into her room.

"Where were you?" I asked.

"Are you the youngest member of the FBI, now? What do you care?"

"I care about you," I said. "I'm sorry if I haven't acted like it much lately."

"You haven't."

"Well, I am now. How was your day?" I let go of her arm, and followed her to the entry to her room. I was not expecting her to slam the door in my face.

I thought about banging on it, but I knew Mom would come out to see what was going on, and I figured there was always tomorrow.

Now I know that's not always true.

Tuesday went about like Monday, and Wednesday went about like Tuesday. Mom kept reiterating the importance of not doing drugs. All she needed was a shirt and she could audition to be the new D.A.R.E. dog. Hope kept ignoring me, and she kept coming in later and later. I expected my mom to do something about it, but she was spending a lot of time in her room, too. Usually having three women in the house is kind of nice. We don't fight over what movie to watch, there aren't any stinky socks around, and everything stays pretty clean. That week, there was a little too much estrogen.

Mom called in sick on Wednesday, but I don't even think she had a headache. As far as I could tell, she did it just to mope around. You'd have thought she'd been rejected by Yale, not me.

On Thursday, when I still wouldn't talk to him, Mason gave me a letter. I held it in my hand for a moment, curious what he might have to tell me, but then I tossed it in the trash. I was done with the drama. Done with the disappointment, just done. I hadn't been able to bring myself to work on my plan, or my negative counter plan at all. I guess, now that I didn't have a shot at Yale, I didn't care much. I should've changed tournaments again to increase my odds of going to state, but a part of me just didn't care about any of it. State or not, why did it matter? It's not like Drew and I really had a chance at winning the whole thing, so it was just another wasted weekend.

When our home phone rang Thursday afternoon, I almost didn't answer. It's usually only telemarketers calling, wanting to extend a warranty that ran out on my car about 35 years ago. I thought maybe it was Drew though, so I picked it up. "Hello?"

"Miss Shelton?"

"Yes, this is Lacy Shelton."

"My name is Harold Zane. I'm a friend of Anders Langston. He told me you would be expecting my call."

"Oh, I figured you'd call my cell phone."

"I did try that," he said, "but you never returned my calls. Your coach, a Miss Harris I believe, gave me this phone number."

Bless her, Ms. Harris had broken the school policy, but I might kiss that drunk old crazy right on her over-lipsticked mouth, I was so happy.

Until I remembered Yale had already rejected me. "Uh, yes," I said. "I'm happy to hear from you, but it's my understanding that you're the recruiter for the Yale debate team. Is that correct?"

"Yes, that's correct. Mr. Langston told me you're one of the finest policy debaters he's ever seen. That means a lot coming from him, and with the way our team did last year, well I'll just say I can't face Harvard again until we find some new talent."

I sighed. "I feel like I should tell you this, before you waste your time coming out, sir. The thing is, I got a letter from Yale on Monday. It seems they decided that while I have very fine test scores and an impeccable GPA, I'm not quite what Yale is looking for at this time."

"Ah, yes," he said, "Yale receives many fine applicants and it simply cannot accept them all."

"Uh, right, that's what the letter said."

He laughed. "Those idiots at the admissions office don't know their knee from their elbow. The good news is that I have a lot of leeway there. If you have somewhat decent grades, the letter you've gotten doesn't matter. I should verify though, you do have decent grades?"

"Yes, sir. I'm in line to be the Valedictorian in a few months."

"Excellent. And your SATs?"

"Fifteen hundred and twenty."

"As I said, one phone call from me will get that mess cleared up. But here's the important part. If you're interested in coming out to debate for Yale this Fall, show me what you've got tomorrow. I'll be the portly gentleman with the plaid pants. Can't miss me here in Texas."

"I look forward to it," I said.

I stayed up all night Thursday working on my case and negative modifications so I'd be ready. It felt like I had a second chance at this one little thing in my life, and I wasn't going to blow it. I was working on pure adrenaline, but I felt good.

Mom didn't get up for breakfast that day. I was a little worried, so I poked my head into her room. "Hey Mom. You okay?"

"I think I've caught the cold that's been going around," she said.

There weren't any tissues on her nightstand or the floor, but there was a trashcan near her bed. Maybe she tossed them all in there.

"Really?" I asked. "Want me to call Mr. Dunmore and let him know?" She had missed so much work lately, she must have been nominated for worst employee of the year. I really didn't want her to lose her job.

"I already texted him."

"Okay."

I turned to leave.

"Lacy, I love you. I always will, no matter what happens this weekend. Sorry I can't come."

"I know, Mom. I'm sorry you're sick. I'm going to try and win this tournament, and I'll bring you the trophy for your shelf, okay?"

"I don't care whether you win trophies. I love you even if you lose every single match from here on out."

"Uh, but I really hope that doesn't happen. Thanks for the vote of confidence, though. It's super. And I love you, too, Mom." Even when you're strange. That's when I heard a beeping. "Hey, what about my phone?"

"It's in my top drawer," she said. "You'll need to charge it."

"I'll plug it into the car charger."

"You can take my car," my mom said. "I think Hope already took yours."

"Okay," I said. "Thanks."

I felt great when I ate breakfast. I felt great when I texted Drew to let her know I had my phone back. I felt okay on the drive to Brazosport High. But, when I got to school, that sleepless night hit me like a baseball bat to the head.

I had arrived a few minutes early, thanks to lucky lights and no traffic, and I sat down by the back of the school to look over my links for the negative counter plan for a minute when I saw him. Spoiled rich Jack. Before I even had time to think about it, I popped out of my car and slung my bag over my shoulder. I practically jogged so that our paths would cross.

He smiled when he saw me and slowed down. "Hey there Theresa."

"Uh, my name isn't Theresa. It's Lacy." He must've been really lit up back at Clear Lake.

"I remember," he said, "but you couldn't get my name right, and I like Theresa better. It fits you, like Mother Theresa, you know?"

I rolled my eyes. "I'm not so perfect." In fact, I could really use an energy boost right now. I know I told my mom I wouldn't use anything ever again, but this was a true emergency. I had a shot at Yale, and even Mom would want me at my best. I was seconds from crashing. I thought about how I'd felt that Saturday night, like I could conquer the world. When I took that one tiny pill, my burning eyes, clammy hands, foggy brain and cotton mouthed exhaustion melted away. I needed it. Just this one last time, and it was a prescription drug anyway. It's not like I'm planning to snort a line of unregulated, cut-with-rat-poison cocaine or anything.

"Actually," I whispered, "maybe you could help me."

He wheezed. "Mother Theresa wants a hit?"

"Not marijuana," I whispered, "but maybe something to boost my energy, and help me think."

"Stop whispering, you weirdo. It looks super weird. I might have something," he said, "but I'd need payment."

That I expected. "I have some cash."

He grinned. "Duh, but that's not what I meant, not today. Right now I need a favor more than cash." He glanced back and forth like he was worried there were cameras in the clouds. We were late enough that no one was around. For all his accusations that my whispering looked crazy, his spastic scanning around us looked unhinged. I thought about just saying I was late and heading inside. Who knew what he'd ask for next?

"No way. I've got cash if you can get me something to boost my energy and focus, but I'm not doing anything for you."

He shrugged. "I don't know you, Theresa, not at all. Why should I trust you out of the blue? No favor, no energy boost. This could be a setup."

"What, like you think I'm working for the cops?"

He laughed. "Or maybe the principal."

I felt uncomfortable. I remember that distinctly. And obviously in retrospect, I should've listened to my conscience and walked off. Or I could've said I'd pay him, but I wouldn't do him any favors. I should've said absolutely not. But I was so trashed that my eyes were burning, and I guess everything seemed more dire than it was. Things weren't so bad yet. I know that now, but it felt like they were. I wanted my mind to move as fast as it had last weekend. I needed that edge, because this was a chance to redeem myself and I'd messed up enough already.

I knew I should have turned him down flat and walked way, but I didn't.

"Fine, what?"

"I wasn't kidding about the setup. The principal's on to me," he said. "He's always after me, but he knows where I've got my stash, I think. I saw one of my regulars in the principal's office. I just need to store it somewhere else today. Just for one day."

I thought about it. I had to be the last person the principal would suspect of drug use. My mom knew I'd taken a pill last week, but no one else knew anything. Come on, the Valedictorian? It wasn't like I was on a suspect list or something.

"Sure," I said. "But how are you going to get it there?"

"You leave that up to me," he said. "You got a car?"

"Sure," I said. "I have my mom's car." I held up the shiny combination clicker and key.

He cursed. "That won't work. It's too fancy, too new. Sorry Theresa, but I can't keep chatting. I got to deal with this."

"Wait, I have another car, my real car. This one's my mom's. My car should be in the parking lot because my sister drove it today."

"You got a space number?" he asked.

"Sure," I said. "Ninety-six."

"Great," he said. "You got a key?"

I nodded, and fished it out of my purse. "You aren't going to steal my car, right?"

"Yeah, Theresa. If I wanted to steal your car, I'd ask for the crappy one." He shakes his head in disgust. "You're valedictorian?" He rolls his eyes. "I could boost your old car in three seconds, if I wanted it, but I don't. I just need somewhere to leave my stash. I'll get it back before school lets out today, and I'll leave your key in the glove box when I'm done, okay?"

"Sure," I said.

He reached into his bag and pulled out a baggie. He

handed me two small, white pills with tiny blue flecks. They looked almost the same as the ones I'd taken from Drew's mom.

"Only take one at a time. No more than one a day, got it?"

I nodded.

"Don't want you keeling over from a heart attack."

I stuffed them into my pocket and practically ran to the front office to do the announcements, my heart racing faster than my feet.

Chapter Fourteen

HOPE

Dear Diary:

I'm lucky I had this journal in my bag, or I couldn't be writing this at all. Although, calling myself lucky in any way today might be dumb. It's been even worse than the last time I wrote. Way worse. Where to begin? Well, I sort of got back together with Dave. Or at least, we were still hanging out this morning. I don't really know what's going on with my life minute to minute anymore.

The day started off so well. I went over to Dave's because I wanted to, well, I wanted to feel good about myself, maybe. It was a stupid idea, but it turned out okay. He's been working hard this whole time with a tutor so he could get his grades up and get back on the team. He just found out he's eligible again. I was surprised by how happy that made me.

I know Dave isn't Mason. He's not as hot or as smart, and he's not as exciting, but maybe that's okay. Maybe my mom's right. Maybe I'm not that complicated, because it was almost a relief to be with someone who I knew wanted me. I didn't really appreciate him before, but he has his good points.

Anyhow, after I found out he was eligible again, I told him he should come to practice. He needs to get in the water. He had been running while he wasn't swimming, but that's not the same. I told him this morning to come swim, but he didn't have all his gear. He had his suit, but he needed a pair of goggles. At the beginning of sixth period, I jogged out to the car to grab an extra pair. I always have a few pairs in the trunk.

I don't know why the principal had someone watching the parking lot, and I have no idea why they thought I looked suspicious, but they did. The parking lot attendant came over to check things out. I explained what I was doing, and he said to go ahead, but he didn't leave. He just stood there.

If I had any idea what was in there, do you really think I'd have just opened it up? I may not be Einstein okay, but give me some credit. I'm not a total moron.

When I opened the trunk, it was full of all kinds of crap. Pills, bags of stuff, a bunch of junk I'd never seen. At first, I thought maybe it was part of some kind of science project for Lacy, but then I remembered she was in physics this year, not chemistry. They don't use powders, and pills and stuff in that, I don't think. At least, I never did in my physics for dummies class last year.

The attendant started shouting and then the police showed up. On school grounds, in the middle of the day. It was crazy. They made me follow them back to the school, while a police officer started taking photos, and stuffing everything into marked blue bags. I was lucky it was in the middle of sixth period, because the way they marched me through the halls, and into the principal's office you'd think I'd just killed someone. At least no one was around to see.

Lacy comes to the front office every day to do the morning announcements, but other than breezing past the front desk to drop off excused absence slips, I'd never been up here. The principal's office was big, almost as big as the front lobby, and half the room was taken up with a wooden desk. The other side was crammed full of shiny, brown wooden chairs. The parking attendant shoved me down into a chair and walked out the door without a single word, but he glared at me as he left. The principal sat in his desk chair, scowling at me. He didn't speak.

"What's going on?" I finally asked.

He stood up and walked around the desk. "Hope Vincent, right?"

I nodded.

"Hope, did anyone ask you to store something for them?"

I shook my head.

"Anyone at all. Did they tell you that they just needed it put somewhere for a day, or even for a few hours?"

"No," I said. "I haven't talked to anyone about anything going in my car."

"Do you know what we found in your trunk?"

"I saw all that stuff, but I don't know what it is." That was true, but it didn't sound good.

"Did anyone else have access to your car? A key? Or did you leave it unlocked?"

"The trunk can only be opened with a key." Before I said anything else, an image flashed across my mind. Lacy with a pill bottle. Mom yelling. Mom freaking out.

Lacy had a key.

What if the bags were drugs, and the drugs were hers? Would Lacy go to jail? She's eighteen, and I'm just seventeen. Lacy's so smart, and she's going to college for sure. I thought about that recruiter. I had a chance at college, but

I'd seen Lacy's letters. She'd not only been accepted to good schools, but she even had scholarship offers to a few. I didn't even have any ideas for a college major. Unless swimming was a major, which I doubted.

Why would Lacy have an entire trunk full of pills?

"Miss Vincent?" Principal Skinner was looking at me like he'd asked me something else and I hadn't answered.

"I'm sorry," I said, "what?"

"We found a lot of illegal drugs in your car, Miss Vincent. This is serious. You don't seem like the type of person to take them, but if I've learned anything in my eleven years as a principal, you never know. You could be in very real trouble if it turns out those are yours. Right now, until you tell us different, that's our assumption."

I looked down at my shoes. "I was just going out to my car to get some goggles for a friend."

"You're quite the swimmer from what I hear."

I nodded.

"I just want to get to the bottom of this. I want to figure out where those came from so we can deal with the problem."

I glanced up at him. "If you find this person, what might happen to her? Or him?"

"She," he paused then and stared at me for a moment, "would be in a lot of trouble."

"Or he," I said.

"Right."

"What does that mean? Trouble like suspended?"

"No, Miss Vincent. Trouble like jail time, or juvenile hall, at the very least. There were a lot of drugs in your trunk. Pot. Stimulants, narcotics. In Texas, the punishment depends on a lot of things. How much was found in your possession is one factor, certainly. Another factor is your age. Even if you aren't eighteen yet, they could choose to try you as an adult if the circumstances merit it. You should be completely up front with me today. The truth is your best defense."

I suddenly couldn't breathe. I thought about Lacy, my brilliant sister. She worked so hard. She did so much. She helped around the house while I was out swimming. She helped with laundry while I went for jogs on the beach. She was always doing homework. She helped *me* with my homework whenever I asked. She always shared what she had, and she gave me whatever I wanted. The cherry on a sundae. The best seat on the rollercoaster. The bigger bedroom.

She came to my swim meet, even when I was being a jerk. I knew she was there, and I kissed Moby anyway. I knew Moby liked her more, and I let her think I'd been with him, and if I was being honest, maybe I thought that would help me win him from her.

She was a really great sister to me. She always had been.

I was the world's worst sister.

But now she needed my help. She was the only other person with a key, so I knew she'd made a mistake, a big one. One that could eat her whole future in one bite. Me on the other hand, well, I loved swimming, and it would've been cool to swim for UT. But once I was done, it wasn't like I had some major career plans I would springboard toward. The next sixty years of my life would be essentially the same, even if I got kicked out of school and went to Juvie for a while. Lacy though, this would destroy her, and she's like a rocket launching into space. The sky's the limit.

I had a chance to fix this if I played this just right. Maybe she would forgive me for being spoiled and selfish and greedy. Maybe she would love me again.

"Miss Vincent, I'm going to ask you one more time before we pass you over to the police. I'm much nicer than them, and I can recommend other options in your case, like diversion if you want to avoid going into police custody. Trust me on this, I'm your best friend right now. Did someone ask you to hold these drugs? Where did they come from? Who else had access to your car today?"

"No one else had access. I share the car with my sister, but I've been the only person driving it for more than a week. My mom will confirm that. We got in a big fight, and she's been getting rides, or driving my mom's car. She doesn't have access to it at all."

"If no one else had a key, then how do you think the drugs got into your trunk?" The principal had returned to his side of the desk. I guess he wasn't so worried about getting me to confide in him, now that it looked like I might be the villain.

It was now or never. This was my shot. I could toss Lacy under the bus, tell him I'd forgotten, that Lacy had a second set of keys. I could swear those drugs were not in the trunk that morning, when I tossed my swim bag inside.

I could have told him the truth and my life would have gotten much easier, much better.

I didn't.

"They're mine," I said. "All the drugs are mine. I've met a lot of people with swimming and I live on the beach. I meet more people that way. I always have a big bag with me. I make a lot of money on the side with that. I was trying to figure out how to get out of it, but I guess you got me before I did."

Principal Skinner sat on the edge of his chair, and shuffled some papers. "Are you sure? Your mother has a good job, and you already have a car. Why did you need money so badly? Why would you sell drugs?"

"I'm sick of sharing a car with my sister. We got in a fight, like I said, and I want my own car. And not a piece of junk. I realized I could make a lot more money if I just sold some stuff, but a little turned into more."

He raised one eyebrow. "Just like that, you decided to 'sell some stuff'?"

"I'm not saying anything else," I said. "Don't I get a lawyer or something?"

"You're a minor," he said. "Once I hand you over to the police, they can't talk to you without your guardian there. She will make decisions about whether you have a lawyer. Who is your legal guardian?"

"My mom, Rosemary Vincent."

"Alright, if you're sure that's your story, I'll hand you over to the police. They'll take you downtown, and contact your guardian to come and meet you at the precinct."

I just stared at him, trying to look penitent, but guilty.

The two men in dark blue police uniforms didn't put me in handcuffs. They even let me keep my backpack with me. I guess they weren't worried about me doing them bodily harm. Strangely, with my police escort, I felt less embarrassed than I had being marched through the halls with the principal and the parking lot attendant.

I followed the officers quietly and quickly, and climbed into the back of their squad car. It had a glass partition between the back seat and the front. I wished for a second that I had a club or something I could pound the glass with, like a movie thug. I didn't, so I just sat there, holding my backpack on my lap. Everything felt surreal, like it was a bizarre dream. They took me to the police station, and then after filling out some forms, they led me over to a small room with a few mirrors. It must be an interrogation room, but no one interrogated me. They just left me to sit in here alone. I'm guessing we're waiting for my mom. If she's got a migraine, we might all be here for a while because she turns off her phone.

I should be mad at Lacy maybe, for putting me in this position. Or maybe I should be angry because I'm pretty sure she and Moby will work things out, and I still kind of wish he'd picked me. If I'm honest, I might wish that more because I hate to lose than because I love him or something. I could be fuming about having to spend my Friday afternoon and evening stuck here waiting for my mom, but I'm not. I feel oddly calm about the whole thing. The cops told me that even if I end up getting booked, the judge will set bail. We don't have a ton of money, but they said it won't be too bad. One of the cops, the older one, said he has a son about my age. He seemed almost sorry to stick me in here, even if he does think I'm a drug dealer-in-training.

Now I just have to wait here until my mom can come and get me out and bring me home. I doubt many kids who are sitting in a police department, waiting for their mom to show up so they can be interrogated about a felony, are in a good mood, but I feel strangely at peace.

You said I'm supposed to work on introductions and conclusions in these journal entries, and so I'll be honest, Ms. Littleton, even if I get expelled. Even if you never read this and I don't graduate. Even if I have to go to Juvie for a while, and I can't swim anymore. Even if this ruins my entire life, this still feels like the first thing I've done right in a long time.

Sitting here, about to be booked for a crime, I finally feel proud of who I am.

Chapter Fifteen

LACY

I had to run to get to the office in time for announcements. My eyes were burning because I was so tired, my lungs heaved from the run, and I felt like any moment, someone would notice the tiny bulge in my pocket and I'd get caught. It was a rush.

I kind of loved it.

After I did the announcements, I walked slowly toward our classroom on the far end of the world. I knew there was a water fountain at the end of the hallway, and I knew that was where I'd take my first pill. After all, I'd need a bit of time for it to kick in. I was already a little shaky in anticipation of the energy I knew would be coursing through my body momentarily.

I leaned over the water fountain and took a drink. I had just reached my hand in my pocket when I heard his voice.

"You can't ignore me forever, you know."

I turned back, and there he was. Mason wasn't wearing the dark jeans and t-shirt that made my heart race. He wasn't even wearing a polo shirt. He was wearing a dark suit. Why was he wearing a suit?

"You can't keep bothering me forever," I said, but there was no force to it, no anger left in me. Now go away so I can take this pill, you idiot.

"You threw away my note." His voice was flat.

"I didn't try to hide that."

"Why?" his voice cracked. I'd known Mason for four weeks today. It felt like a lifetime, but it wasn't actually very long. He was always so confident, so cocky, so sure of himself. This guy, standing here with uncertainty in his eyes, I didn't know this guy.

I sighed, too tired to fight with him anymore.

"What do you want Mason? I'll give you two minutes, and then I just want you to leave me alone."

"Two minutes," he muttered under his breath. "I don't want two minutes. Two hours probably wouldn't be enough." But then he straightened, and he said, "I'll take it. Two minutes."

"You just wasted fifteen seconds," I said. "Better get on with it."

"I was afraid," he said. "You thought I didn't know whether I liked you or your sister. I'm so sorry I put you through that, but you need to know it wasn't about you at all, or Hope either. It was about me."

"Well that's refreshing," I said. "And not at all cliché. It's not you, it's me. Really?" I tried to walk past him, but he took a step to the side to block my path.

He shook his head. "That's not two minutes, and I'm not done yet."

I sighed, but I stopped walking.

"I know it's cliché, and I know you don't want to hear it. I know it's all too late, but from the very moment I saw you, I've wanted to ask you out. I've wanted to kiss you. I see you, Angelica. You're brilliant and vulnerable, confident and unsure, funny and cutting, loyal and infuriatingly driven. I see all of you, and you're stunning. I can't look away, even when you're mad at me."

I look down at the dirty floor tiles because I can't breathe and I can't look at him, because what if I did, and then I believed his cheesy lines? I can't do it, not again.

"Liking your sister, asking her out, it was easy. Like everything in my life has always been easy. I knew she'd say yes. I knew she wouldn't ask me to do anything I didn't already want to do. I knew I could swim, and she'd cheer. I could complain about my parents, or the move, or anything at all and she'd smile and say something trivial. I'm not trying to belittle your sister, because she's a really great girl, and a talented swimmer, but Hope isn't you, she's not even close."

"No," I said. "She isn't much like me. I think we've established that." I tried to walk past him again and when he reached out for me, I wanted to scream. Because I'm not Hope. I'll never be simple or uncomplicated or easy, or just bubbly and fun and energetic. I'm not my sister. "It's been two minutes. Please let me go."

He pulled back like I'd burned him. "You scared me, Lacy, because from the second we met, I couldn't imagine how I'd survive if you left. You changed my life that very first day. You told me I could do something, and then you showed me how, and you stepped back and watched while I did it. Instead of taking the credit, you cheered me on. Instead of showing off, you built me up. I've never had anyone do that, not ever."

I looked up at him this time, and his eyes burned into mine.

"I wanted to ask you out the next Monday, but I couldn't do it. What if you said no? What if you liked someone else? For all I knew, you and Drew were together."

I laughed out loud. How could Mason know?

He shrugged. "There was obviously something intense between you two, and I was scared what. When you ditched me before the awards ceremony to go find her, and came back alone and super upset." He shrugged. "I didn't know, okay? The bottom line was, for the first time in my life, I was terrified I'd screw things up, and then I was angry with myself for not asking you out. When I saw Hope that afternoon, I needed something simple, a sure thing. She clearly liked me, and she was exactly the kind of girl I've dated in the past. I asked her what she was doing the next day, because I wanted...I don't know what I wanted. Sometimes people do stupid things, things they know they shouldn't do. I guess you don't, but not everyone is like you. Not all of us are perfect all the time."

I thought about the pills in my pocket. "None of us are perfect all the time."

He smiled at me, and it felt like someone had thrown open a window and the sun was shining again. "I just want another chance at all of it. Please? I have my signed permission form. I'm wearing a suit. I'm ready to do whatever you want. I'll even debate with you and not flirt at all, if that's what you want. Just let me back in. Give me another chance to at least be your friend."

I wanted to hug him. I wanted him to spin me around and kiss me. But I couldn't do it, not yet. I kept seeing him kissing Hope. I kept thinking about how he said he liked me, but he asked her out. I couldn't quite trust him. But I could trust him enough to take him to this tournament. But this time, I had to do it right. "I want to debate with you. The recruiter couldn't make it last week, and he's going to be there today. I didn't get into Yale, but he told me on the phone today he can change that. The thing is, Drew's my partner. I won't screw her, not if she's here."

I heard her voice from around the corner of the room

and I wondered how much she'd already heard. "It's fine, Lace." Drew's head popped around the doorframe. "I've been thinking about it since I saw him show up in a suit today. You can debate with him. I don't mind. And if it can get you into Yale, even better."

I was smiling before, but now I'm beaming at both of them. Mason grabbed my laptop bag and my clothes and carried them down the hall to the classroom. When he stepped inside, Drew followed, but I paused by the door long enough to pull the pills out of my pocket and drop them into the trashcan. I didn't need speed, not anymore. I had enough adrenaline to survive on my own.

When I walked into the classroom, Drew put her arm around me. She leaned against my ear and whispered, "I just want you to be happy, but you need to know that if he hurts you again, I'll kill him, and I don't want to hear you whining about it afterward. Fair warning."

I grinned ear to ear. "I believe you. No whining."

Mason looked from Drew back to me, and said, "See? Weird vibe."

"It's a best friend thing," I said. "But it's fine."

He shrugged and smiled.

I spent the next twenty minutes explaining the changes I'd had to make to the case and counter plan.

"It's a brilliant solution," Mason said. "And the case is even better now."

Drew, leaning back in her chair, popped her gum. "Dude, all I can say is, I'm so glad I don't have to try and make sense of that crap anymore."

I rolled my eyes. "You're going to miss it."

She leaned forward so her chair flopped back down. "Maybe a little bit. But I'll come today and watch."

I was almost proud of Ms. Harris when we climbed on

the bus for Alief. She seemed sober, and when the bus driver cancelled, she offered to drive the bus herself. Normally I'd object, but she had a bus certification from a long time ago, and she had been sober all week. Maybe going to jail had helped her gain some clarity. I actually remember thinking that maybe I should've tried some jail time myself, instead of just wallowing.

I was an idiot.

My phone hadn't taken much of a charge before we got to school. By the time the bus came, it was bleeping at me. I motioned to Ms. Harris and told her I was going to leave it in my car to charge. She shrugged. I ran over and plugged it into my mom's car, and jogged back.

I sat next to Mason on the bus trip over, answering his questions about how my changes would impact the cases I knew other teams were running. I showed him the link quotes I'd come up with, and I went over the two revised kritiks we could run on any alternative energy plans, in addition to our counter plan. Drew sat across the aisle on the bus, chiming in with comments now and again and popping her gum.

The rest of the tournament on Friday went smoothly. Mason picked up like we'd never left off, explaining the revised and improved plan as though he'd written it himself. I relaxed more than I ever had, with prep time to spare each round now that I wasn't writing Drew's rebuttals and answering her cross examination questions for her, and wasting time recovering from her botched answers.

Mason and I won three rounds in a row, and before I knew it, we were in our last round of the day. When our judge walked in, my heart sank. Drew and I had lost with this screwball just before Christmas. He claimed to be "tabula rasa", or a "clean slate" judge, but he wasn't, not really. Before I could say anything to Mason, the guy started talking.

"My name is Mr. Kumar. I've been judging debate since before you kids were born, and I'll be judging after you've graduated from college I'm sure. I've seen debate fads come and go, and I'll be honest. I hate them. Just give me a good, solid plan, and show me your argument skills."

My friend Anastasia on the other team had made it to semis at state last year, but I didn't know her small, nervous Indian partner. They were affirmative, which meant they set the tone for the round. Her partner raised his hand and in a querulous voice asked, "What's your judging paradigm?"

"I'm tabula rasa. I say I don't like gimmicks, but if you argue them cleanly, I don't care what you use. Just give me something to sink my teeth into."

Mason glanced at me and I shrugged. At least we were negative this time. Our case was a lot more radical on the affirmative, since it didn't really propose anything.

When Anastasia got up to read their nuclear power plan, I hesitated. Should I pull up some standard disadvantages? This was the easiest case to link to pretty drastic harms, what with Chernobyl, etc. Or did Mason and I stick with what I had prepared? I was vacillating in my head when Mr. Langston and a large, dark-skinned man I assumed was Harold Zane walked in and sat near the back of the classroom.

I tried to listen to what Anastasia was saying, but it was so hard to focus. I needed to decide what to run, but my brain was so tired it was stalling. I jotted a note down for Mason on a post it note. "What do we do? Traditional? Or anti-anthro?"

He glanced at the note and wrote back, "You're the boss. I trust you."

Great. One of the most important things in a debate round is reading the judge and I'd completely bombed that two months ago. When he had said tabula rasa in December, I'd believed him. I'd run some pretty radical kritiks at the time, and crashed and burned with them. I didn't want to make the same mistake, but I watched the judge for a moment. He was taking notes in earnest, nodding his head. It made me wonder. Was it the judge's bias that tanked us two months ago, or was it me? Maybe I hadn't been convincing enough? He might be traditional, but if he was open at all to the concept of something new, I would deliver it this time like I couldn't have two months ago.

I handed Mason a post-it that read: We're doing it.

He nodded at me and gave me a cheesy thumbs-up.

I stood up, counter plan ready. My throat closed when I looked up at Mr. Zane, but then I glanced at Drew, sitting just behind the judge. She held up a paper with the following words written on it: Just Breathe. You've got this.

I took a single deep breath and smiled at her. She was right. I had this. I focused on our 'tabula rasa' judge and began reading. I had some of the quotes memorized, and I glanced up during those to see the Judge's demeanor. He seemed entirely open to our bizarre approach, which was good. I tried to forget the stakes, but I couldn't quite get Mr. Zane's penetrating gaze out of my head. Even so, I nailed it during cross-examination.

When I sat down, Mason reached over and squeezed my hand under the table. He didn't let go and a zing flew through my body that woke me up entirely.

The rest of the round deteriorated into a bit of a brawl, but Mason managed to pull it back out, and sum up beautifully. We all sat in silence while we waited for the judge to say something. Anything. Most judges announce at the end who they're voting for, and give some kind of explanation.

Mr. Tabula Rasa didn't do that. "It's been a pleasure to judge this round today. You've all done an excellent job of rising to my request that you debate issues, that you use good rhetoric, and showcase your speaking and reasoning abilities. You haven't made my job easy, but the best rounds don't. I look forward to seeing you all in the future."

He stood and walked out. My heart sunk. Did we lose? Had we won? Mason took my hand again, this time not bothering to keep it under the table. When I stood up, he still didn't let go. Mr. Langston and Mr. Zane approached us.

"That was a very fine round," Mr. Zane said, his deep voice booming. "You should both be quite proud. From what I understand you don't have many resources at Brazosport, which makes that round even more impressive."

"And I'm impressed with how you reworked your case to function on the negative as a kritik," Mr. Langston said. "And used the Open Evidence Project to bolster instead of undercut it."

"Thanks," I said. "And thank you for coming to watch us."

Mr. Zane's smile showed a mouth full of enormous, white teeth. He could have been on a dental advertisement. "It was my pleasure. My friend Anders is almost never wrong when he tells me he's found someone worth my attention. He certainly wasn't this time."

"Thank you," Mason said, "we appreciate that."

"I'm sure you won that round," Mr. Langston said. "Unless that judge was a complete moron."

I smiled. "Thanks. I was a little worried, honestly. He said he was tabula rasa, but he hasn't been completely progressive when we've seen him in the past."

"Reading judges is hard," Mr. Langston said, "but maybe

the best thing you learn as a debater. I use the same skillset with juries now."

"Exactly," Mr. Zane said. "Nicely handled, I thought."

"Lacy spent a lot of time reworking the case so it would hold up in spite of another school that set out to ruin it," Mason said. "She has a brilliant mind."

"That she does." Mr. Zane rubbed his short beard a time or two and then said, "I know Miss Vincent here has applied to Yale, and they've botched up her acceptance letter. She will likely have to submit a revised application through my office. What about you, young man? Have you finished your application to Yale yet?"

Mason shook his head. "No, sir. I was planning to attend University of Texas on a swimming scholarship."

Mr. Zane appeared to evaluate Mason's size with appreciation. "University of Texas is a fine school if swimming is what you're after. But I'd hate to break up such a promising pair of young talent. I hope you'll consider sending me an application as well. Yale has a swim team with very fine water, I'm sure. I bet they'd welcome you there, too."

"I'll think about it, sir."

"You do that," Mr. Zane said. Then he socked Mr. Langston in the arm. "You didn't tell me I was going to have to convince them to take my scholarship, you sly dog."

"I didn't know," Mr. Langston said, glancing at me. "This is the first I've heard about it."

"Oh well," Mr. Zane said. "The best ones always have other options. It takes them time to realize we're the best one." He turned to me. "And you, what else are you considering?"

"I've been accepted to Duke, Stanford and Princeton. I'm still waiting to hear back from Harvard."

He shook his head. "Of course you are. Those snobs

love to make people wait. If you join their team instead of mine, I might cry."

Imagining this huge black man in plaid pants crying made me want to giggle, but I didn't. "I can assure you sir, Yale is my top choice."

He clapped me on the arm. "I appreciate your enthusiasm. Okay, here's our next step. I'll send you an official offer letter, contingent on your graduating with the same grades as you have now, etcetera, etcetera. Then you'll need to resubmit your application, but this time to my office. I'll send it through the proper channels and we'll be in business. I should warn you, I only have three full tuition scholarships to offer, and I've offered two. That means I can only offer you each a half tuition scholarship. You might qualify for financial aid, but I don't get involved in all that. Now, if your boyfriend here doesn't end up accepting my offer, we can talk. I'd prefer to keep the two of you as a team since you seem to work very well together, but I don't want to lose you either, young lady. And if you're as good as you say at swimming Mr. Montcellier, I might be able to coordinate with them to see if you could do both. Maybe they'd throw some money at you too. I doubt they can offer the same resources as University of Texas, but I'm sure they'd love to bring a fellow like you on."

It seemed almost strange when I walked out of that room on my own two feet instead of floating out on a cloud. Mason looked a little stunned, like he'd been smacked between the eyes. I worked very hard not to ask him whether he was considering Mr. Zane's offer.

Drew threw her arms around me the second Mr. Zane and Mr. Langston were gone. "I'm so excited," she said to me. "I knew you could do it. But now that you have, I can tell you my news! I got accepted to Yale last week."

I looked into her earnest blue eyes and realized something. "I'm such a horrible friend," I said. "And you're the best friend ever."

She looked down at her black boots. "I didn't want to tell you, not when you didn't get in. But then Mr. Zane called and I thought, it would be so cool if we both went together."

"You could've told me," I said. "I would've been happy for you."

"It wasn't fair," she said. "My mom, my grandpa, my uncles, they all went there. They care about dumb stuff like that and it wasn't fair they let me in, but not you. Your grades and SAT score were better."

I shrugged. "You still could've told me. I would've been happy for you."

"I know," she said, "I know you would've, but I thought maybe if I waited, we could be happy together. And look, I was right."

Drew hugged me again. I was such an idiot for taking her for granted. When I finally did let go, Mason was gone.

She and I walked to the cafeteria, but the rest of our classmates had already headed out to the bus. When we reached it, I saw Mason sitting near the back. I squeezed Drew's arm and headed for the back of the bus to see what was going on.

Mason was big enough to fill up the bench, almost entirely. He had shifted so I was looking at his back.

I shoved on him. "Hey. Let me in you big ox."

He turned toward me. "I figured you'd want to sit by Drew, your future roommate."

I reached down and grabbed his arm and pulled on it, hard. I might as well have been pulling on the bench seat. He didn't budge. "Get up, you big baby."

He stared at me, sulking for a moment. But then, he stood up and I slipped past him. I could've sat on the edge of the seat like I had earlier, but I had done that to talk to Drew and Mason at the same time, and it left half my butt hanging off for the entire ride. This time, I only wanted to talk to Mason.

I patted the seat next to me. "Sit."

He did.

I thought about how he'd taken my hand. Twice. "Why would I want to sit by Drew?"

He shrugged. "You seemed to have a lot to celebrate earlier."

He was pouting. Mason, my big, confident partner and world-class swimmer was pouting. I reached up and put my hand on his face. "*We* have a lot to celebrate."

He turned away and my hand fell back. "By my calculations, you're better off if I don't take Mr. Zane up on his offer. Full scholarship versus half."

"You big idiot. I don't care about that. I never expected any scholarship at all to Yale. My mom has saved money for our college funds. I can afford to pay half their tuition, and what I can't afford, I can take out loans for. Stop acting like a meathead and look at me."

Mason finally turned to face me. What I saw in his eyes surprised me.

"What are you nervous about?"

"I can't go to Yale."

"Why?" I asked. "You heard Mr. Zane. They have a great swimming program. I bet you'd be their superstar. Actually, they might offer you another partial scholarship! I bet their program needs you way more than UT's does."

"It's not about swimming."

"Then what?" The bus jolted out onto the main road, and I fell against Mason's enormous chest. He wrapped one arm around me, and pulled me back upright. He was so big and so talented, and everyone wanted him. "What could you possibly be worried about?"

"You're Yale caliber. You should've gotten in on your own, without debate. You got into Stanford and Princeton and Duke. And Drew, she got in too."

I shrugged. "I didn't get into Yale. They rejected me."

"You probably have perfect test scores. I heard you're going to be the Valedictorian. It didn't even occur to me to apply to any of those Ivy League schools."

"Mason, what are you trying to say?"

"I only applied to a handful of schools, Lacy. University of Texas, Michigan and Florida."

"What do those even have in common?" I asked.

"Texas is the number one swimming school in America. Michigan, California and Florida are next. I didn't apply anywhere on the basis of my scholastics."

"You're smart Mason, one of the smartest guys I've ever met."

He turned away again. "Not Ivy League smart. I'm jock smart. I wouldn't survive at Yale."

"You're Ivy League smart," I said softly. "I knew that the second we met."

His head snapped back toward mine. "You believe that?"

"No," I said. "I don't believe it. I've seen it, and I know it's true."

He smiled at me then, a real smile, a warm smile. He put his arm back around me and I curled up against him. I fell asleep a few minutes later, and didn't wake up until we reached the school. Mason and I were the last two people off the bus. He carried all my stuff and his own. He walked me over to my mom's car in the bitter evening cold and loaded my bags into the back. I put the key in and turned it on, pressing the seat heater button immediately.

"Where's your dad?" I asked.

"I just texted him," Mason said. "He'll be here in like five minutes."

"Oh," I said. "Wait in here with me, then."

Mason climbed into the car next to me. It wasn't much warmer inside, but I wasn't about to drive off and leave him standing out here alone. Ms. Harris was doing better than I could ever remember, but she was already gone, and the bus had already headed for the bus barn. Such a responsible chaperone.

"What will your parents think about the Yale offer?"

Mason chuckled. "My dad will be over the moon. He'll try and force me to take it. He's so bitter now that his base-ball career is over. He thinks he wasted his time on baseball and he should've done something that would have left him in a better position now, at forty. He basically has to start all over. He's taking online classes to try and get a degree in graphic design. I guess it's embarrassing for him that my mom's supporting us."

"And your mom?"

"She'll probably still want me to go to UT. It's the number one swimming program in the country. She wants an Olympic Medal more than anything. She thinks the endorsements and the accompanying fame will set me up forever. And she said I'll be smarter than my dad was and I'll save what I make."

I think about Mason's looks, his eloquence and I realize his mom's probably right. He'd be an idiot to go anywhere but the place that will get him closest to his gold medal.

"What do you think?"

He looked at me for a moment without speaking. Then he said, "I don't know what I think. Before today, I just assumed I'd go to University of Texas."

"What changed today?"

"I realized I don't want to be without you in a few months. I don't want to be without you, ever." I had a steering wheel, boxing me in. He sat on the other side of a gear selector from me. It was still so cold that our breath made a fog in front of us. Nothing had gone right, not since the day we met, but it didn't matter, because we were right together. Mason, the strong, absurdly gifted swimmer, and me, the nerdy, hotheaded debater.

We had so little in common, but I couldn't seem to stop moving toward him, no matter what was in the way. We were both facing forward in our seats, and I thought this had to be the worst place for a kiss in the history of ever, but he leaned toward me, and I turned toward him, and I realized I was wrong. Anywhere we were, that was the best place for a kiss. When his lips met mine, the world exploded all around me. I didn't feel the steering wheel. I didn't feel the cold. I didn't worry about Yale or the University of Texas or the distance between where we were and where I wanted us to be.

There was only Mason and me. I was filled with a joy I couldn't contain. The two of us became something more together. Unstoppable. I don't know how long we kissed, but when I finally pulled back, my seat was burning hot, and the windows were steamed instead of frosted. Even then, I didn't want to stop, but I'd noticed something. Something insistent, something annoying.

My phone was beeping.

I felt dazed when I finally sat back in my seat. I clicked the seat heater off, and then I reached for my phone. Thirteen missed calls. Ten voicemails. Fifty text messages.

What in the world was going on?

If I could go back in time, would I want to notice those messages before Mason and I kissed? I don't know. I honestly can't say whether it would be better not to have ever had such a perfect moment, or better to have it, knowing it would be utterly ruined seconds later.

Because when I listened to my messages, that's when I found out. See, my sister Hope had gone to jail, charged with possession of drugs I had selfishly allowed to be placed in her car. But that wasn't even the worst of it. Not by a long shot.

I close the laptop and slowly look up toward Dr. Brasher.

"I've finished right up until the day she died. I won't write anything else until you comply with a reasonable demand."

"I'm in the middle of a guardianship evaluation here," Dr. Brasher says. "I'm going to need to see what you've written, and then we can talk about what you want."

"I've spent every single minute I wasn't in school right here in your office since practically the day it happened," I say. "I need to see her. Not tomorrow, or after you've perused this, or called the police. I want to see her now. Right now."

"She's in care right now. She can't just drive over here."

I shake my head. "Then I'll delete everything I've written. I'll smash this laptop to bits if I have to. It's not like the replacement cost is high. You'll have to tell the Court your opinion without the benefit of my side of things for the last few days. If that's what you want..."

Dr. Brasher pursed his lips. "Why? Why do you need to see her first?"

I look down at the laptop. The one on which I've confessed to a felony. Possession of almost ten pounds worth of illegal drugs, and the reason for it. Intent to use illegally acquired prescription drugs. "I need to know what she wants me to do. I need to know what to tell you about the end. I can't screw this up, not again."

Finally, Dr. Brasher nods. He walks to his desk and picks up the phone. He speaks so softly that I can't hear what he's saying, but after that he sits in his desk and says, "It may be a few minutes. She's not located very close to here."

I wait. My stomach fills with butterflies. No, not butterflies. More like hornets. I haven't seen her, not since it happened. I don't even know what I'm going to say. I don't know what she wants, or what I want. I honestly can't see a single clear path out of this mess.

When Hope walks in the door and I see her gorgeous face for the first time in what feels like weeks, but is actually only a few days, I feel my eyes well up with tears. I want to run up to her and hug her tightly. I want to tell her that I know it's all my fault. I want to apologize for everything, for being so selfish, for not taking care of her like a big sister should and for leaving her to deal with my mess. But most of all, I want to tell her I'm sorry that our mother died.

Because of me.

Hope's stuck in foster care now, maybe for quite a while, also because of me.

I expect her to turn toward me with anger, loathing, or maybe even pity. Instead, when Hope looks at me, she looks as broken as I do. She looks at me with love, sorrow, and maybe even guilt.

"I'll leave the two of you to talk for a moment," Dr.

Brasher says, and for the first time since I stepped into his office, I like him.

Before I can figure out what to do, Hope rushes toward me and wraps her arms around me. Something in my heart thaws then, and I can breathe for the first time in days. "I'm sorry," I say. "I'm so sorry for everything."

"No, I'm sorry." Hope finally pulls away and sits down on the sofa. I sit down next to her, and she takes my hands in hers. "I ruined everything. I don't know what I was thinking, spending every single minute at Dave's after that Cypress meet, making you feel guilty, never telling you that Mason liked you, and that he turned me down. Kissing him. I let you be miserable just because I was, and I wanted to hurt you."

"I'm sorry you were miserable. I never should have stayed up all night before the Alief tournament, or told Jack he could put his drugs in our car... in your car."

"Who's Jack? I've been wondering where those came from. I knew you couldn't be selling yourself."

"If you knew it was my fault, why did you let them think it was you?"

Hope smiles bitterly then. "It was my fault you were in that mess. I'm sure you only got drugs again because you didn't know how else to win, since you and Mason weren't talking. I knew it was my fault, but that's not the only reason I did it. I did it because the principal kept going on and on about how bad it would be if I weren't a minor, and I thought, crap. Lacy's not a minor. Thank gosh I still am." She shrugged. "Besides, I'm not the one on my way to the Ivy League."

I shake my head. "I'm not either, not after all this."

Hope jumps up from the sofa. "Why not?"

"How could I be?"

"Why wouldn't you be? I took the blame. They think

they were my drugs. They're just giving me probation. I've been back at school, just like you, only they make me go talk to a counselor during lunch. That's why you haven't seen me there. Which means things are fine for you, right?"

I grit my teeth. "Yes, they're too fine. Mom committed suicide because you got arrested for my drugs, the drugs I let Jack store in the car. Meanwhile, I get off scot free." I look at the shabby carpet, ashamed to meet her eyes. "I've petitioned to be your guardian. That's why I'm here. I need an evaluation to determine whether I'm fit to be a 'guardian of your person' until you turn eighteen. That's what they call it."

Hope beams at me. "That would be wonderful! The Boones aren't a bad couple, but I can tell they want to transform me from a criminal element into an upright young lady and it's exhausting. They want to parent me, and they don't get I had a parent, a perfectly wonderful mother."

Our eyes meet and I can feel tears form in mine. "How did we miss it?" I ask. "How come we didn't know she was depressed?"

Hope shrugs. "I don't know. I guess it seems obvious now, but I didn't even know it was really something that people had, as like a disease. I thought it just meant they were sad a lot."

I close my eyes. Dr. Brasher had given me a checklist. Mom had lots of symptoms. Talking about death, lying around doing nothing for days sometimes, debilitating intermittent health problems, which for her was her headaches, and mercurial mood changes. If I'd known what I was looking for, I'd have realized it for sure.

"We should've figured it out and made her take something. They have medicine for it."

Hope shakes her head. "She'd never have taken it. I actually wonder whether maybe she knew."

"What do you mean?" I asked. "In some cases, many cases, the medicines can completely repair the brain chemistry, according to the book Dr. Brasher gave me."

Hope bites her lip. "You know how she was about any kind of drugs. We never took anything. I guess Dad didn't die of a car accident after all."

"What are you talking about?"

She hangs her head. "I should've told you. I should've told you that morning we both snuck in, but I was so angry, and I thought maybe you'd been out with Mason. I wonder whether it might have made a difference."

"What are you talking about?"

"Mason came to the house to wait for you, the night you went to Drew's, the night you stole her mom's pills. Mason waited at the house for a long time, talking to Mom. I don't even know how long. I saw his car, snuck toward the window and heard them talking, so I didn't go inside until later. I kind of listened in for a while first."

"You eavesdropped? Like, literally, from under the eaves?"

"I'm not sure what eaves are, but yeah, I sat under the window in the porch swing. Lacy, she told Mason a lot of things, stuff I didn't know. Like how Dad died, and it wasn't in a car accident. He died from a drug overdose, and it wasn't his first problem with it."

My mind's spinning at a thousand miles a minute. Drugs? Dad? Mom had never said a word. "Why wouldn't she tell us?"

"I've thought about that a lot," Hope says. "I think it might have been to spare us at first, or because she was embarrassed. Or because she was worried it would come back to plague us. Like in our rebellious years, if we were curious about Dad, maybe we'd experiment."

"She was always saying she couldn't bear losing us," I said. "And then I came home with drugs."

Hope nods. "And then she hears that I'm arrested for drug possession. She hadn't been doing well for the past week, too. I think maybe it just was the last straw."

I can't process it. I can't believe it. I knew when I spoke to Jack that morning it was a mistake. I knew I shouldn't have stayed up all night, but it felt like it was my only hope for the future. Then I saw Jack and I thought, hey, what could I lose? People take pills specifically for focus, prescribed by doctors. Manufactured with FDA approval. They weren't really that bad. It seemed like a tiny risk.

I figured Mom killed herself because of me and Hope and our fighting, but now I know for sure.

I killed my own mother.

I'm suddenly sobbing and Hope is patting my back, and saying something, but I can't even tell what. I have no idea what she's saying, and I can't even think about it, not now. I can't be her guardian. It's my fault she needs a guardian at all.

I don't know how long I'm crying, and I don't know what Hope says while I am. I do know that eventually, Dr. Brasher comes back into the room.

"Is everything okay?" he asks.

I manage to choke back my sobs and try to pull it together. I haven't even asked Hope whether she wants me as a guardian, and I'm beginning to think I'm not fit.

"I need a few more minutes, please," I say.

He turns toward Hope, clearly looking for some indication of what's going on. She nods too, and he steps back out.

"I asked them to bring you in here because I needed to

ask you something." I glance up at Hope and just looking at her big blue eyes makes me want to cry again, but I don't. I can't, not right now. I'm not sure how long we have, and I need to know what to ask for.

"I'm going to admit that it was my fault there were drugs in the car," I tell her. "I can't let you take that from me. I have to own up to it."

Hope shakes her head violently. "No, you can't. Promise me you won't."

"I have to. It was so brave of you to take the blame, but it's not fair and it isn't right. Even if you're willing to do it, I can't let a lie like that stand."

"It's already done, though. There won't even be charges once I turn eighteen. They weren't going to do anything at all, except that I wouldn't tell them anything about where they came from." She mumbles. "I didn't know where they came from to tell them, anyway."

"I'm doing this, Hope. It's the right thing to do. It might not be on your record, but as an athlete, you'll forever have to answer questions about drug use and drug charges. Are you sure this won't follow you?"

She bobs her head. "I'm sure. And even if it does, that's what drug tests are for. I don't care."

I think about Hope peeing in a cup while someone stands behind her watching. I shake my head. "I care." I take her hand. "If I've learned anything from all this, it's that lies come back again, even well intentioned ones. I'm petitioning the Court to let me be your guardian. I can't be a good guardian if I let you lie for me."

"You won't be my guardian at all if you don't!"

I shake my head. "Then I shouldn't be. The more I think about it, I wonder whether I'm fit anyway. It was my mistake, and I'll fix it myself. But what I needed to ask you was whether you even want me for a guardian. After what happened to Mom, after I..." I wipe away an errant tear. "I doubt they'll even approve me, not after all this, but if they do, we could stay together for the rest of the school year and all summer. Do you even want that? Be honest. I can take it if you don't."

Hope hugs me again. "Of course I do." She pulls away.

"Who knows? Maybe they'll believe me when I tell them I threw those drugs away, and that it was a mistake I'll never make again, but if they don't, well at least you can stay with the Boones, and you'll be fine."

"Wait," she says, "what about Yale?"

I tilt my head sideways. "What do you know about Yale?"

"I know you didn't get in, but that you wowed the debate coach from Yale so much, they offered you a scholarship."

"How do you know about that?"

"Mason told me," she said.

"He did?" I stomped down on a bit of irrational jealousy. I see him every day at school, but he hasn't said whether he's doing an application for Yale and I haven't asked.

"I see him at swim team every day, Lacy."

I think about how Hope is willing to risk her future for mine. The same girl who, not two weeks ago, refused to step back and let me date a guy she liked. She's changed. "The thing is, Yale wasn't an option a week ago, and if it goes back to not being an option again, then so be it."

"You say that now, but the point is, if you let this stand, you can go. But if you tell them everything, maybe not."

I think about it. She's right. I'll probably have a record after this. They could actually convict me of a felony. They've already put Hope on probation and she's entered a plea. I didn't ask her to, but maybe it's for the best. I could take care of her, be her guardian, and be a good sister to make up for all the bad if I just change a few lines. No one has to know, except for me and her.

But that's enough.

I can't do it, because it would eat at me. Every single day. Some lies are too big. They're so big they consume your life. Like our mom lying to us. It obviously ate at her like a cancer. Maybe it caused her headaches, or worsened her depression. At the very least if she'd told us, we would have known to stay clear of drugs entirely, no matter what. She could have taken medication, too, if she hadn't been so afraid of it, and if we knew what happened with Dad we might have seen her aversion in another light and pressed it. Who knows?

She didn't tell us though, because she never trusted us with the truth. She's gone, at least in part, because of her own lie.

When Dr. Brasher comes back inside, I don't send him away, not this time. "I'm ready." I look at Hope sadly, and I pray that this doesn't destroy our lives even more, but I can't let her take this bullet for me.

This time, I'm prepared for him to know the ending of my story. I'm ready to revise my ideas about the future to exclude New Haven if I have to, and I'm ready to own up to my mistakes. Ignoring the things I did wrong landed me in this mess to begin with. I open the laptop and slide it over to him.

Chapter Seventeen

HOPE

It takes Dr. Brasher quite a long time to read whatever Lacy wrote. I don't know whether he reads slowly, or whether she'd just written an awful lot. Knowing her, she probably wrote like a million pages. When he finally finishes, he doesn't look at either of us. He closes the laptop and exhales loudly.

I glance at Lacy, and she shrugs. She doesn't know what he's thinking either.

"The drugs had nothing to do with you, Hope?"

I shake my head.

"Why did you tell Principal Skinner they were yours?"

"I'm a minor. I didn't want Lacy to go to prison."

"You didn't know about her deal with Jack, though. As far as you knew, the drugs were hers."

I nod.

"And you still told the police, the principal, everyone, that they were yours?"

I nod again. "Lacy has a bright future, Dr. Brasher. She shouldn't go to prison for felony possession, like Principal Skinner said she could if I told."

Dr. Brasher leans back and laughs.

"I don't see what's funny about this," Lacy says. She's wearing her, 'watch out or I'll kick your butt' look.

"Lacy, you've been scared to admit this, that you spoke to Jack about letting him put his drugs in your car, and even gave him your key?"

She nods. "Yes. I know it was wrong."

"But you never took the drugs he gave you?"

She shakes her head. "No, I didn't, but I gave him a key. I told him he could store them in my property."

"You did, and aiding a criminal is a serious issue, but it's not a felony, not under these circumstances."

"It's not?" she asks.

He shakes his head, and my chest feels so much lighter, I wonder that I don't float up in the air like a birthday balloon.

"Oh good!" I say.

"The real crime," Dr. Brasher says, "is that I've written up my recommendation to the Court. I was going to tell them that there wasn't a strong bond between the two of you, and that you might complete your grieving and finish the school year better alone, in separate domiciles."

Lacy's mouth drops open and I feel just as shocked.

"I love my sister," I say.

"I can see that," Dr. Brasher says. "I can see it clearly now that I know the whole story. I'm going to recommend the Court perform a drug test on your hair, Lacy. It should show only one usage of Adderall, and if it does, I'll recommend they drop charges and allow you to be placed as your sister Hope's guardian. You will almost certainly be required to testify against the boy who asked you to hold the drugs for him."

Lacy's smile fills the room, and my heart soars. "Really?"

"You obviously have a deep bond, one that matters.

After something like your mother's passing, you need those bonds more than ever." He walks over to his desk and shuffles some papers. "Unfortunately I can't do anything about it tonight. Hope, you'll need to return home with the Boones, but if the judge agrees with me, you two could return to your home as early as tomorrow night."

I feel like the world is spinning around me. No record, no foster care. The future is wide open, and maybe Lacy will be okay, too. I want to dance and sing. Of course, when I sing it sounds like the seagull in *The Little Mermaid*, so I don't, but I want to.

"One last thing." Dr. Brasher hands Lacy a file folder. "I pulled these a few days ago. That's your father's arrest record. Your mother had to post bail quite a few times for him. The last time, she didn't go to post bail. She went to identify his body. I can't imagine how hard that would have been, or what agony she suffered trying to do the right thing by the two of you. Addiction runs in families. She was probably terrified you two would eventually follow the same path. It ate away at her, and combined with her depression, well. Make sure, for her sake, you don't ever get involved in any form of drug use."

Lacy doesn't speak, and neither do I, but I think Dr. Brasher can tell we're listening. I don't intend to ever walk that road. I wish my mom was here to see that.

"It's not your fault, you know."

I look up at him. He's talking to both of us.

"There's nothing either of you could have done that would have saved her, not at this point. You couldn't have been expected to know the clinical signs of depression, not at your age. I included her medical records in that folder as well. You'll see she was diagnosed on two separate occasions, but refused to take any medication. Wherever she is now, I will promise you one thing, and you need to believe me. She would not want you to carry around that guilt."

Whether she wants it or not, I don't know. I do know that I can't quite erase it, but I'll make sure I keep my eyes out for anyone else in the future. And I'll badger the crap out of them to take their medicine, every day if I have to.

"But if I hadn't told Jack he could store those drugs." Lacy shakes her head.

Dr. Brasher takes a step toward her. "Your mother didn't even listen to the voicemails on her phone before she died. She had no idea any of that happened. Sometimes depression worsens for no reason at all. It's a medical condition, Angelica, and it was not your fault. Not a bit of it."

A tear runs down Lacy's face then, and she leans forward and hugs Dr. Brasher. She practically whispers the next words. "Thank you. For your patience. For your understanding. For everything."

He smiles as we leave. "Keep me apprised of where you go after graduation," he says. "I'm really interested to know."

"I will," Lacy says. "I've got a new application for Yale to finish tonight, now that it looks like I might be going after all."

The Boones are waiting outside, matching looks of concern on their faces. They're good people; they just aren't my people. I hug Lacy tightly before I let her go and head back to their home with them. That night, before I go to bed, I check my email. I haven't checked it in over a week, and I have a lot of junk mail. I never should have signed up for People magazine's updates.

The most recent email isn't junk, though. It's from Lacy. "Finished a first draft of my admissions letter. Tell me what you think." I click on the attachment.

Dear Admissions Board:

I used to think that who we were was somehow a product of our essence, something you might call a soul. I thought that people were who they were, and you couldn't change them. This past week has altered my paradigm. I now realize that our lives are nothing more than a sequence of decisions, all of them small, but they send ripples out all around us. They weave together to form the fabric of who we are. If I choose to eat two pieces of toast every morning, and I consume healthy vegetables and fruits, with meat in moderation, I will likely be thin and healthy my entire life. If instead, I choose to eat Snickers bars for lunch, and wash them down with a soda, I'll likely become sickly or weak. It won't happen overnight, but little by little, day by day, my health will deteriorate. Sometimes we make decisions so incrementally that we don't even realize where they're taking us.

A few months ago, I applied for admission to Yale. I applied to many places, but your school has always been my top choice. I received a rejection from you a little over a week ago. Following that letter, I made a sequence of bad decisions, and the result was that my life began to spin out of control. I can't pinpoint exactly when it began, but I know I shouldn't have let a drug dealer store his stash in my car. I shouldn't have gotten in a huge fight with my sister over a guy we both liked. I definitely shouldn't have stayed up all night working on a project, and then contemplated taking prescription drugs improperly the next day to compensate for my exhaustion. All of those things were bad choices, potentially ruinous ones, but the decision that impacted my life the most last week, the one that got me thinking about all of the repercussions of each choice we make was one I didn't even make. Notwithstanding my helplessness, I've agonized over it, I have wailed, and moaned and yes, I have even cried. Buckets of tears, if I'm being honest.

My mom chose to end her life two weeks ago today.

At one point, I partially blamed my sister. When I learned more about the circumstances, I shifted all of that blame to myself.

On several occasions, I've been furious with Mom for leaving me. After the benefit of a few weeks' thought on the horrible, tragic decision my mom made, I've come to the conclusion that the only person we can blame for any decision is the person making it.

I am to blame for fighting with my sister. I am to blame for bad judgment in letting an acquaintance put illegal substances in my car. I am to blame for almost taking amphetamines, but in the end, I threw the pills in the garbage. That's the same thing we must do with our guilt over other people's decisions and our own mistakes, every time the guilt resurfaces. Sure, I might have recognized the signs of my mom's depression and prevented her death if I'd been less caught up in my own problems, but I didn't. I could have caused her less stress in the past week, if I'd known what the results would be, but we cannot live our lives out of fear of what may happen. Sometimes the consequences of our decisions spiral far beyond our ability to predict.

Of all the things that went wrong in my week, I'm to blame for all but one. I refuse to accept the blame for my mother's mental illness and the horror that followed. What I promise to bring to Yale, if Mr. Zane convinces you to accept me, is an ability to make each decision now, small though they may seem, with the attention I know those decisions deserve. I hope that with my unique perspective, I can help other students to learn to do the same. It would be my distinct honor to debate on Yale's team, if your esteemed institution will have me.

Sincerely,

Angelica Shelton-Vincent

I type a reply right away. "Lacy for President. :)"

Chapter Eighteen

LACY

Time still confuses me.

Some things go on and on. For instance, an hour at the dentist drags on forever. The two weeks leading up to Christmas lasts for months, and the hour my mom used to make us wait to open presents while she made breakfast stretched into eternity. Conversely, when we went to Disneyland, a day passed in a snap. In timed tests, the sixty minutes fly by.

Some days when I wake up, I feel like my mom should be smashing her snooze button, or sitting in the kitchen, hunched over a cup of coffee. The grief slaps me right in the face, fresh and new. Those days are hard. Other days, it feels like I've been so long without her that I've forgotten what she looked like. Those days are the hardest.

No matter how much time passes, I feel a familiar pulling at my heart every time I think about her, which I do often.

I still wonder sometimes whether she'd have survived if I'd been born a few weeks earlier. After all, I would have graduated a year before and never even met Mason. If Hope had been born a few weeks later, she might have been on the junior varsity team, and she might not have caught his eye. If Mason had shown up just one day later, he wouldn't have come with me to that tournament when Drew was late, and we might never have dated. He'd already have been securely smitten by Hope at that point, and I'd never have tried to mess with that. Sometimes I wonder whether my mom would still be alive if Principal Skinner hadn't put the parking lot attendant on alert for anyone going outside during school hours, Dr. Brasher's reassurances she never saw the voicemails notwithstanding. The only answer I can find is that, no matter how many seconds we scraped together, I'll never know what would have happened.

My mom might still be alive, or she might not. Either way, I can't let other people's agency impact the choices I make today. And I want to make every second I have count.

Which means, when my alarm goes off at six am, I don't hit the snooze button. I groan and roll out of bed. My feet land on Moby's tail, and he yelps with displeasure. That wakes up Hope, of course, and she rubs her eyes.

"If you hadn't insisted we get a dog, we could be in the dorms," I grumble.

"You still could have. I'm at Gateway Community College, remember? We're living here so you can room with me, not because of poor little Moby." She leans down and rubs him, then blinks several times. "What time is it?"

"Your first class isn't for hours yet," I say. "Go back to sleep."

"Good luck at your meet," Hope mumbles.

I don't remind her it's a tournament. Some things are just hardwired. Mason still calls tournaments meets sometimes, too. I take a shower and pick my favorite suit, a charcoal grey with pink pinstripes. I just got it back from the dry cleaners.

My phone buzzes and I check it. It's a text message from Mason. JUST LEAVING. SEE YOU IN FIVE.

Crap, that barely leaves me time to walk Moby before I need to leave. I rush into the kitchen and reach for a granola bar.

"In a rush?" Drew asks.

I sigh. "I guess I was in the shower too long."

She holds out her hand. "I'll take the mutt for a walk for you."

I grin at her. "Thanks." She pretends to hate him, just like she still pretends to hate Mason, but she actually loves them both.

Drew and I walk out the door at the same time, me in a suit, and her in jogging pants and a long sleeved shirt. New Haven is stupidly cold.

Mason is just pulling up in his blue Audi. Graduation present from his parents. He whistles at me, and I grin.

"No one looks as great in a pinstripe suit as you do," he says.

Drew rolls her eyes at us and walks away.

I climb into the car and look at Mason's suit. "Except maybe you." I sigh. "I thought we discussed this. We look silly when we match. Like tweedle dee and tweedle DUMB."

"If you telling me not to do it is 'discussing it,' then yes, we did, but, I like it," Mason says. "I'm not changing. Besides, my suit is black and white, while yours is charcoal and *pink*. That's not too matchy."

Mason is every bit as infuriating now that we've been together for months and months. And he's still swimming, so I have to sit on my hands and wait for his free weekends. I don't mind too badly. Actually, Mr. Zane is the one who complains about it the most.

Even though Yale isn't number one in the country, their program is number twenty-five, and I guess that's good enough. We work our debate schedule around his swimming one, and as far as I can tell, he's on track for the Olympics. Even his mom is satisfied with his progress. I'm not sure how he finds time to study, but somehow he's hanging in there. He likes to say, "Bottom of the class at Yale still graduates."

When I think about time these days, it's usually to count good things. It just so happens that on the very day I learned my mom had died, I also found out that Mason liked me, and we kissed for the first time. I know that my mom would be delighted to see how happy I am now. I try to focus on the things that bring me light and joy, and not the things that cause me pain.

For instance, it's been eight hours since Mason last said he loves me. Coincidentally, it's also been eight hours since I last kissed him. It's been two days since our last date, and a week since we went on a triple date with Hope and her boyfriend Chad, and Drew and her girlfriend Anica. That was less awkward than you might have guessed. It's been almost two months since Hope turned eighteen and I was officially not her guardian anymore.

"Are you worried that I forgot?" Mason asks.

"Forgot what?" I smile.

"Well, I didn't. I know it's your birthday today. I didn't want you to think I forgot it, just because we have a big meet against Harvard today."

"Tournament." I grin. "It's so sweet you remembered."

"Hope texted me every single day for the last week like

I'm mentally deficient." He rolls his eyes. "I've given this a lot of thought, and I wanted to give you something special. Something that will tell everyone we know how much I care about you."

It will tell everyone how much he cares? Um... I scrunch up my nose. Oh, no. Please tell me my sweet boyfriend is not about to propose. Please, oh please, no. Maybe if I turn it into a joke, he'll realize it's a bad idea. His parents got married in college, but we are nothing like his parents. And we're freshman. And that's insane. Think of a joke, Lacy!

I spit out the first thing that comes to mind. "I am SO not getting a couples tattoo."

He rolls his eyes. "Too white trash, I know. I'm lucky you put up with my monstrosity as it is."

"I like your Moby Dick tattoo." I reach a hand over and trace it across his back.

He kisses my hand, and then places a small box into it. My heart stalls. I swear if he's proposing to me our freshman year in college, in a car no less, I'm going to turn him down flat. He will just have to be man enough to deal with that.

I feel sort of ill, but I open the box anyway with a forced smile on my face. I look at the ring contained inside and my feeling intensifies. I don't even merit a diamond? Then I glance at Mason, at the hopeful smile on his eager face and I can't stand it.

"Are you proposing?"

He gapes at me. "Excuse me?"

"What is this?" I shake the box at him.

"No, I'm not proposing." His eyes widen. "Did you want me to?" He looks as horrified as I feel. "I designed a ring for you that symbolizes our relationship."

I start to laugh, and I can't stop. There are tears

streaming down my face. "This is so how we do everything. No, I didn't want you to propose, but Mason, you told me you loved me, and you had something that would tell the world how we felt, and then you gave me a ring. And not even a big old diamond."

Finally he sees it. He starts to laugh, too. "Wow, you thought I was proposing, and that I sucked at it. No," he chokes out. "I was thinking how you're Lacy, and I'm Mason. I wanted something to reflect both of us. I talked to this jeweler, and we came up with three interlocking rings, one for each of us, and one for how we're more together than apart, you know like synergy. They fit together like a mason would put stones together, but when they're together, they look like lace, see?"

He turns the rings, which are now soldered together, but I can see the separate rings: one white, one rose, and one yellow gold. Now that I'm not panicked about a proposal, I can see how delicate and beautiful they are.

I lean over, and this time, I'm the one pressed against the gear shifter. Mason shifts to move around the steering wheel and his beautiful face gets nearer to mine, one inch at a time. Even now, after eight months, it still feels like the world shifts around me when his lips meet mine. I don't know how long he kisses me, but I know it always feels like Disneyland, not the dentist. I'm never ready for it to end.

The good news is that even when it does end, I know it's not The End.

If you enjoyed Already Gone, please leave me a review on Amazon! It helps tremendously!

Also, feel free to join my newsletter by filling out your

email address on my website: www.BridgetEBakerWrites.com.

Also, I've included the first chapter of my YA Post Apocalyptic novel, Marked. If you like it, the entire series is available on Amazon! All three books are free in KU, or only $3.99 (per book).

CHAPTER NINETEEN

I'm a big, fat coward.

I've known this about myself definitively since one month before my sixth birthday. The night I lost my dad.

Case in point: I'm just shy of seventeen. I've been in love with the same guy for almost three years. Even though

I see Wesley a few times a week, I haven't said a word. But tonight I have the perfect opportunity to do what I've always feared to try. Tonight, to celebrate our upcoming Path selections, all the teens in Port Gibson play a stupid, risky game.

Spin the Bottle.

I glance around as I walk toward the campfire in front of me. Only thirty-five kids turned seventeen in the past year, so of course I know them all. My best girl friend, Gemette, waves me over. I try to squash my disappointment at not seeing Wesley. When I played this scene in my brain earlier, I was sitting by him.

"You gonna scowl at the fire all night, Ruby?" Gemette pats a gloved hand on the slab of granite underneath her.

"You couldn't have saved us one of those seats?" I point at the smooth, flat stumps on the other side of the fire. I sit down and shift around, trying to find a flat spot.

"I think what you meant to say was, 'Thanks, Gemette. You're the best.'"

Her straight black hair reflects the campfire flames when she tosses it back over her shoulder. It's against the Council's rules for hair to cover your forehead. Gotta make it easy to see anyone who might be Marked. Except tonight, no one's following the rules. Everyone's wearing their hair down, and Gemette's silky locks frame her face beautifully. I envy her sleek hair almost as much as I covet her curves.

"My bum's already hurting on this," I mutter.

"If you weighed more than eighty-five pounds soaking wet, it wouldn't bother you so much."

Instead of curves, I've got twig arms and a non-existent backside. I shift on the huge slab, trying to find a position that doesn't hurt. I arch one eyebrow, not that she can see it in the dark. "I weigh ninety-two pounds, thank you very much."

Gemette snorts. "That proves my point, you bony butt."

She leans toward the fire and picks up the glass bottle lying on its side. She tosses it a few inches up into the air before catching it again.

"Be careful with that." That bottle's the only reason I'm sitting here, sour-faced, stomach churning.

Slowly the remaining seats around the fire fill up. Wesley shows up last. There aren't any seats left, but before I can convince Gemette to squish over, he grabs a bucket. He turns it upside down and takes a seat a few feet away from everyone else. I guess that's fitting. His dad's the Mayor of Port Gibson and a Counsellor on the CentiCouncil, so Wesley's in charge by default tonight. He'll probably take over for his dad one day, which isn't as glamorous as it sounds since less than two thousand people live here.

He looks around the fire, and his gaze stops on me. He bobs his head in my direction, and I shoot him a smile. I'm glad he can't hear the thundering of my heart.

Although we're all huddled around a campfire, and I've known most of the kids here for years, we maintain carefully measured space between us. Tercera dictates our habits even when we're rebelling. Which we're only doing because it's a tradition.

Maybe Tercera's made cowards of us all.

"Are we starting?" Tom's sitting to my left. His parents are both in Agriculture and he's Pathing there, too. He has broad shoulders and tan skin from working outside most of the day. Gemette likes him, and it's easy to see why. Of course, he's nothing to Wesley.

I glance across the fire in time to see Wesley stand up. He

straightens the collar of his coat slowly and methodically, like his dad always does before a town hall meeting. Wesley loves doing impressions, and he's usually convincingly good at them.

"I'd like to take this opportunity to welcome you all to the Last Supper." His voice mimics his father's, and he touches his chin with his right hand in the same way his dad always rubs his beard. Wesley himself is tall and lean with long black hair that he's wearing down, for once. It falls in his eyes in a way I've never seen before, and I feel a little rush. I want to touch it.

Wesley smirks. "I know you may be less than impressed with the culinary offerings for our gathering, but as I always say, Tradition has Value." He cracks a grin then, and everyone laughs. "Seriously though." He drops the impression and returns to his normal voice, which I like way better anyway. "I know the food sucks, but this whole thing started with a bunch of teenagers who were sick of rules and ready to throw caution to the wind for a night."

I look down at the three or four-dozen nondescript metal cans with the tops peeled back, resting on coals. Another few dozen are open but sitting away from the fire. Presumably they contain fruit or something else we won't want to eat hot.

Wesley leans over and snags the first can, his gloves keeping him safe from the heat. "I hope you'll all forgive me, but this was what we could find."

"This is a pretty crummy tradition." Lina reaches down and grabs a can with mittened hands. Her dark brown hair falls in a long, thick braid down her back, like it has every single time I've seen her.

"Traditions matter, even the silly ones. They help pull us together as a community, which is valuable when fear of Tercera yanks communities apart. We're stronger when we aren't alone. Thinking every man should look out for himself hurts all of us." Wesley takes his first bite right before Lina. I grab a can of baked beans.

The food really is as bad as it looks, but at least it's not spoiled.

Wesley talks while we eat.

"As you already know, we come from a variety of backgrounds. Before the Marking, Port Gibson housed approximately the same number of people, but not a single person who lived here before the Marking survived. We cleaned out the homes, burned some to the ground and rebuilt, circled the city with a wall, and made it our own. The Unmarked who live here are Christian, Muslim, atheist, black, white, Hispanic, Russian, German and Japanese. I could keep going, but I don't need to. Before the Marking, these differences divided humanity. Now, we know that what truly matters is what we all share. We embrace the traditions that bring us all together, because we're more alike than we are unalike."

I swallow the last spoonful of baked beans from my can and set it down on the ground by my feet. I'm almost the last one to finish eating, but several half-full cans are scattered around the campfire. A few people grab a can of fruit. I prefer the stuff my Aunt and I process and can ourselves, so I don't bother.

I rub my hands together briskly. Even in mittens, my fingers feel stiff. It's usually not too cold in Mississippi, even in January, but a late freeze has everyone bundled up. The Last Supper's supposed to be a chance to rebel, but I'm grateful that everyone's as covered as possible. It means I won't look as cowardly for keeping my mittens on. My aunt is Port Gibson's head of the Science Path, so I know all about how Tercera congregates first in the skin cells, even before the Mark has shown up on the forehead in some cases.

The wind moans as it blows through the trees, and we all huddle around the meager fire. Even though the flames have died down to coals in most places, it burns hot. My face roasts while my back freezes. The bottle lies stationary on the weathered flagstones by the fire where Gemette set it, light glinting off of the dingy glass at strange angles.

The quiet conversations die off and the nervous laughter ends. Eyes dart to and fro among the thirty something teenagers gathered.

"So." Evan's voice cracks, and he clears his throat. "Who goes first?"

"Thanks for volunteering," Wesley says.

I suspect no one else asked for just this reason. All eyes turn toward poor, gangly, redheaded Evan.

Evan gawks momentarily. Even though he and I work in Sanitation together, I don't know him well. I haven't been there long enough to guess whether he feels lucky or put upon. He sighs, and then leans forward and tweaks the bottle. It twists sharp and fast and skitters to the right, spinning furiously.

I really hope the bottle doesn't stop on me, and I doubt I'm alone in that thought. Evan's funny in a self-deprecating way, but he isn't smart, and he definitely isn't hot. I bite my lip, worried about what I'll do if it does stop on me.

It slows quickly and finally stops pointing to my left. I sigh in relief, which I belatedly hope no one heard.

Tom gasps, and then in a raspy voice says, "No way. I mean, you're nice and all Evan, but I'm not . . . I don't . . ."

"Yeah, me either. Chill, man." Evan laughs. "So, does it pass to the next person over?" Evan raises his eyebrows and glances at me.

I want to protest, but my throat closes off and I look down at my feet instead.

Evan stands up. "So Ruby . . ."

He may not have saved me a seat, but Wesley jumps in to save me now, thank goodness. "That's not how it works. If you get someone of the same gender, and neither of you . . . well, then your turn passes to him or her. Which means you sit down Evan, and you spin next, Tom."

"Who made these rules?" Evan grumbles as he sits.

Gemette smiles. "They make sense, Evan. I mean, it's not spin the bottle and pick best out of three. Your way, you'd basically pick someone in the circle who's close and kiss whoever you want."

Evan shrugs and glances at me again with a smile. "Sounds pretty okay, actually."

Tom snorts. "I don't hear Ruby complaining about Wesley's rules. I'd say that's your answer, man."

I look back down at my shoes, but not before I see Tom's wink. Jerk. Evan must feel idiotic, and I definitely want to sink into the ground.

I bite my lip again, this time a little harder. Tom's an obviously good-looking guy, but I have no interest in kissing him. I hope his wink was a joke about Evan and not some kind of message.

Cold air blows past me as Tom leans forward to spin the bottle, his body no longer blocking the wind. One thing jumps out at me as he reaches for the glass bottle. In spite of the cold, Tom isn't wearing gloves. He must've taken them off at some point. He's either a daredevil or an idiot. I'm not sure which.

Tom spins the bottle less forcefully than Evan and rocks back and forth as the bottle circles round and round. His eyes focus intently on the spinning glass as if he can somehow control where it stops. I wonder who he's hoping for and look around the circle for clues. Andrea seems particularly bright-eyed. My eyes continue to wander. One gorgeous, deep blue pair of eyes in the circle stares right back at me. Wesley. I've looked at him a lot over the past few years, but this feels different somehow. A spark zooms through me, and I quickly stare at my feet.

No luck for Andrea tonight, or Gemette. The bottle comes to rest on Andrea's best friend, Annelise, instead. She and I were in Science together a long time ago. Her dark brown hair hangs loose, framing high cheekbones and expressive chocolate eyes. She frowns. Tonight doesn't seem to be going right for anyone so far.

"Now what?" Annelise's voice shakes. "We just kiss, right here in front of everyone?"

"No, of course not," Gemette snaps.

"Who made you the boss?" Evan frowns. Judging by his sulky tone, he's still mad about losing his turn earlier.

"Unfortunately, I'm the boss," Wesley says, "and she's right." He points to a dilapidated shed at the top of the hill. "You two go up there."

"Romantic." Tom rolls his eyes as he stands up. He rubs his bare palms on his pants. Gross. At least I know I'm not the only nervous one here. Tom and Annelise trudge a path through clumps of frozen brown grass toward the rundown tool shed.

What a special memory for their first kiss.

Gemette sighs and I pat her gloved hand with my own. I'd feel worse for her, but Gemette likes every decent looking guy in town, including a few boys a year younger than us. She'll recover from missing out on a special moment with Tom.

I glance again toward Andrea, an acquaintance from my time in Agriculture. She and Tom trained together for years. She may have liked him as long as I've liked Wesley. She looks into the fire while her foot digs a messy hole in the soil. I wonder how I'll feel if Wesley spins and gets Andrea. Or worse, Gemette. I'll have to sit here and twiddle my thumbs while I know he's in there kissing a friend. My stomach lurches. Coming tonight was a stupid idea. I clearly didn't think this through.

No one speaks to distract me from my anxiety. The shed isn't far. We could easily eavesdrop on them if the wind would shriek a little less.

"How long does this take?" Evan asks.

"Who the heck knows?" Gemette points at the bottle. "Impatient for another crack at it?"

Kids around us chuckle.

After another few awkward moments, Gemette grabs the bottle and gives it a twist. "No reason we have to wait on them."

"Sure," Wesley says. "Whoever it lands on can go next."

"Wait," Evan asks, "whoever it lands on goes next as in it's their turn to spin? Or goes next as in Gemette's going to kiss them?"

The bottle stops before anyone can respond, pointing directly at Wesley. His perfectly shaped brows draw together under disheveled black hair. Gorgeous hair. His lips form a perfect "o". His bright blue eyes meet mine again.

My heart races and the baked beans sit like a lump in my belly. I shouldn't have come. Of course Wesley will want to kiss her. Gemette's gorgeous, curvy, and smart. Ugh. Am I going to have to sit here while my best friend kisses the guy I like twenty feet away? This is all my fault. If I'd only told Gemette, she'd beg off.

I bite down a little harder on my lip and taste blood this time. I really need to kick this particular habit, especially with kissing in my future. Maybe. Hopefully. I'm such an idiot.

Wesley clears his throat. "I think I'm going to sit this game out. I'm more of a moderator than a participant."

"No," I blurt out. "You can't. You're here, you're seventeen, you have to participate." What am I doing? Why am I shoving him at my friend? But if I don't make him play, I'm flushing my chance to kiss him down the toilet. I want to cry.

"Well, then I guess it's my turn to spin." His deep voice sounds completely different than any of the other kids here tonight. My stomach ties in knots when I hear him speak, which is ridiculous because I've heard his voice a million times.

I glance at Gemette. She looks disappointed and I want to cry with relief, but I don't blame her. He could've kissed her but didn't pursue it. I imagine most any girl here would be disappointed. He glances up and his eyes lock with mine again. Caught. I start to shiver and try to stop it. This look is different somehow from any before, like something shifted. Wesley clears his throat, looks down at the bottle, gracefully reaches over, and snaps it between his fingers.

It spins evenly, not moving to the right or the left. It spins on and on, and I wonder if it'll ever stop. It slows, whirling a little less with each rotation, the butterflies in my stomach swooping and swirling with each pass.

Until it finally stops. On me.

My eyes snap up reflexively, wide with shock. Wesley doesn't even seem surprised. He simply stands and inclines his head toward the shed.

"Isn't it still..." I clear my throat. "Umm, occupied?"

"We can wait over there." He gestures at the hill to the right of the shed. One side of his mouth lifts in a smile and I feel an answering grin form on my lips. Which makes me think about what we're about to do with our lips.

Swarms and swarms of butterflies flutter in my chest.

"Sure," I say.

I stand up, and without even thinking, I wipe my palms

on my jeans. They aren't even sweaty and what's more, I'm wearing mittens! I really hope no one noticed. Okay, more specifically, I hope Wesley didn't notice. Gemette holds something out to me when I stand. I can't tell what it is from feel alone, thanks to my thick mittens, and in the dark I have to squint to make it out at all. A tube of something. "What—"

"Lip gloss," she whispers. "A gift from my mom. I was going to use it, but looks like you need it more, you lucky, lip-biting brat." She winks.

I'm glad Wesley's still across the fire from me and that it's dark. Maybe he somehow miraculously missed both the palm wipe and her wink.

I walk as slowly as I can toward the old shed, partially to avoid tripping, but also so I won't look overeager. I try to hide my face while I apply the fruit-scented lip-gloss so that Wesley won't notice. It's dark, but I don't want him to be put off by dry, scratchy lips, or worse, dried blood. Gemette's a good friend. I feel guilty for overreacting earlier when I thought she might kiss Wesley. Not super guilty, but you know, a little.

Neither of us speaks a word, but I feel the eyes of the other teens follow us toward the shed. We're only a few crunching steps away when the swinging door flies open and Tom and Annelise barrel out. I jump when it bangs shut behind them.

Tom looks as ruffled as I feel, his eyes darting back and forth. He ducks his head and reaches down to take Annelise's hand. They walk out and away from the fire and the rest of Port Gibson's teens. I can't tell where they're headed, but somewhere far away from here.

"Did you know almost a third of the couples in town trace their start to the Last Supper?" Wesley asks.

"No way."

He shrugs. "We've only been an Unmarked town for seven years, so it's even more impressive. Not all of them are matched up from a bottle spin, but I think the game helps people realize how they feel."

A thrill rushes through me. Does Wesley feel the same as me?

My hand reaches for the door handle and collides en route with his. I'm wearing mittens, of course, and he's wearing shiny, brown gloves, but a thrill runs through me when we touch, even through layers. He doesn't move his hand away, but instead draws my hand in his and pushes the door handle back in one fluid movement. My heart skips a beat and time stops. When the door's completely open, he slowly releases my hand. I lower my eyes and step over the threshold into the rundown little building.

Although there's clearly no power, and consequently neither heat nor an overhead light, the walls at least cut the wind. It's at once both warmer and quieter. Two tall candles burn softly on a pile of rusted metal boxes in the corner. Someone prepared this dump, I realize. I wonder whether it was Wesley. The flames provide enough light that I can see his face. His dark brows are an even more startling contrast to his dark blue eyes than usual, accentuated by his hair falling in his face.

"So," I say. "Here we are."

Wesley looks at me from less than a foot away. The shed's small and crammed full of moldering farm implements. The air around us practically hums, but that isn't new. It's always like the moments right before a lightning storm when he's near. Supercharged almost, like the electrons around my body might fly off at his slightest touch. The difference is that here, away from the town's work projects, away from my family and his, it feels like anything really could happen.

Wesley's so close I can smell him, the same citrusy, woodsy smell I've secretly savored for years. It's even stronger tonight, like he put on more of whatever it is he usually wears. I breathe deep, and all the memories of him re-imprint on my brain. Scrubbing, sanding, painting, digging, cleaning, hammering. Projects his dad made him attend, but I suffered through to be near him. When I'm with him, I belong somewhere for the first time in a decade.

When we become adults next week, Wesley's mandatory attendance at work projects ends. Wesley steps into his role as an administrator, and I'll become part of Port Gibson's janitorial crew. It's now or never if I want to make any kind of permanent place with Wesley.

I never thought I'd be close to him like this, and I know I may never be again. I lean toward him and tilt my face upward, eyes closed, ready for what comes next. Maybe I'm even a touch impatient. I have waited for this for years.

Except I keep waiting, and then I wait some more.

Not a single thing happens. The trouble with being ridiculously small is that Wesley, who's on the tall side anyway, towers over me. Even with my face angled up, his lips are pretty far away. I can barely make out his expression, but it looks guarded.

Maybe he doesn't know how to do it?

No way. Wesley must know. I mean, it's not hard, right? You just push your lips onto the other person's mouth. Why isn't he doing anything? This is the moment. THE moment!

Until it passes. And then another moment falls on top of it, and another. All passing. Even the butterflies in my stomach get bored and go look for flowers elsewhere.

I'm not sure exactly how much time has elapsed, but the seconds drag, heavy with my growing frustration. Soon, someone will bang on the door. "You've been in there forev-er," they'll say. "Make room for the next couple."

I want to smack them in their eager faces.

I know I don't have much time, and I want to say some-thing, anything. I need to tell him how I feel, say the words, take a gamble. But like it always does, my tongue shuts down. My throat closes off. The words stick inside my throat. Why am I such a coward? Our perfect moment withers and dies. Tears well up in my eyes, and I can't breathe.

Wesley isn't similarly affected. He steps back and says, "We don't have to do this, Ruby. It's not safe at all. I don't know why my dad even lets these dinners happen."

"Why'd you spin the bottle in the first place?" I hear the desperation in my voice, but the words pour out in spite of myself. "I know you, and you know me. How's it dangerous for us?"

He takes another step back, his expression registering surprise. "People get Marked, Ruby. It still happens. Every few weeks, in fact. Maybe I'm Marked. You don't know. It happens, even here, even with all our rules. It may take years to die once you're Marked, but it's inevitable."

I roll my eyes. "Well I'm not Marked, if that's what you're worried about." I point at my forehead. "See? Clear."

"We shouldn't be taking these risks." Wesley scowls. "Not now, not right before our real lives begin. This whole thing's supposed to be a time to say goodbye to being a kid, not act like an idiotic five-year-old, breaking rules for no reason."

Our real lives? Maybe he never thought it felt right, the time we spent, the way we are together. Maybe I never belonged with him at all. "Why'd you even come, then? Why follow me in here if you're not going to kiss me?"

Was he hoping for someone else? Was he stuck with me

and looking for any excuse to bolt? Am I Evan in this scenario?

I look up, but I'm too close. The hair cascading over his face obscures my view. I want to touch his hair; I want to kiss him; I want to tell him I love him, and that I always have. My fingers and toes and everything connecting them zings in spite of the bitter cold, in spite of the indifference of his words. Energy spins round and round in my body, a closed circuit with nowhere to go.

"Look, Ruby, I don't know what to say . . . but the thing is . . ." He sounds torn, confused.

Suddenly, I don't want to hear "the thing," whatever it is. I've been talking to Wesley for years, talking and talking, and working alongside him, but I don't want to talk to him anymore. I know what I want and I'll never have a better chance to play things off as part of a game, if he feels like I now suspect he does. The notion of an excuse appeals to my cowardly heart. I can't speak the words, but I won't stand here and do nothing, not anymore, because he's the real life I've longed for.

I stop thinking and step toward him instead. He tries to step back and slams up against the back wall. I quickly take one more step and use my gloved hand to pull his head down to mine. I push my lips against his. In my haste, I push too hard and pull a little too fast. Our teeth smack into each other and my tooth knocks against my own lip, splitting it wide open again.

It's the opposite of magical.

I look up at Wesley instinctively. He has blood on his mouth, but whether it's his, or mine, I can't tell. And if it's not awful enough already, Wesley stiffens from head to toe like I mauled him, like I forced him into something torturous.

A tear rolls down my cheek and I inhale deeply. I won't

cry over this. I can't, because there's no way I can play it all off as a game if I bawl my eyes out. I turn away from him. If I can't stop the tears, at least he doesn't need to see them. When did this go so wrong? I should be calm, cool, in control. I need to laugh it all off and tell him friends can't be expected to kiss well. Whoops.

Except my heart won't listen to the screaming from my head. I'm not calm. I'm the opposite of cool. I've lost all control.

He grabs my shoulder and tugs me around. I turn, but my eyes stay glued to the ground, too ashamed to meet his gaze.

"Ruby, look at me."

He puts two gloved fingers under my chin and lifts. His head comes down then, but slowly, too slowly. My heart stops pumping and I worry it might never beat again. His lips brush mine gently, then with more pressure. I ignore the discomfort of my torn lip and lean into him, connected to him in a way I can't explain. I need more air, but I want less, because that means more space between us. If this never ends, maybe it'll erase the moments that preceded it.

Suddenly, he lets me go and steps back. Emptiness fills the space where he stood. I reel again, sucking air in and blowing my breath back out to steady myself.

When I raise my eyes, our gazes lock. All my sorrow from before is gone, replaced with a feeling like I'm flying, soaring, floating on top of the world. His sapphire blue eyes reflect candlelight back at me. He's breathing as deeply as I am; he's as affected as me. I can't look away from his strong, almost hawkish nose, his square jaw, his flashing eyes and thick black lashes. I continue to stare as Wesley reaches up and brushes his unkempt hair away from his eyes.

I almost faint.

Such a simple movement. Small in the grand scheme of things, but also vast, earth shattering, all encompassing. My dreams crumble. My world spins out of control. He moves his hair off his forehead, and suddenly things make sense. His reticence to touch me, his skittishness, but also his quick recovery. Once he knew it was too late, he didn't hesitate to kiss me. Because we'd already touched.

There, on his otherwise perfect forehead, is a rash. Before it wouldn't have mattered. Before the Marking no one would care. Acne on a teen, a reaction to hair product. It shouldn't matter that his forehead has a blemish. It shouldn't terrify me, but it does. Because that small rash means Wesley is Marked, and in under three years, he's going to die terribly.

And now, so am I.

———

If you want to read more, click here: Marked!

ACKNOWLEDGMENTS

My mother continues to be my biggest fan. Thank you for all your unfailing support.

My husband is my biggest supporter, in every single way. I would be nothing without you. You may not have a tattoo, but you're every bit as cool as Mason.

My kids are amazing, and they force my books on their teachers and friends. Keep it up, tiny sales force. Cutest pushers ever.

My friends are wonderful. Esther, Shauna, Jennifer, and the Writing Gals. Thanks for moral support, beta reads, promos, and on and on. Your support is transformational and means everything to me.

ABOUT THE AUTHOR

Bridget loves her husband (every day) and all five of her kids (most days). She's a lawyer, but does as little legal work as possible. She has a yappy dog, backyard chickens, and a fish. She makes cookies too often, and believes they should be their own food group. To keep from blowing up like a puffer fish, she kick boxes every day. So if you don't like her books, her kids, or her cookies, maybe don't tell her in person.

ALSO BY BRIDGET E. BAKER

Marked: Sins of Our Ancestors Book One

Suppressed: Sins of Our Ancestors Book Two

Redeemed: Sins of Our Ancestors Book Three

Finding Santa: Almost a Billionaire Book One

www.ingramcontent.com/pod-product-compliance
Lightning Source LLC
Chambersburg PA
CBHW050337190726
48284CB00007BB/2040